THE SECRET JOURNEYS OF JACK LONDON

—————————— * ——————————

THE SECRET JOURNEYS OF JACK LONDON

———— ✳ ————

BOOK I:
THE WILD

BY **CHRISTOPHER GOLDEN & TIM LEBBON**

WITH ILLUSTRATIONS BY
GREG RUTH

HARPER

An Imprint of HarperCollinsPublishers
NEW HANOVER COUNTY PUBLIC LIBRARY
201 Chestnut Street
Wilmington, N.C. 28401

The Secret Journeys of Jack London: Book I: The Wild
Text copyright © 2011 by Christopher Golden & Tim Lebbon
Illustrations copyright © 2011 by Greg Ruth All rights reserved. Printed in
the United States of America. No part of this book may be used or reproduced in
any manner whatsoever without written permission except in the case of brief
quotations embodied in critical articles and reviews. For information address
HarperCollins Children's Books, a division of HarperCollins Publishers,
10 East 53rd Street, New York, NY 10022.
www.harpercollinschildrens.com

Library of Congress Cataloging-in-Publication Data
Golden, Christopher.
     The wild / by Christopher Golden & Tim Lebbon ; with illustrations by Greg
Ruth. — 1st ed.
     p. cm. — (The secret journeys of Jack London ; bk. 1)
     Summary: Seventeen-year-old Jack London makes the arduous journey to the
Yukon's gold fields in 1893, becoming increasingly uneasy about supernatural
forces in the wilderness that seem to have taken a special interest in him.
     ISBN 978-0-06-186317-2 (trade bdg.)
     1. London, Jack, 1876–1916—Juvenile fiction. [1. London, Jack, 1876–1916—
Fiction. 2. Adventure and adventurers—Fiction. 3. Supernatural—Fiction.
4. Survival—Fiction. 5. Wolves—Fiction. 6. Gold mines and mining—Fiction.
7. Yukon—History—19th century—Fiction. 8. Canada—History—1867–1914—
Fiction.] I. Lebbon, Tim. II. Ruth, Greg, ill. III. Title.
PZ7.G5646Wil 2011
[Fic]—dc22   2010007475
                                                                                                    CIP
                                                                                                    AC

Typography by Sarah Hoy
11 12 13 14 15   LP/RRDB   10 9 8 7 6 5 4 3 2 1
❖
First Edition

For our children, Nicholas, Daniel, Ellie, Lily, and Daniel.
Life is a wild adventure. Hear its call. Have no fear.

CONTENTS

The function of man is to live, not to exist.

—Jack London

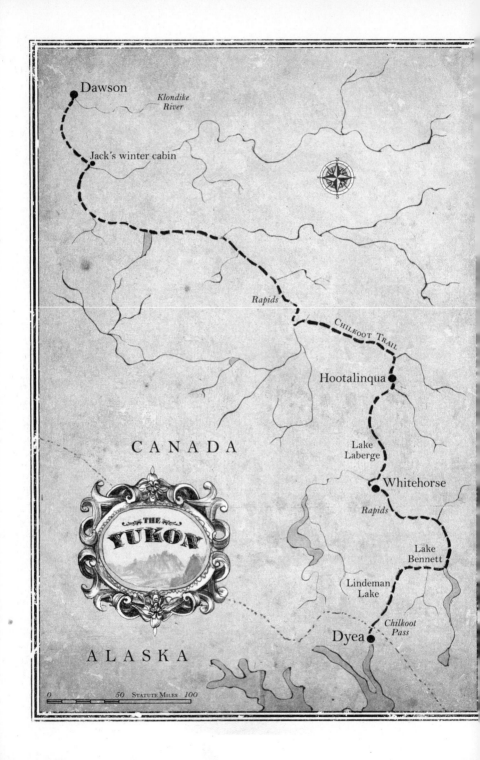

Dawson

*Klondike
River*

Jack's winter cabin

Rapids

CHILKOOT TRAIL

Hootalinqua

CANADA

Lake
Laberge

Whitehorse

THE YUKON

Rapids

Lake
Bennett

Lindeman
Lake

*Chilkoot
Pass*

Dyea

ALASKA

0   50 STATUTE MILES 100

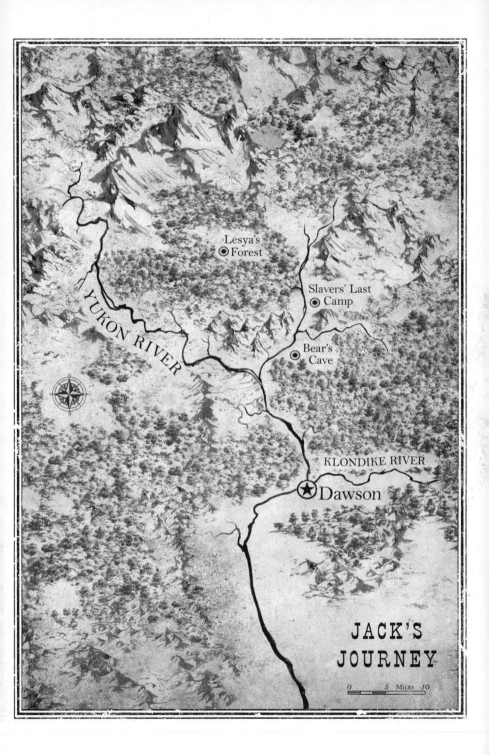

Lesya's
Forest

Slavers' Last
Camp

Bear's
Cave

YUKON RIVER

KLONDIKE RIVER

★ Dawson

JACK'S
JOURNEY

0   5 MILES 10

I've never been much of a writer, but I've always been able to tell a tale. Got Jack London to thank for that. He made me realize that stories are all about heart and soul, not words and spelling, and he had heart and soul aplenty.

Jack saved my life many times. Once, he did it for real, beating off two evil men who were ready to kidnap me and take me off into slavery. There were other times down through the years, and for most of them he wasn't even there. It was the thought *of Jack that helped me. The idea of his courage, his outlook, his philosophy that life is for living, not just existing. And his conviction that there are so many unknown things that can never be fully explored in one single life. Some of them are wondrous, some terrible. Jack saw both.*

I became an explorer because of him, of the spiritual as well as the physical. And I like to think that in some small way, I helped him in his own journeys.

It's well-known what became of him. One of the greatest writers we've ever had, he could spin a yarn like no one else, and imbue it with a power that was almost . . . well, supernatural. But much as some thought what he wrote about was the life he'd lived, I knew the truth all those years, because he'd told me: He could never, ever tell of his real adventures. They were too personal for him to put down on paper, and much too terrible. Some of the things he saw just weren't for human eyes.

But he never told me I *couldn't tell.*

Jack died far too young, but in his forty years he lived the lives of many men. And he died knowing there's more here in this world than we can or should understand.

That's part of the reasoning behind me writing this down at last. I'm an old man now. Who will it hurt to learn the truth? Will anyone even believe? In these modern technological times when the fantastic doesn't seem quite so fantastic anymore, and the wilds aren't quite so wild, I think these stories, terrifying though they are, need telling.

They're a warning, and I think we need reminding.

These, then, are the true stories of Jack London.

His secret journeys.

Hal Sawyer

San Francisco

June 1962

CHAPTER ONE

INTO THE WILD

J ACK LONDON STOOD on the deck of the *Umatilla* and looked out upon the docks of San Francisco, wondering how long it would be before he saw the city again. He had been born with a wandering heart, and he embraced adventure, unafraid to face the dangers often presented by journeys into unknown places. When the *Umatilla* sailed out of the port of San Francisco, he would be bound for the Yukon, leaving civilization behind for the wilds of the frozen north, where rumor claimed vast quantities of gold awaited discovery and any man could become King Midas.

Yet gold represented only one part of the Yukon's allure for Jack. Given the chance, he'd have gone purely for the sake of going, dared all for the sake of daring. And there was the idea in his adventure-yearning heart that those northern wilds were waiting for him.

Now he leaned against the *Umatilla*'s railing and breathed in the smells, took in the sights, and listened to the sounds of chaos and excitement around them. Never had he seen such a mixed group of people. Every race, every nationality, every creed was represented here. Even with the scent of the ocean so strong, dozens of other odors drifted on the breeze. On the dock, a vendor sold roasted nuts. A man at Jack's shoulder reeked of cheap whiskey. Others gave off the strong smells of spices or smoke or food, and several stank from need of a bath. Jack had been a tramp, oyster pirate, and convict, and had been friends with men who hadn't bathed properly in decades, but he shuddered to think what the ship's quarters would smell like by the time they reached Alaska.

He'd heard whispers that the steamer had twice as many passengers as it was licensed to carry, and he could well believe it. Having stowed their equipment in the ship's hold themselves, Jack and Shepard, his aging and ailing brother-in-law, had shouldered their way through a bustle of gold prospectors, from sailors and rough-handed laborers to the sons of the wealthy elite who were setting out to seek their own fortunes.

Now, from the ship's railing, they prepared to bid farewell to San Francisco.

"No need for good-byes," said Shepard. "It'll still be here when we get back, same as ever." He looked side-long at Jack, and his usually glittering eyes seemed wan and empty. "Do you think we're going to change?"

Jack thought of the hardships ahead of them. He'd lived seventeen eventful years, and for him the future was a vastness of opportunities, calling to him with a voice like the wind across the desert, or the echo that sang through trees heavy with the weight of a blizzard's snowfall. He thought of that voice as the call of the wild, and it set Jack's heart pumping like nothing else.

"We'll change, James, but only in a good way," he replied at last. "Adventure makes a man grow." He refrained from voicing that other possibility: *Adventure can kill a man.* But he could see in Shepard's eyes that he knew the brutal truth of things.

James Shepard was a big man made small by sickness. His eyes still held the vigor of youth, but his body betrayed the cruelness of time, lined and worn by successive assaults and currently defending against this one final attack. His heart was weakening, but his mind remained as strong as ever. Jack had always liked the gray-haired, gray-eyed Shepard; though much older than Jack's sister, Eliza, the man seemed to make her happy. Eliza's happiness meant everything to Jack.

And though Jack knew the dangers inherent in Shepard's making this journey—and he knew that Eliza knew, as well—the older man held all the finances. Jack hated staining adventure with the taint of money, but that was the stark truth. Besides, embarking upon this journey, Shepard seemed more alive than he had in a very long time. That could only bode well for all of them.

Leaving port at last, waving madly at the well-wishers on shore, Jack had never been so excited. Ahead of them lay sixteen hundred miles of ocean, wild rivers, snow-covered mountains, treacherous passes, and some of the most inhospitable country known to man.

He was embarking upon the greatest adventure of his life.

But to achieve greatness, one must sometimes risk pain.

The voyage from San Francisco took eight days, and despite the overcrowding aboard the *Umatilla*, the time passed quickly. Jack kept a close eye on Shepard and was pleased to see that the man lost none of his resolve during the journey.

When they aproached Dyea, sailing toward the breathtaking views of mainland Alaska, rather than seeming worse for the trip Shepard shone with a new vitality. His heart might no longer be pumping blood with its former vigor, but its essence remained strong.

He was embarking upon the greatest adventure of his life.

The two men jostled for space at the railing as the ship came into port. One of the reasons Jack had been so pleased with the *Umatilla* was that it could actually land them at Dyea, thanks to having a shallower draft than some larger ships. Most had to settle for docking in Skagway, near the entrance to White Pass, which could be even more treacherous and time-consuming than the perilous route Jack intended to follow.

"Where are the docks?" Shepard asked. He coughed into his fist and then spat a wad of phlegm over the side.

At Jack's tender age, most young men tended to ignore the cautions of their elders. Impulsive and quick-tempered, he had never been an exception. But where this trip—and gold—were concerned, Shepard behaved more like an excitable boy than Jack himself. So when he heard that wary tone, Jack frowned and studied the shore.

The crew began to drop anchor with no dock in sight. Jack could see the beach from here, and smoke rising from chimneys in the town beyond, but nowhere for them to put in. Small boats were already heading out toward the *Umatilla*, locals intent upon earning a little money helping to off-load the ship.

"Excuse me!" Jack said to a grizzled crewman—a pale, drawn figure about thirty years of age—who tried to hurry by even as Jack accosted him. "Where's the dock?"

The man tugged his arm from Jack's grasp. "No docks in Dyea, kid. You'll land on the beach."

Shepard cleared his throat, sounding like an angry bear as he clamped a firm hand on the crewman's wrist. "Now hold on. That's lunacy! It'll take hours to get all the supplies out of your hold, sorted, and off the beach before the tide comes in."

A dangerous glint had appeared in the crewman's eyes, and he glanced down at the grip Shepard had on him.

"James . . . ?" Jack began, looking around to make sure no one else would jump into the fight. He reached around to the small of his back, where he'd tucked a small, sheathed knife.

Shepard released the man's hand but did not back off.

The crewman smiled. "If you're worried about the tide, you'd better hurry."

With that, he rushed off through the crowd, many of whom appeared to have been aware of this little detail, though others were only just now learning. A chorus of complaints rumbled across the deck, but there was nothing any of them could do about it. They'd come too far and spent too much money to turn back now.

If Jack had thought the preparation for the journey a breathless scramble, it seemed nothing in comparison to the chaotic rush as the *Umatilla*'s more than four hundred passengers attempted to get their supplies and equipment onto the beach, and from there to higher ground. Would-be prospectors, who'd been dubbed "stampeders" by the press, cursed one another and fought for space aboard the many small boats ferrying goods and people ashore.

Many of the men and women must have become lethargic during the voyage, and some already seemed to be having second thoughts about the journey they'd set out upon. Jack, on the other hand, felt as though he might burst into song as he and Shepard sat in a small rowboat, clinging to packs full of their most vital belongings. Though only late August, it was already growing cold up here, but Jack was warmed by the thrill of adventure.

During their last few days in the city, he had used Shepard's money to buy equipment and provisions. Adequate clothing was a necessity: heavy mittens, hats, fur-lined coats and trousers, warm underwear, boots with thick grips and straps to seal them against the ingress of water and snow. He purchased tools with which they could chop trees and construct boats and cabins, a year's supply of food in sealed containers—dried, preserved, and pickled. Camping equipment was vital, and Jack had the money to buy two of everything, including tents and blankets, shovels, ground-sheets, and the Klondike stoves that would keep them warm whilst camping, cook their food, and give them light.

He had also packed his all-important books. Jack never traveled without at least some work of Melville's, and *Moby-Dick* rode in his pack now.

He breathed in the Alaskan air, caught the scent of the wild, and after eight long days aboard ship, felt ready to run the Chilkoot Pass. All of the preparations here in Dyea would only make him more anxious to begin. If he could have set off that very day and left all the supplies behind, he would have done so, and eagerly. But though he had come to the northlands to dare much and would not be discouraged by whatever obstacles might be put in his path, only a fool took unnecessary risks.

Best to be cautious, and smart. There was a lot riding on this expedition.

A grin stretched his lips as the rowboat slid onto the shore of Dyea Beach. Jack took two steps—quite used to the sway of the surf by now—and then stood on dry land for the first time in more than a week. He turned to watch Shepard climb out of the boat and nearly offered his brother-in-law a hand before realizing the man would never take it. To do so would be a sign of weakness.

Once on land, though, Shepard threw his head back and breathed deeply. Jack expected another of his ragged coughing fits to follow, but it did not come. An auspicious sign. Shepard peered up the beach toward the smoke rising from the town's chimneys and nodded as if to himself.

"Let's get to work, boy," Shepard said.

Boy. That dreaded word. Yet today, Jack did not object. Perhaps it was merely a term of endearment, or the way the old soldier chose to remind himself and his young wife's stepbrother which of them was in charge here. It didn't matter. Jack would not be broken by the frozen north, and certainly, despite his often quick-draw temper, he would not allow himself to be irked by a single word.

And so they set to work.

With Jack as the runner and foreman and Shepard as the paymaster, they quickly corralled a group of willing locals. As their equipment began to arrive on the beach in crates and packs, those enterprising Tlingit Indians carried them to higher ground and arranged them neatly in a spot Jack had chosen. Trusting no one but themselves, Jack remained on the beach with their equipment while Shepard oversaw its safe delivery.

The tide came in fast that afternoon, and three large crates were partially dampened by the encroaching surf. Jack exhorted the men to work faster or they wouldn't be paid a dime, and the last crate he half dragged several feet to avoid having the contents swamped before it, too, was finally hauled away to safety.

Halfway through the job, the price changed. The Indians charged twenty dollars an hour when the tide was low—already an astronomical sum—but as the waves grew closer and the tide rolled in, the price went up to fifty dollars an hour.

"They ought to have been pointing guns at us, asking that price!" Jack fumed, indignant, as the men raced away to enrich themselves from the plight of some other passenger.

Shepard seemed barely to have heard him. The man wore a smile Jack had never seen on him before, not even in his most tender moments with Eliza.

"I've sent a boy ahead to secure rooms for tonight," Shepard said. "We'll depart at first light."

Then he noticed Jack studying him.

"What are you staring at?" Shepard demanded.

"You look well," Jack told him, surprised. "Ready for adventure?"

Shepard appeared to give the question a moment's thought. Jack had expected a lighthearted reply, a rallying moment before they set about engaging more Indian porters to carry their equipment into town, but his brother-in-law seemed apprehensive.

"I'm sixty-one years old, boy, and God gave me a weak heart." Shepard gazed at the packs and crates piling up all along the beach. "At night, I dream of gold. It might be the only thing keeping me alive."

Jack nodded. "Fair enough. Let's go find some."

Having engaged Indian porters to carry their supplies and equipment to the hotel—and paid handsomely—Jack and Shepard shouldered their packs and walked from the rocky beach up toward Dyea proper. The word *town* was generous. The single main street and few outlying homes and buildings were more a settlement than anything remotely permanent. Coming upon it from the coast, Jack had a queer moment of disconnection and felt as though they had found themselves not in Alaska but in Deadwood, during that town's run of gold fever.

The sky had been a crystalline blue when the *Umatilla* dropped anchor, but on the shore a light mist seemed to hang permanently above Dyea, and the plumes of chimney smoke from the settlement only added to the gauzy veil that obscured the eastward view. They could see the outline of icy hills in the distance, but as they started along the main street, their focus remained on the town.

On the right they passed a row of nearly identical barnlike buildings, each with a small window just below its peaked roof and with a shop entrance below. Jack glanced at the signs: YUKON TRADING POST, U.S. POST OFFICE,

COUGHLIN-LANDRY HARDWARE, DUTCHER BILL'S SALOON.

The left side of the street seemed more familiar, with a brightly painted façade on a stand-alone structure whose sign read only DANCE HALL. Beyond that stood Hayley's Hotel, a big box of a building—clapboard like all the others—with its sign painted right on the side wall.

"Looks like it's about to fall down," Shepard muttered.

"I've slept in much worse," Jack said, thinking about railroad sidings and jail cells. "It'll be nice to have a soft bed for a night, especially since it's going to be a long while before we encounter another. And a bath wouldn't go amiss for either of us."

Shepard grunted in amusement. After eight days at sea, they both stank. "First we have to get there."

It was an excellent point. The entire street was a muddy mess of hoof- and boot prints, and furrows cut by wagon wheels. In some places the dirt had dried and hardened into ridges, and in others water filled the crevices.

As they navigated the runnels and potholes, mud sucking at their boots, Shepard's breathing grew labored under the weight of his fifty-odd-pound pack. Jack gave him a surreptitious glance and saw that rather than glowing red with exertion, his brother-in-law's face had paled. Before long, Shepard would be unable to carry his own pack.

"You doing all right?" Jack asked.

"I'll manage," Shepard muttered.

They'd been amiable traveling companions all through the voyage, but now a growing tension enveloped them. In all the world there was no one Jack loved as much as his stepsister, Eliza. She had practically raised him, and against her wishes, and with full knowledge of the man's deteriorating health, he had plotted with her husband to embark upon this adventure, knowing that Shepard was able and keen to finance the entire journey himself.

Perhaps Jack had been selfish, but there was nothing to be done for it now. Besides, Shepard was a willing and insistent partner.

Jack tried to assuage his guilt by considering the other purpose for this adventure: to aid his mother. On the day of their departure, Eliza had revealed to him that their mother was close to losing her home. She had relied on Jack's income for a long time, and his recent month-long absence—a stretch in jail for vagrancy, though none of his family knew of it—had caused her to fall deeper into debt. She had even returned to conducting séances and other rituals as a spiritual medium, an absurdity that she touted as the truth and that made Jack distinctly uncomfortable. He had persuaded himself that it was nothing more than a charade and a fraud. So though the woman had little love in her heart—all the nurturing he had needed as a boy he had found in Eliza—still she was his mother. If he found gold, she would be able to keep her home, and to abandon the charlatanry of spiritualism. Yet that seemed a distant concern right now; it was Shepard who worried him most.

But Shepard had his own mind. He was a man, not some sickly child to be coddled, and Jack believed that every man must be master of his own fate. Nevertheless, he dreaded having to deliver the news to Eliza should calamity befall her husband.

Eyes front, chin high, Jack marched across the muddy ruin of Dyea's main street toward the boardwalk in front of Hayley's Hotel. Only when he had stepped up onto the wood and kicked mud from his boots did he glance back to check on Shepard's progress.

The man had stopped a dozen feet back.

"James?" he said.

Shepard's face had gone slack and he stared eastward with wide eyes, bent slightly forward to manage the weight of his pack. He'd been pale before, but now he looked dreadfully sick. He blinked, coughed lightly, and then set off into a deeper fit of coughing that bent him double. The old soldier let his pack slip from his back and fall into the mud.

Jack dropped his own pack on the boardwalk and ran to Shepard's side.

"What is it, James?" he asked, gripping the man's

elbow. "You're all right. Try to catch your breath."

Shepard was shaking, his skin hot, and blood freckled his lips and chin. He'd been ill almost ever since Jack had known him, but he had never seen the older man looking so frail.

"James?" he said again, softly.

James nodded and took several long, steadying breaths. He stared to the east, wheezing and coughing some more, eyes watering the entire time. Still bent double, hands on his knees, he gestured with a nod.

"Is that it, boy? Is that the pass?"

Jack turned to see that the mist had thinned, providing a clearer view of the nearby hills. It might be August, but they were in Alaska, and to the east white walls of ice rose up from the land like the forbidding landscape in a dream of endless winter. The gap in the ice, visible only as a shadow from here, was the Chilkoot Pass. The trail that would take them to Dawson City began at the foot of those frozen cliffs.

Even from this distance Jack could make out the dark line of men and horses trekking up the Chilkoot Trail toward the forbidding pass—men with dreams of gold, and the Tlingit Indians making their own fortunes just getting the stampeders and their gear over the mountains.

Shepard started coughing again, and this time when he wiped at his lips, Jack saw a larger smear of blood.

It did not bode well. Dark thoughts of resentment and frustration flitted at the edges of Jack's mind, but he pushed them away. They had made a pact, the two of them, and Jack London always kept his word.

He put a hand on Shepard's shoulder. "I'll help you every step of the way. I'll get you there, so help me God, or else we'll share an icy grave. And I don't mean to die, so that means we'll both have our stake on the Klondike come spring, and bring back a pile."

At last able to breathe evenly, Shepard gently pushed Jack's hand away.

"I've been a fool," he said, words burning with a fury obviously reserved for himself. "I won't allow you to become one."

"James," Jack said, "you've come all this way."

"Yes, and now I have to go all *that* way." He looked again at the pass, eyes wide. And even as he watched, Jack saw James's expression change from fear to resignation to sorrow and regret.

Shepard slowly stood upright. He shouldered his pack, taking deep breaths. And finally he turned his back on the frozen mountains.

"I've got to get back to the beach before the *Umatilla* sails for home," Shepard said. "I'll bring your love to Eliza and your mother."

Jack said nothing. Shepard would clearly brook no argument.

"I've invested a great deal in this journey," the old soldier went on. "More than money, you understand? Every wish I've ever made. I'm leaving them all here with you, and I expect you to carry them to Dawson and beyond. Don't let me down, boy."

Jack shook his head. "Of course I won't."

"See you don't," Shepard said. And with that he left, trudging back through half-frozen mud toward the shore, leaving Jack with all their supplies and equipment and enough determination for both of them.

Jack watched him go and hoped he would make it home in good health, so that Eliza would not have to grieve. He found himself untroubled by the idea of making the journey alone, for most of his life's journeys had been undertaken as solo ventures, even when he was surrounded by others pursuing their own paths.

Shepard walked to the edge of town and vanished on the road down to the beach without once turning to look back. The moment he was out of sight, a huge grin broke out on Jack's face. He felt a strange elation growing within him. Freed of his obligations to and concern for Shepard— and, yes, shorn of the guilt he'd been feeling at bringing the older man along—he felt more confident than ever in his course of action.

He turned to look up into the mist at the Chilkoot Pass. He felt it drawing him almost physically, and he was tempted to run there now and climb it all tonight, supplies or not. Throughout the voyage they had heard tales of men who had died on the trail, and thousands who had faltered and turned back. Shepard had wilted at the mere sight of the ominous terrain.

Not Jack. The frozen north would not defeat him. Only death could stop him now.

CHAPTER TWO

MARCH OF THE DEAD

THE WORD AROUND DYEA was that a man with no des-
tination could have camped on the Chilkoot Trail
for months without wanting for anything. Warm
clothes, dried and salted meats, canned beans, guns for
hunting, tents . . . the trading post and the hardware store
down in Dyea would have gone out of business if the stampeders landing by the thousands on the beach had but
known that they could pick up all the supplies they needed
right on the side of that trail. Especially on the westward
side, making the climb up to 3,500 feet, where frigid winds
buffeted travelers even in late summer, abandoned gear lay
everywhere.

And if the desire was for fresh meat, the cruel terrain
of the Chilkoot Trail provided that in ample supply. Horses
collapsed of exhaustion, broke their legs in crevices, or

fractured their spines falling backward when the trail became too steep. Some were put down to end their misery, while others were left to die in agony by hard-hearted men who stripped them of their saddles and went on, not wishing to waste a bullet.

Without Shepard accompanying him, Jack made the decision to travel light. Opening crates, he sorted through food stores and put aside essentials. Much of what they had brought on the voyage he sold to the proprietor of Hayley's Hotel. Shepard's clothes he traded to a burly, bearded fellow named Merritt Sloper, whom he'd met on board the *Umatilla*. Sloper had a particularly fine skillet and several bags of coffee with which he was willing to part, provided Jack wouldn't refuse him a brew if their paths crossed on the trail.

The deal struck, Jack took an extra blanket from Shepard's supplies and then went through his own clothes. By the time he fell asleep that night, he had set aside, sold, or given away three-quarters of what they had brought with them. More confident than ever, contentedly exhausted, he fully expected to sleep through to dawn.

When he woke in the middle of the night, disoriented, he sat up and breathed in the darkness. *I'm in Hayley's Hotel in Dyea*, he thought, and then heard a groan.

Jack held his breath. He had never been afraid of the

dark, but he had learned to respect it.

The groan came again: a floorboard, protesting under a weight that should not be there. Whoever walked tried to do so quietly.

"Who's there?" Jack whispered.

A door drifted open where he did not remember seeing one before. He was so unsettled that it took a few seconds before he saw the hand splayed flat against the wood, and a few seconds more before he followed it back along the arm, across the shoulder, and to the face hanging behind it in the gloom.

"Mother?" he asked. With recognition came the familiar smells of home—stale cooking and incense.

"There will be doom," his mother said, but not in her own voice. The tone was flat, cool as ice, almost disinterested. "Doom in the north, a cry of death in the great white silence, and the spirits will bear witness." She entered the room, and Jack caught his breath. *That's not my mother,* he thought, and though the idea was ridiculous—the woman standing before him *was* his mother, with her hair, face, and nightdress—he could not shake the idea. There was something disquieting about her appearance, as if a stranger hiding beneath her skin was trying to force itself out. She was dreadfully stiff, skin almost translucent and the shade of freshly fallen snow.

There was something disquieting about her appearance, as if a
stranger hiding beneath her skin was trying to force itself out.

He had seen something like this before. She had told him it was her spirit guide speaking through her. He had never before believed a word of such foolishness, and he hated her false spiritualism. She fooled people with it, preyed on their suffering, and—

Is she fooling me now? Am I here, or am I at home? He thought he was dreaming, but such knowledge usually granted the dreamer control. Here, *he* was the one being controlled.

"Get out of my room," he whispered.

"Something follows," his mother said, smiling. It was a sickly expression, and it did not touch her voice. "Yet still you'll die in the snow, cold . . . and almost alone." Then she turned and left.

It was a few minutes before Jack could leave his bed, but when he approached the door, he found a blank wall. He touched it, and it was only wood. *I'm awake now for sure*, he thought, and after returning to bed he could not return to sleep. He watched dawn cast its cleansing light over Dyea.

Unsettled by the nightmare, yet determined to let daylight blanch it away, Jack was the first to leave town that day on his way toward the Chilkoot Pass.

He'd left Dyea with two horses carrying his kit, his own pack twenty pounds lighter than it had been the day before.

His shoulders were padded so the straps did not cut into him, and he'd set off at speed as the sun rose over the white peaks, the crack of Chilkoot Pass gleaming on the horizon.

That had been four days ago.

Now his eyes watered at the stench of rotting horseflesh beside the trail, and he kept as much distance as possible from the others jostling for position as they climbed. He'd been making excellent time, outpacing most of the white men and even some of the Indian carriers, who were used to the terrain and the climate.

He kept his focus fixed on the mountaintops, his goal in sight, and kept to himself. Several times fights had broken out, and he'd had to guide his two horses around the stinking combatants as well as others who had slowed to exhort them on, grateful for the distraction of potential bloodshed. Jack had never been one to shy away from a fight, but he could already feel a cold bite in the air as he climbed higher and higher, and feared winter would arrive sooner than any of them had bargained for.

The debris of surrender littered the sides of the trail. He passed men who had given up and were making their way back to Dyea, eyes downcast in defeat. They had failed and were ashamed, and Jack vowed that he would never be one of them. Such failure must be hard to live with, and there was no sense of relief in their bearing, even though their physical hardships were behind them.

As he walked on, the trail rising higher, the going steeper, memories of his dream flashed across his mind. He often dreamed of his mother, sometimes fancies of the perfect relationship they had never had, more often interpretations of her lovelessness and occasional cruelty. She could be a stone-hearted woman: When Jack was a boy she had often exhorted his stepfather to beat him when he misbehaved, and the only affection she gave to Jack came on days when he managed to bring a paycheck into the house. And there were those times when she'd made him lie on the kitchen table during a séance and called upon the spirits of the dead to damn him for some boyish wrongdoing. Even back then he'd never really believed, but she'd done her best to ensure that the process scared him.

"The spirits are closer to you than you think," she'd say. "And if you're bad, I can *invite them in*."

For days after these séances he'd be angry and resentful, sad at his mother's treatment of him. And come sunset and bed, alone in the dark, he'd also be terrified that perhaps she was right. Now he could hardly bear to think of it. And yet despite all this she was still his mother, and he loved her.

Such musings confused Jack, and he became angry at those confusions.

He cursed and led his horses to the side of the trail. He had crested the top of the pass whilst buried in introspection, and that moment of success had passed uncelebrated. Damn these melancholy thoughts—they would not do here!

He decided to make a brew and let the hot coffee mark the moment the rest of his journey began.

"Just the man I was hoping to run into," a voice said.

Settled into a windbreak he'd built by piling up his pack and hauling boxes and satchels down from his horses, Jack looked up from his small fire into the ruddy-cheeked, smiling face of Merritt Sloper. The man had frost in his ginger beard and a thick cap pulled down over his ears, so he looked like some deranged Father Christmas.

"I suppose you want a cup of coffee," Jack said. He could not hold back a small smile. He was comfortable in his own company, but right now he welcomed the company of another, even someone he knew only vaguely.

"I thought you'd never ask."

"I hope you brought your own cup," Jack told him. "I've only got the one."

Sloper grunted as he settled onto the ground beside Jack, shucking off his own pack. He banged his gloved hands together, pulled the gloves off, and held his palms out to the small fire. Primarily, however, his attention was on the small black coffeepot that Jack had propped beside the fire.

Sloper dug a tin cup from his pack. As Jack poured him half a cup of strong coffee, another man approached, this one holding the tether of a horse.

"Damn it, Merritt, you could have waited for me!" the man chided. Thin and bespectacled, he had the air of a fussy schoolmaster gone to seed.

"The smell of coffee drew me on, friend Jim," Sloper replied with mock penitence, hanging his head. "Do not curse me for my one indulgence." Then he shrugged an apology, sipped his coffee, and let out a loud sigh of contentment, settling more comfortably on the crusty snow, closing his eyes.

"You left me with the horse," Jim began, then lowered his voice. "Those two fellows from Texas have been eyeing our supplies ever since the last of their own horses died, and you—"

"Besides!" Sloper said, eyes springing open. "We made it over the top! Despite all your doubts, my friend, here we are! I hadn't the energy for a victory dance, but a cup of coffee is celebration enough."

Rolling his eyes, Jim gave up. He led his burdened, exhausted horse over beside Jack's two, knocked a peg into the snow with the heel of his boot, and tethered the beast to it.

Then he held out a hand, leaning over the fire. "Jim

Goodman. I believe we arrived on the same ship."

Jack smiled and shook. "Jack London. I remember you."

A rush of good feeling filled him. Odd as they were, here were two men hardy enough to crest the Chilkoot Pass, to face the challenge and not turn back. In the short time since he had set out from Dyea, he had seen enough failure and breathed in enough death to last him a lifetime. Now he found the companionship of these two men very welcome indeed.

"I don't suppose you have another cup of coffee," said the morose Goodman.

Jack shook the pot. "Only a drop, I'm afraid. Merritt took the last of it."

Goodman's shoulders drooped. "Of course," he said, as though used to being left out.

Suffused with this new feeling of bonhomie, Jack reached for his pack. "Actually, there's more where that came from. I'll fix us another pot."

"Really?" the two men said together, both raising their eyebrows in surprise.

"Why not?" Jack replied. "We made it to the top, boys. We're in this together now."

After almost a week spent climbing the Chilkoot Trail, Jack's bones ached and his muscles burned, but he felt alive in a way he believed few people would ever experience. Unshaven, unwashed, he nevertheless perceived himself as clean, somehow purified by the icy mountain air and his own backbreaking efforts. Away from his mother and her spiritual charlatanism—but more important, away from every job he'd ever had, every version of himself he'd ever tried to create—at last he could strip away the world's expectations and find the man within.

Who is Jack London? he wondered, certain that this journey would bring him the answer.

Seen from the top of the pass, the remainder of the trail seemed like a gift. It leveled out and then began a gentle descent toward distant canyons.

"How far to Lake Lindeman?" Sloper asked.

Jack cocked an eyebrow at Jim Goodman, for he himself had heard varying estimates.

Goodman did not hesitate. "Nine miles."

"We'll be all right," Jack said, gesturing around them. "Nobody's turning back after making it through the pass."

And it was true. The traffic all trudged in the same direction now. There were still bits of abandoned equipment on the sides of the trail, and looking ahead, Jack could see at least two dead horses—poor beasts that had handled the worst of it but couldn't go a step farther—but for the most part, the prospectors were getting on with it.

"But we need to hurry," he said.

The laconic, gloomy Goodman seemed to come awake at that. "Hurry? I'm just happy to be alive."

Ahead of them were two men, German by the accents he'd heard, who slowed down a bit as if to eavesdrop. Holding the leads of his horses tightly, Jack slowed his own pace, and Sloper and Goodman followed suit.

"Maybe there's enough gold for everyone," Jack said. "Maybe the whole of the Klondike is El Dorado. But I look at every man on this trail as competition, and you'd do well to think the same way."

Merritt Sloper scratched at his thick ginger beard. His normally jovial expression had faded into an almost child-like sadness. "Even us, Jack? Are we competition?"

Jack grinned. "You sure are, boys. But with us, it's a friendly competition. And listen, there's another reason we need to hurry. Winter's coming on."

Goodman scoffed, pushing his glasses up on the bridge of his nose. "Winter! Jack, in case you hadn't noticed, it's always winter up here."

"You know what I mean. It'll all be frozen soon. If we don't get to Dawson before the rivers freeze, we may never make it."

"It's barely September," Sloper said.

"I talked to a fellow on the climb up, a Tlingit tribesman,

who told me the signs were pointing to an early freeze. He said that once, when his grandfather was a boy, the rivers froze in the middle of August."

Goodman tutted, gripped the lead of his weary horse, and picked up the pace again. "Impossible."

Sloper, though, gazed at Jack with worry creasing his brow. "Is that the truth?"

Jack loosened his grip on the leads and followed Goodman, with Sloper beside him and the horses behind. "I mean to survive this adventure, Merritt. Survive, and go back to California with a mighty pile. You visit an inhospitable land, you have to rely on the wisdom of the people who make it their home. Besides, can't you feel it? The wind makes my teeth rattle."

Sloper nodded at this, and when the trail widened a bit, the three men walked abreast. They spoke of home and of their dreams, of books and adventure. Jack entertained them with stories of his time as an oyster pirate, and of riding the rails with hoboes and brawling on the docks. He chose not to mention his thirty days in prison.

His two companions managed to surprise him, however, when he discovered that neither was much older than Jack himself. Sloper, a stonemason, was twenty-five, a decade younger than Jack had presumed, while Goodman—who actually *was* a schoolteacher—had recently celebrated his twenty-second birthday. The two men hailed from Illinois, not far from Chicago, and had become acquainted due to a long friendship between their families. While their personalities could not have been more different, Sloper and Goodman had the rapport of lifelong friends, yet they easily and willingly incorporated Jack into their dynamic.

They camped that night in the shelter of a copse of trees, stacking their belongings around three sides to try to protect themselves from the worst of the wind. After tending to his horses first, Jack sat with his two new friends around the campfire. They shared coffee and dried fruit, cooking a weak stew that tasted better than it had any right to taste, and then Jack felt exhaustion overtaking him. He fell asleep blinking up at the stars, imagining the time to come when he would spend his days panning for gold.

At some point this daydreaming slipped away, and he was adrift in his own subconscious. The relative peace with which he imagined the prospecting passed away also; men were killed for the best claims, and wild creatures came from the forests to snatch away the unwary, leaving behind only bloody red smears in the snow. But such a mundane dream death did not stalk Jack.

There was something else.

He dreamed himself working upriver from the main strike in Rabbit Creek, existing on his own with little more than a campfire and a torn, tattered tent. He panned by day and read by firelight at night, and all the time something lurked at the edges of the flickering illumination of the campfire, watching. It followed him across the landscape, one day observing from the heights of a great mountain, the next day spying on him from the darkness beneath the trees. He could never make out what it was, but the sense of foreboding was terrible.

And it was only at night that he saw it. Eyes like fallen stars stared at him from the shadows, waiting for the opportunity to pounce.

In the late morning of September 8, the three men came at last to the shore of Lake Lindeman. Goodman's horse had collapsed the night before, and it was Sloper who put the animal out of its misery. With the echo of the gunshot ringing out along the trail and across the green-black mountain slopes, Merritt Sloper finally lost his smile.

Nor did it return the next morning when they came in sight of the lake. The scene ought to have been beautiful. Lake Lindeman sat nestled in a basin surrounded by white-capped mountains whose foothills were thick with dark pines and powdered with a light snow. Around the lake grew scrub grass, and at other times animals must have come to the water to drink and nibble at what little vegetation grew there.

But a vast swath had been cut out of the pine woods around the shore of the lake. Stampeders worked like an ant colony, cutting trees and sawing timber. Men unwilling to go farther had set up a nice business for themselves building boats and rafts and selling them at outrageous prices.

"We'll be flat broke before we even get to Dawson if we pay that," Goodman said, anxiously cleaning his glasses with a kerchief he kept in his front pocket.

The three of them stood with Jack's two horses, now carrying the additional weight of Sloper's and Goodman's equipment, and watched the buzz of activity on the lakeshore. There were planks and boat frames everywhere, and a couple of acres' worth of sawdust that covered the ground like snow, the sweet smell of pine in the air.

Thunderous hammering and the ragged sound of saws on wood resounded, along with shouts and laughter and the crash and crack of more trees being felled. They watched a new boat set off across the lake, and it immediately began to leak.

"We're not paying that," Jack said.

Sloper scratched his red beard and glanced nervously at Goodman. "You don't mean to walk around the lake, Jack? We'd be better off turning back."

Jack shot him a harsh look, raising his chin. "I set myself a goal, Merritt. I mean to keep it. My whole life, I never turned back from anything, and I won't start now."

He opened a long satchel that hung from the saddle of the gray mare he'd bought in Dyea. From within he drew out a leather case, and from the leather case an ax.

"Besides, I don't think you boys were listening to the stories I told you. I've been on boats my whole life. Why, I spent so much time at the docks and out on the bay that they used to call me the Sailor Kid."

Jack slung the ax over his shoulder and took up the horses' tethers again. "Now you go and talk to the men who already have boats, the ones who are putting them in the water. See if you can't buy us another ax or two, and a saw. That'll cost a lot less than a boat. Then come and find me. I'll get started felling some pines."

Goodman slipped his glasses back on, fixing them as though not quite sure if he could see Jack clearly.

"Are you suggesting that we build our own boat?"

Jack tipped him a wink. "You catch on quick, Jimmy."

Sloper had taken his jacket off and hung it over his arm. The sun felt warm today, at least by comparison to what they'd grown used to. It would be a long while before they were truly warm again.

"If you say you know boats, then I believe you, Jack,"

the burly stonemason said. "And I'm not afraid of a little work. But you were worried about the winter coming. Won't this delay be costly?"

"I won't lie to you, Merritt," Jack said. "This is an unfortunate complication. But the boatbuilders down there on the shore have a long line of customers ahead of us. If we work hard and don't make mistakes, building our own boat might actually be faster than waiting for them to make one for us."

With that he left them to their own tasks, walking toward the line of trees with the horses behind him, whistling happily with the ax slung over his shoulder. He could see in his mind the boat he would build, every plank and joint. And he knew what he would name her.

The *Yukon Belle*.

First the lake, then Thirty Mile River, and if they wanted to make it to Dawson before the big freeze, they'd have to shoot White Horse Rapids as well. He'd chosen not to mention that to his companions, however. The word was that most men who'd attempted to ride the rapids had died or at least half drowned and given up. No need to frighten them before they got there.

After all, as Jack had told them, he'd been around boats all his life. A little rough water didn't scare him.

How bad could it be?

CHAPTER THREE

THE *BELLE*

OUR DAYS TO BUILD, and the *Yukon Belle* was a good boat. Jack saw that, and it made him proud, but he also knew that there was a greater test than Lake Lindeman yet to come. And sometime soon, he would have to tell Merritt and Jim just how treacherous the next stages of their journey would be.

They crossed the lake in good humor, taking turns rowing and bailing. Two of them would row at a time, sitting side by side on the rough plank seat, while the other member of their small team tried to prevent too much water from leaking into the boat. Their feet were quickly awash, but constant bailing kept the water down to an acceptable level. Jack had built several thick struts across the boat widthwise, and their equipment was propped on these, held up out of the water he'd known they would inevitably be taking on. Though it was the first boat he had ever built, he was an experienced sailor, and he was confident that theirs was the best craft currently crossing the waters of Lake Lindeman.

They'd left the horses behind, exchanging them for tools and a good helping of food kept by the boatbuilders camped along the lakeside. Jack had been sorry to see the horses go. They were strong beasts, and he had a feeling that their strength would be missed by the three men.

The lake's surface shimmered with thin ice.

"We're breaking through easily," Merritt said. The ice barely whispered along the boat's rough hull.

"For now," Jack said. He pulled at his oar, enjoying the rhythmic movement and the warm strain on his muscles. "Don't forget, many others have already come this way."

"We're doing well," Jim said. He was bailing, his clothes soaked and his brow dripping sweat. Jack thought he had never seen the schoolteacher so happy.

"As I said," Jack said, "for now. But there's hard waters ahead, friends."

"Rapids," Merritt said. "We heard about them. We'll need to portage, then—"

"No," Jack said. "It'll take too long, and it's too danger-ous. High cliffs, uncharted land. You know the lay of the land ahead of us? You've studied it?"

The two men glanced at each other; then Merritt shrugged.

Jack sighed. "The White Horse Rapids," he said. "Very rough, very dangerous. A lot of people have tried to shoot them. Some disappear, some wash up dead. Lots turn back."

"There's no turning back here," Merritt said, and Jack was impressed by his confidence.

"But you've built us a good boat?" Jim asked. "You know the water?"

Jack examined the *Yukon Belle*. Water lapped around his feet, and with Jim paused in his bailing while they talked, the level was rising quickly. The bow was sharp, the stern square, but the draft was deeper than he would have liked. The rough boards nailed and tied together to form the hull were already distorting as the timber took on water.

"Yes, she's a good boat," he said. And he rowed in silence for a while, silently thinking ahead to the dangers they faced.

The thundering water formed a violently foaming, snaking ridge along the base of the canyon. It was monstrous. The ground shook, the air was heavy with the roar, and spray cooled Jack's skin like the touch of ghostly fingers. He was thrilled to his primal core, and terrified as well, a blend of sensations that he had experienced before and would likely know again. His soul cried in exultation at the adventure ahead. One day, he knew, such yearning could be the death of him.

There were other people on the riverbank, some in groups, several more alone. They watched the grand and fearsome river, and Jack wondered how long they had been standing here, men and women rooted to the spot by the terror of what lay before them. He had the strange image of them being frozen, slowly turning to stone as the waters crashed by without any consideration of the passage of time. One day, perhaps, the river would shift its course enough to start abrading these statues of humanity, if the spray did not wear them away beforehand. And here they stood now, testament to both fear and determination: They could not go forward and refused to turn back.

Jack prepared the *Yukon Belle* before the observers. He felt good. He sensed their eyes upon him, and perhaps somewhere in their perception of him as a madman was respect.

"Merritt, you take the bow." He gave Merritt a paddle. "You rafted in the Amazon, you told me."

"Yes, but—"

"Then you'll be our lookout." Jack could see the older man's dread, but to pause now would be to retreat forever.

"Jim, the oars. Just row, keep us moving, keep the power flowing from the boat to the water, not the other way around. I'll be at the stern, steering." He regarded the boat where it bobbed close to the bank. "For now, let's get all the stuff as low as it'll go."

"It'll get soaked," Jim said.

"Better that than keep its weight high and let it flip us over."

The three men worked together, and Jack actually sensed the fear that exuded from the other two turning slowly to excitement. It was something about taking action, *doing* instead of just standing there watching like the many other prospectors lining the riverbank. But he also thought it was something to do with camaraderie. They were doing this together, and they felt like a team.

When they cast off, the people on the bank began shouting advice. "Keep to the ridge in the middle!" someone shouted, and the same words came from elsewhere. Jack wondered just how many foolhardy people the observers on the bank had seen on their way, and how many of them had ever made it through the rapids to the Thirty Mile River, and the upper Yukon River beyond.

For now, though, such musings were best cast from his mind. The river had them in its grasp, they had surrendered to its direction and fury, and to survive was all that mattered.

At first the water had an oily appearance, fast flowing but unbroken by protruding rocks. The *Yukon Belle* slipped along comfortably, with Merritt in the front giving calm direction and Jack switching the tiller from side to side to steer the boat. The canyon walls rose around them, the banks disappeared, and the water was funneled into narrower and narrower chasms.

The river raged and roared. The cliffs flashed by, and Jack glanced up to see the shadows of people watching from the cliff edge, or perhaps they were simply the disinterested leanings of trees. Either way, he felt alone with his friends and the river.

They powered through the first violent patch of rapids, the boat slicing through waves and shuddering as it scraped across a shallow patch of buried stones. Jack felt the vibration through his knees and tried not to imagine what would happen if the rough boat was pulled apart by rocks.

"Left!" Merritt shouted, and Jack tried to edge them that way. A domed rock flashed by on their right, the river foaming angrily around its head.

Jim's eyes were wide with terror behind his little teacher's glasses, which were spattered with spray from the tumultuous river. He stared past Jack, back the way they had come, and perhaps he was wishing he'd never set foot in this boat. Jack grinned at him, but Jim seemed not to see the expression.

Jack felt his pulse racing, heart thrumming inside him. Every nerve ending tingled, and he forgot to breathe as he concentrated on trying to keep to the central ridge of water. It was fastest here, but it was also the clearest route through the rapids. That was his hope, at least. In reality, he knew that the bottom could be ripped from the boat at any moment.

In those moments, Jack had never felt so fearful and yet so alive. His grin spread farther across his features, so wide that it hurt his face, and he whooped with amazement. For several seconds it seemed as though he had left his body, as though he observed himself from someplace above or behind the world. Though nature raged around and against him, he felt as though he could command it, as if he were not a pawn like Odysseus but the river's master.

Then he heard Merritt shout and glanced over just in time to see the big man's arms whipped around and the remains of his paddle flipped up into the air, disappearing behind the boat. The rock that had surprised Merritt and snapped his paddle ground against the boat's hull, growling angrily as the water pushed them past. Jack hauled on the tiller just in time, and then they were through the rapids, bow turning slowly toward the left wall of the canyon as the waters around them seemed to relax their hold.

"Good God!" Jim said, gasping.

"Damn, that was close!" Merritt said, and he laughed as he slapped Jim on the back.

"Don't get lazy yet," Jack said. "Plenty more to come." *And worse*, he thought, but saying that would benefit none of them. He had not mastered the wild yet, but he was damned if he'd let it defeat him.

As they drifted down the river toward the next section of rapids, the men had time to appreciate their surroundings. It was a wondrous place. The steep canyon walls were speckled white here and there where snow had built up on ledges. The cliff tops were mostly bare, but in places trees hung over the river valley, as if considering leaping in. Birds circled in the gray sky above, and the sound of the river filled their ears. Here it was a gentler flow, yet still it shushed from the canyon walls and echoed back, a constant whisper that would know no silence. Jack felt at peace in such danger, and he asked himself again, *Who is Jack London?* He thought he was still a long way from the answer, but it felt as though the river were drawing him closer.

"This place is spooky," Merritt said from the bow of the boat. He was looking around the canyon, past Jack, then ahead at where they were going, and if he'd been a dog, his hackles would have been up.

"It's too damn noisy to be spooky," Jim said. He was cleaning his glasses, wiping the lenses with measured strokes with his handkerchief. "And too cold."

"Keep your gloves on, Jim," Jack said. "You'll need every nerve in your hands when we hit the next rapids."

"I'm without a paddle," Merritt said. He kicked the top off one of their food boxes, splitting away one of the boards and carefully bending the nails so that they were not protruding. All the while he was looking around, like prey watching for its stalker.

Jack looked around as well. And as the roar of fresh rapids grew in the distance, realization struck him like a punch to the gut: *I'm being watched.*

He did not think, *We are being watched.* This was all him. He felt a great focus upon him, and the more he glanced around in growing panic, the less idea he had of where such attention was coming from. The cliff tops seemed too high, the rough walls of the canyon too far away. He even looked down into the dark waters, half expecting to see the faces of drowned men rising to leer as he rode the river to his death.

"Jack, Jim," Merritt said. "Here we go again."

And the river broke its back, drawing the little boat and its passengers into its raging wound.

———

Perhaps it was the thought of being watched—perhaps it was the unsettling idea that he was observing himself from afar—but every moment of that experience imprinted itself on Jack's mind like a photograph: the whirlpool, the Mane of the Horse, the wolf.

The wolf most of all.

They plunged into the next set of rapids, working as a team as much as they could, though Jack was aware of their woeful unreadiness for the trip they were undertaking. Merritt sat in the bow, guiding them with his impromptu paddle. Jim shipped his oars and sat awash in the base of the boat, keeping his weight as low as possible. And Jack knelt at the stern, leaning on the tiller, doing his best to edge the boat this way and that. In reality, though, the boat found its own path through the rapids, scraping and gouging past and over rocks. He felt the craft being injured all around him, cracked and battered and split, and the fact that it held together made him proud.

A strange calm descended upon him, that of a man awaiting judgment.

They rose between two large rocks, riding the water where its volume drove it upward, and past the rocks the boat tipped and fell down toward a violent, swirling pool below. *Whirlpool!* Jack had time to think, and then they were caught. The boat was trapped in conflicting currents, shaken this way and that, and water poured in from all sides. Jim started ineffectually bailing, and had it not been so terrifying, Jack would have laughed. Instead he grabbed on to the boat's hull, racking his brains for a way to escape. He shouted in terrified exhilaration, but the water was so loud that he could not even hear his own voice. He was soaked to the skin and freezing cold, but something at the heart of him kept him warm.

He looked left and right, and up at the cliffs, and though he still felt eyes upon him, the watcher was elsewhere.

The boat slid sideways. For a second that felt like minutes, it tilted on its side, and Jack expected them all to spill into the raging torrent. The boxes and bags would follow them, pushing them deeper down until the vicious current dragged them across the riverbed, braining them against submerged rocks worn smooth by millennia. As Jack fought the tiller, trying to steer them out of the whirlpool's grip, he caught Merritt's eyes and realized that the big man had something of Jack in him—he was resigned to their fate but delighted that they had tried.

Then the *Yukon Belle* righted itself and turned its nose downstream, curving away from the whirlpool and continuing on its journey. Jack shouted for joy, and this time he heard both his own voice and those of his companions.

They took their positions again, aware that they were not yet out of the fire. Jack was exhausted, dripping wet, and freezing cold. If it hadn't been for his exertions in keeping the boat aimed toward the center of the river, his clothes would be freezing around his body, and he might even be at risk of frostbite. But rather than freezing, he steamed. It was an odd sight watching vapor rise from his body, but it also gave him a thrill. It was almost *otherworldly.*

He glanced left and right, watching for the watcher. He searched deep to identify the strange sensation he felt, wondering whether his own thoughts were perpetuating the belief that unseen eyes were upon him. But then he remembered Merritt's observation that this was a spooky place, and the screaming water whispered things he could never understand.

They followed the canyon deeper into wilderness, riding the wildest stretch of the river, which had been named the Mane of the Horse. And the river bucked like an untamed horse, lifting their boat and tossing it from crest to crest as though it were made of balsa wood and contained nothing. Jack wondered at the weight being thrown around, and it was beyond his calculation. Jim stared at him with something approaching madness, and Jack could only guess at what he saw. *A madman myself,* he thought. *Sprayed with the river, battered by the boat. Is the gleam of gold still in my eyes? Or is there the look of a watched man about me?*

Merritt shouted something then, and his voice was stolen by the river's roar. He glanced back at Jack, eyes wide, jaw hanging open, and Jack looked beyond his friend, at the rolling back of the river funneled between two banks of rock ahead of them. It narrowed to half its original width in the space of a dozen feet, and the pressures and energies forcing the water through that narrow gap were immense.

Just ride the crest, Jack thought, and he leaned on the tiller.

The boat sailed through, almost as if it were apart from the raging torrent below and around it. And on the other side, drifting down into a comparatively calm stretch, Jack lost control. One second he was fine, steering and commanding the boat like the boatbuilder and sailor he was. The next moment the craft was no longer his. The sense of smooth passage left them, and the *Yukon Belle* was tilting sideways down the river, cresting each wave with a sickening sway, impacting each trough with a head-rattling thump. Wood creaked and cracked, and Jim fell sideways as a splinter as long as his arm broke from the hull and scored across his face. Two inches higher and Jim would have lost both eyes.

"Jack!" Merritt called, but Jack would not look his way. He was too annoyed at himself, too involved in trying to bring the craft back under his control. The river had them clasped in its torrential hand, and it was only a matter of time before it spilled them and their belongings into the water or dashed them against the ragged banks. Either way would be the end of them, and as the water splashed his eyes, Jack saw his mother between blinks, sitting at the table and smiling over the final meal they had shared together.

The spirits will go with you was the last thing she'd said as he'd left, more spiritual foolishness masquerading as affection. Yet as he remembered them now, those words seemed to whisper through the river-water spray.

Jack glanced about. There above, on a cliff under which the river tore itself apart, stood a wolf. It was the largest wolf he had ever seen, its gray fur mottled with streaks of dark brown, muzzle shorter and stumpier than usual. Its ears were pricked up and forward, and all its attention was focused on Jack.

Only on Jack.

"You . . . ?" he whispered, leaning toward the wolf with his right arm outstretched. As his body shoved against and shifted the tiller, the boat creaked and rolled, and with a rush they were reconnected with the river, going with the flow rather than fighting against it.

Jack glanced at Merritt and Jim and saw the two men

It was the largest wolf he had ever seen.

were grinning at him. Merritt said something in praise of Jack's boatmanship, but Jack looked away again, back upriver at the rock they had now passed by. The wolf was gone. He scanned the bank, but the creature was nowhere to be seen, and already Jack doubted himself. The canyon here was narrow, the cliff walls sheer. Where there were banks, they consisted of boulders tumbled down from above over time, abraded by the river to suit its own shape. From what he could see, there really was no way down here for an animal of that size.

They sailed on, shooting more rapids and moving farther toward the Thirty Mile River. Jack no longer feared the waters. Something was guiding his way, and he could not shake the idea that seeing the wolf had caused him to shift the tiller at just the right moment.

That wasn't me, he thought, though he tried to smile at the men's praise. *None of that was me.*

The farther they moved from the deadly rapids that should have killed them, the more unsettled Jack became.

CHAPTER FOUR

THE DEATH OF HIM

WHEN THEY CAMPED THAT EVENING, Jack was quiet and withdrawn. The wolf preyed on his memory. He had felt watched for a long time, and now, though the sensation seemed to have passed, he could still sense that lupine influence in the land around them. This was an altogether wild place, and while he had it in his mind that his presence could affect his surroundings, the idea that the opposite might be true was troubling. In a struggle of man versus nature, he felt sure, man—a man of determination and conviction such as himself—would be victorious. Now his certainty wavered.

Merritt and Jim were confident and upbeat. With the three of them sitting around a fire and drying their soaked clothes, Jack's two companions made jokes and talked of the journey to come. Jack nodded in the right places, and now and then he mustered a smile, but he stared into the fire's insides and tried to shake the idea that things were changing.

Perhaps it was the cold, and the winter bearing down on them faster than ever. Merritt and Jim still doubted Jack's observations—surely they had weeks yet—but he felt things winding down. There had been ice on the Thirty Mile River when they reached the end of this leg of the great Yukon, and though thin and brittle, its presence had troubled Jack. They still had a long way to go, and he knew very well how their journey could be disrupted if and when the river froze.

"Why so glum, Jack?" Merritt asked. "We did well today. Rode the beast and tamed it, eh?"

"Tamed the wild horse!" Jim said, and the men chuckled. They had their mittened hands wrapped around metal cups of coffee, and the smell of the brew hung fragrant in the air. Their breaths hung also, clouding the still atmosphere with every exhalation, every word spoken.

"You know why," Jack said. "I'm worried about that ice." He stood and paced around the fire. "I'm worried about how cold it is now. Worried about the frost in our beards, the cold in my toes, the numbness in my hands. We don't reach Dawson before the first freeze, we might just be stuck for months. And I don't like our chances without shelter."

"Jack—," Jim began, but Jack went on. Talking made him feel better; voicing his fears, perhaps, or maybe it was simply the act of concentrating on something other than that wolf.

"If we *are* stuck, where will we stay? We won't be able to camp—what little camping gear we have will become our tombs. So maybe we find an old cabin in the forest and make use of it. What will we eat? Our supplies might last through a winter, but barely, and that'll leave nothing for afterward."

"This doesn't sound like you, Jack," Merritt said quietly.

Jack thought angrily, *You've only known me a matter of days!* Never mind that though he was the youngest among them at seventeen, his friends seemed to look to him for leadership. But the big man's words rang true. And Jack knew that there was no better way of forging close bonds than by tackling hardship together.

He sighed and shook his head. "It isn't me, normally," he said. "Maybe I'm just tired."

"Then let's sleep," Jim said.

Merritt nodded. "Then up at dawn, and on the river all day. We'll get there, Jack, just you see."

Jack smiled as he turned away, but that expression soon dropped from his face. He left the fire and ventured into the woods, stomping through the snow that would likely be much deeper very soon. He needed to relieve himself, but he had other reasons for leaving the camp. He scanned between the trees, sniffed the air, and closed his eyes as he tried to sense the thing that was following him.

But if it *did* follow, it remained at a distance.

They spent the next day on the river, but by the time they needed to land again to eat and dry their clothes around a fire, Merritt and Jim were no longer so confident. The river was perhaps a mile wide in places, and the farther they paddled with the flow, the more ice built up around them. Cakes of ice crushed and ground together, and the river had a new sound, like the grumble of a giant slowly falling asleep.

They camped on the bank that evening with the river growling past them, but Jack vowed that from now on they would remain on the water until they reached Dawson. He reckoned it was maybe a hundred miles farther, and the chances of reaching it before the river ground to a halt completely . . .

Well, maybe they'd be lucky. But even Jim and Merritt were quiet that evening, staring into the fire and clasping their coffee mugs. Ice built up on their stubble and eyelashes, and the cold seemed to leach heat even from the fire.

On the river the next morning, Jack barely had need to steer.

"That way!" Merritt said, pointing ahead and to the left. Jack saw the clear channel and the sharp, raised chunks of ice guided them toward it. When they struck a cake of ice, it nudged them in the direction of the flowing water. All around them was the crunch and low rumble of colliding ice masses, and here and there Jack could still hear the comforting gurgle of water. But the sound of the river had changed completely now, and he feared their time was near.

"We'll get there," Jim said, rowing when there was room between ice chunks to dip the oars. When there was not room, they relied on the water's flow to drift them along.

"Of course we'll get there," Jack said. "There's just no saying when."

The great ice chunks hid the banks of the river from view, sculpting themselves into otherworldly shapes as they clung together, freezing, water splashing up only to become whorls and ridges of ice. Occasionally Jack glimpsed trees between the rearing chunks, but more often it was simply ice and water, and around midday a steady snowfall began, which limited their vision even more.

Since that time on the rock, there had been no sign of the wolf. But Jack could no longer believe that he was alone in this vast wilderness. What that feeling meant he had no idea, but he had yet to share it with the other two men. Jim, a teacher, would likely think him foolish. And he feared that Merritt would think him mad.

And perhaps he was. Ever since Dyea, the feeling had been growing that something out here was waiting for him. *Expecting* him.

That afternoon, with the sun barely breaking the horizon, the river slowed more than ever. Merritt stood at the bow, fending them away from chunks of ice and toward water passages that grew narrower and less common. Still they moved forward, but at a much slower rate than before. The boat nudged ice. Clumps of snow fell into the craft, and Jim scooped them up and tossed them back over the side. Ice cakes pressed into the boat to port and starboard, and several times Jack heard the straining of timber as immense forces clamped upon the hull.

Jim no longer needed to bail, because most of the water in the *Yukon Belle* had frozen.

"Stuck fast," Merritt said at last. He did not turn around to look back at Jack, and neither did Jim look up. Jack could blame neither of them. On the contrary, he had respected their enthusiasm and believed that he would have been feeling the same if it were not for the wolf.

A sense of foreboding hung over him like the sword of Damocles.

"Keep shoving," Jack said. "Maybe it's just this part of the river. Perhaps it's just a bottleneck."

This time Jim did look up, and Merritt glanced back.

Half an hour later, with a deafening grinding sound that set Jack's teeth vibrating, the river moved on with a surge. Ice broke apart, water gurgled up from beneath the floes, and their little boat found itself a fast channel again.

"To Dawson, boys!" Jack shouted, whooping and waving his hat in the air. He quickly replaced it when his ears grew numb, and though he knew that this was but a brief respite—they would not reach Dawson this side of winter—he suddenly felt a rush of confidence once again. So what if they did have to winter somewhere around here? This was part of the adventure he had vowed to give himself, the grasping of life instead of watching it drift by—

To his left, across the layers of ice and snow, something dark marred the whiteness. Jack looked, but already it was gone.

Hiding.

There was a tributary called the Stewart, close to Upper Island and barely seventy miles from Dawson. Where the Stewart converged with the Yukon, the ice floes piled together and caused a jam that quickly turned as solid as land. Their time was up. They managed to haul the *Yukon Belle* up onto the ice before she was crushed, and then came the long, laborious process of dragging the craft onto the snow-blanketed riverbank. There was no shelter out here on the ice, and if fate dictated that they had to build their own hut for the winter, then they would have to do so immediately, and use the wood from the boat as a start. The air was colder than ever, and Jack knew a man's fingers could freeze solid without him even noticing. When it grew even colder, spit would freeze in the air, they would lose the use of their fingers, and then they would die.

The boat was heavy, weighed down with their supplies and the ice that had frozen around them, and even with three of them pulling, it took some time to reach land. Luckily they had drifted close to the bank before the ice trapped them for good, and by the time evening arrived, they were ashore. They collapsed close to the boat and built a fire, Jack gasping a silent prayer of thanks when the first dancing flame rose up.

Sometimes he tried to cast his imagination back to the first people, who needed fire for warmth and security, keeping at bay the cold, the darkness, and predators that would come to take them in the night. He had lived on the road, slept in ditches and railway cars, and gone hungry many times, but despite that Jack was like most other people he had encountered in his life—used to light and heat, food and water, all of it available virtually on demand. The daily lives of those first people, cave dwellers and savage hunters, was difficult to contemplate. There was a barrier of language and understanding, but also an obstacle thrown up by the advances of civilization.

Even hunkered down around the fire, welcoming its heat and light, he could barely connect with his ancestors of many thousands of years ago. Here, he and his two companions relied on these flames to survive. And yet beside them lay the boat with its food and guns, furs and prospecting equipment, saws and axes. Into this wilderness they had brought the tools of civilization, and Jack felt like a stranger here.

They dried their wet socks and boots, warming their feet and hands, but with every breath Jack knew that they would have to move soon.

"We could split up," Jim said. "Take a different point of the compass each, meet back here in an hour."

"That's crazy talk," Jack said. "If you fall and break your ankle, Jim? Merritt, if you collapse under the weight of ice on your beard?" They all laughed, but it was a subdued humor.

"I can feel the wild all around us," Merritt said, glancing beyond the reach of the fire's light. *Is he still spooked?*

"I can feel the wild all around us," Merritt said.

Jack wondered, but Merritt said no more.

"We'll be all right," Jack said. "We were all wild once. But man rose up from his primitive origins, conquered the wildness both within him and without. We have minds, gentlemen. Thoughts that separate us from the lower animals. Passion and ingenuity enough to tame the wild, and to survive. But only if we respect its dangers. I say we leave the boat here, take only essentials for now, and head toward Dawson City. I figure we're seventy miles away at least, and we'd be dead in ten. But the closer we get to the city, the more likely we'll find some sort of shelter."

"Trappers," Jim said. "Prospectors."

"Are there Indian villages around here?" Merritt laughed.

"I think they'd have more sense," Jack said. "And besides, I doubt they'd welcome three soft prospectors. No, it's up to us to get through this on our own. It's a challenge, that's all. You up for it, boys?"

He saw a glimmer of annoyance pass across Jim's features at his use of the word *boys*, but then all three of them clapped hands and huddled closer around the fire, eager to get moving.

Jack was very aware of the darkness behind him. And if it hadn't been for the fire stretching the skin of his face and glittering in his eyes, he would have been swallowed by the darkness before him as well. Hope was kept alive by the flames. Beyond them, in this cold, brutal wilderness, the coming months could bring anything.

Yet still you'll die in the snow, that vision of his mother had told him, *cold . . . and almost alone.*

"No," he vowed, rocking on his heels. "No, no." Jim and Merritt glanced at him, but neither of them spoke, or even seemed perturbed by Jack's muttering. It seemed that all three men were considering their own fates that evening.

They found an abandoned fur traders' cabin. It was built into the base of a steep hillside, protected from the worst of the winds. It consisted of two large rooms, and in the center of one they found an old Klondike stove. Jack had left his own stove way back in Dyea, and it was a welcome sight for all of them. An hour after arriving, they had a good fire going, and there was even a lean-to behind the cabin beneath which a pile of logs had been drying for some time. The wood spat and sizzled, but it burned well enough. The cabin grew warmer, and the three men could go about without gloves and hats.

Over the course of the next few days they brought all their possessions up from the boat. It was a three-mile hike across the base of a hill and down to the river, and after each excursion they had to rest for several hours to gather their strength. The journey along the treacherous rivers had weakened them more than they realized, and it took many days for them to regain some of their lost energy. The cabin was just big enough for the three of them; they used one room for storage and sleeping, and the other was where they spent most of their days talking, cooking, and dreaming of the gold they would find come spring.

Young though Jack was, he sensed the two men looking up to him. This appealed not to his pride, but rather to his intellect. He had always felt himself the leader of their little team, and their time in the cabin confirmed that. He had his books, and he took to reading long passages to the other two men. Darwin's *On the Origin of Species*, Milton's *Paradise Lost*, and others, each of which seemed particularly pertinent to the situation they found themselves in. For their part, Jim and Merritt welcomed Jack's readings, and the men often spent a long time after each discussing the merits or otherwise of the passage.

"Godless heathen," Jim muttered after Jack read yet again from Darwin's book.

Jack blinked in surprise and glanced at Merritt.

"You're not a fan of Mr. Darwin's?" Merritt asked.

"Fan?" Jim said. He sat up, becoming more animated than Jack had seen him in hours. "The man denies centuries of teaching. He shuns God, who put him here, gave him his ship, the means to explore, the knowledge to—"

"And God gave him his intelligence?" Jack asked. "A mind to inquire?"

"Of course he did," Jim said. "It was Darwin's choice to misuse it."

Jack leaned forward, ready to say some more, but he bit back his words. For him, God was as real as many other things he had never witnessed, and he wasn't ignorant enough to dismiss him out of hand. But similarly, a work of such scientific genius and aesthetic beauty as Darwin's book—his theories bold, extravagant, and challenging— should not be shunned. If God had given Darwin such a mind, he had surely meant for him to use it.

"So where's *your* book?" Merritt asked, voice raised in surprise and growing angry.

"I have it all up here," Jim said, touching his temple. "And I believe it here." He tapped his chest.

"Well, if Darwin was right and it's survival of the fittest, I'll see you get a good burial," Merritt snapped.

Jack stood and raised both hands, imploring the men to calm down. He changed the subject quickly, reading another long passage from *Paradise Lost*, exaggerating his reading voice to try and break the icy atmosphere with warm humor. But the first of many tensions that would build through the winter had found root in that cabin.

The weather grew worse. The temperature dropped, the cold now freezing the men's breath, crackling their saliva if they spat. Often when they woke in the morning, ice had frozen on their beards and glued their eyelashes together, so they had to warm their eyes before they could open them. Snow fell day after day, and when it stopped several weeks into their stay, it was three feet deep and crunching underfoot.

That first morning without blizzard, Jack was more determined than ever to capture them something to cook and eat. He and Merritt went farther than they had before, staying out longer, and they returned past midday with a skinny rabbit. As Jack started gutting and skinning it, Jim asked why he was so cheerful.

"I've spent another year living in this amazing world," Jack said quietly. He could hardly feel his fingers, and the knife slipped from his hand several times.

"It's your birthday," Merritt said.

Jack nodded and smiled.

"How old?" Jim asked.

"Eighteen. I feel eighty." He looked up from the rabbit, and the two men were staring sadly at him. *What?* he thought, but he glanced down at his hands again and knew. He was the only one of the three of them who, in the depths of their despair and more and more convinced that this winter would be their last, could still find wonder in their surroundings. The other men recognized only harshness and impending death. Jack saw beauty.

"Happy birthday, Jack," he whispered to himself.

Jack took to walking on his own. It was against his own earlier advice, and the other two objected vehemently, but Jack would have his way. He always carried a rifle, ready to shoot any game he saw, but he was never fast enough. There were snow rabbits and squirrels, but they always avoided his sight once the barrel was pointed their way. In truth, though, Jack did not venture out from the cabin to hunt. He went on his own because something was happening to him, and the more it happened, the more he relished the experience. He was falling in love with this wilderness. The cold hurt his bones and made his muscles slow and heavy, but inside him a new warmth sparked to life.

The landscape was incredible. He came to see it as the great white silence, because if he stood still out in the snowfield, all he could hear was his own breathing and the thudding of his own heart. There was not a breath of wind out there, as if the air itself were frozen into immobility. The land slept beneath the thick carpet of snow. Sometimes it snowed some more, but other times the air was crisp and clear, and even though the sun didn't rise so high above the horizon, he could see a long way. Closing his eyes, standing out in the snow, he always knew from which direction his watcher observed.

Because it was still there. Jack had grown used to its presence, though never comfortable with it. He had not seen the wolf since that incident on the river. But here in the wild it felt like an echo of the land, a manifest wildness that observed him perhaps as an invader, and certainly not as an equal. He felt examined. He felt insignificant, less than a forgotten breath exhaled by this place. And for someone of such a strong mind, the sensation was curiously welcome.

Sometimes he thought it was death waiting to take him away. The end was ever closer; he understood that as well as his two friends back in the cabin. The chances of their surviving were becoming starker by the day. And he remembered what that vision of his mother had said: *Doom in the north, a cry of death in the great white silence, and the spirits will bear witness.* He watched for this spirit watching him and dreaded meeting its eyes.

Yet in some ways, Jack was more contented than he had ever been before. *This is where I belong,* he would think as the weeks and months went by. *I'm a stranger here no more.* He thought that perhaps his spirit had always dwelled here in the wild, watched over by the wolf and whatever it represented, and that it had taken eighteen years for his body to find its way here. Perhaps that explained his constant wanderlust, and the way he had always felt unsettled, until now. He felt whole for the first time in his life, and though he was nothing compared to the greatness of this place, that pleased him.

He might be one snowflake in a billion, but he was starting to know himself at last.

CHAPTER FIVE

AWAKENINGS

O N THE DAY JACK LONDON died for the first time, the snow came without warning.

He was out on one of his walks. Almost twelve weeks had passed with them sheltering in the cabin, and they had fallen into a routine. Jim and Merritt would hunt together in the morning while Jack prepared the cabin for the coming day. He would cook whatever they caught or, if they caught nothing, he would prepare a meal from their dwindling supplies. Then they would talk for a while, sometimes over a coffee, and Jack would venture out for his daily walk. The two men rarely questioned him about where he went or what he did, and Jack would never tell them.

But behind the routine lay the dawning comprehension that the three of them were going to die. The supplies would not last for much longer, and when a few days came during which they caught nothing to eat, they'd start growing weak. The weaker they became, the harder the hunting. The cold would bite in more. The darkness would haunt them. Jack saw this knowledge in his friends' eyes when he looked at them, and it hung heavy when the three of them talked together.

He struggled to fight off the feeling, but his acknowledgement of the fear seemed to bring that thing watching him from the wilderness much closer. He looked for prints in the snow and listened for distant howls. *A cry of death in the great white silence.*

He had walked up the hillside. Far up, with the cabin out of sight below, he had spent some time in the shelter of a fallen tree, looking out over the great river valley and trying to imagine a world without people. It was not a difficult scene to conjure, and the sense of loneliness unsettled him more than he could have expected.

He thought of Eliza back at home and hoped that James had returned to her safely. He thought of his mother and wondered whether the house was still hers.

And then the blizzard came in.

Like a predator stalking its tender prey, the storm broke silently over the head of the hillside and started shedding its load into the valley. The first flake drifted down in front of Jack and he glanced up, expecting to see a small creature disturbing the snow-laden branches of the tree above him. Another flake landed on his cheek, another on his nose, and then it was snowing wildly.

He was unconcerned at first. The way to get back to the cabin was to continue downhill as far as he could, so he was not worried about becoming lost. They'd had a decent breakfast that day, so his body was warm, busy digesting the rabbit meat. He carried a rifle.

And then he saw the shadow in the snow, passing from tree to tree just out of sight above him on the hillside.

He started running downhill. The snow fell more heavily, completely silent and unflustered by even the hint of a breeze. He glanced back, but already he could barely see more than a dozen paces. Working his way downhill, looking back every few steps to make sure nothing was closing on him under cover of the snowfall, Jack did not see the hollow scooped from the hillside until it was too late. The ground disappeared beneath him, and for a while he was held in space. There was no sensation of falling. It was as if the snow bore him through the air. And then he hit the ground, snow cushioning the impact, but still the wind was knocked from him, and he banged his head against a buried stone.

Looking directly up at the lip of the hollow as he blacked out, Jack saw a gray shape leaning over and staring down upon him.

———

When he came to, he knew he was dying from the cold.

Yet still you'll die in the snow, cold . . . and almost alone.

No! he tried to say, but his lips were frozen together.

He tried to move, but his arms would not obey his commands. He looked down across his body, and it was buried. He blinked quickly to clear snow from his eyes. His lashes were heavy with ice.

No, he tried to say again. His mouth opened, and ice sprinkled into his throat.

His mother was with him. She walked in from the silent white distance, visible even though the snow still poured heavily from the sky. She looked sad, but there was condemnation on her face as well, and when she opened her mouth, he knew that she was going to blame him for everything.

And then the wolf was there again, Death, standing between Jack and the image of his mother. It snarled, and she turned away. Then it disappeared into the blizzard once more, leaving him alone.

Cold.

Dying.

Jack felt his heart slow, as if the blood were freezing in his veins just as the waters of the mighty Yukon had drawn to an icy standstill. He had read that the last sense to leave a dying man was hearing, and when he opened his eyes he saw nothing; when he drew in a breath he smelled only void.

In the distance, just as his hearing faded into oblivion, he heard the mournful howl of a wolf.

Jack came back from nothing, rising out of a different sort of white silence with a huge gasping breath, as though waking from an awful dream. Pain clutched at his chest, a giant's fist pressing down upon it, crushing, and then abruptly it pulled away. He breathed in ragged gulps of air, all his senses rushing back to life, and with every breath his nostrils filled with the stink of blood and his throat gurgled with it.

He choked, let his head fall to the right, gagged, and spat.

Blood. There could be no mistaking the iron taste; the rich, meaty odor; and beneath it the smell of animal fear and death. He could not feel his hands or feet—he was paralyzed, a prisoner inside the frozen slab of flesh that his body had become. But he was slowly growing aware of a warmth trickling down his sides and spreading across his chest. In some places it soaked through his clothing.

Savaged, torn apart, not even given the dignity of a frozen death . . .

Steam rose from his face and throat, and as he managed

to crane his neck slightly, thoughts dull and sluggish, his eyes widened. The blood that coated his tongue and filled his nostrils, that warmed his face and neck and chest, was not his own. His heart might have stopped—in the back of his mind he believed it had, though for how long he could not guess, and how the cold might have preserved him he did not know—but the weight upon his chest came not only from pain.

The rabbits had been torn open, their steaming entrails spilled onto Jack and strung along his arms and legs. They had bled all over him and now covered him in a heap of dead flesh. And there were things other than rabbits as well, including a pair of owls, three wolverines, and a ravaged cougar nestled against his left side. A rush of fear and revulsion swept through Jack, and his vision blurred.

The stink was rich in his nose, the taste in his throat causing him to gag slightly. But he did not retch; he hadn't the strength for it. In the deep perpetual gloom of that Yukon winter, he studied the dead things. Those that had spilled off him to lie in the snow had frozen rigid by now, dried blood rimed with ice. They had been replaced by fresher kills. Replaced *on purpose*. Their lives had been stolen to save him, their blood warming him and—hideous as the thought was—*feeding* him.

Once more the darkness encroached upon his vision,

but he dared not close his eyes again. If he did not move, he would die here. He knew that. Here was meat, and in the meat, life. He had been given a chance. He had a hunting knife in its sheath at his hip, as well as flint. *Get up, Jack. You have to build a fire, or you're done.*

His right hand tingled with a trickle of warmth. Though his fingers were numb, he thought he felt the brush of fur on the frozen skin. With deep concentration, he tried to lift his hand, and though his limbs felt like lead, he just managed it. But he would need more than dull clubs made from frigid fists to survive, and so he tried to move his fingers.

Pain lanced up into his hand and all the way to his elbow, like red-hot wires feeding through his veins. Jack cried out, but the only sound that emerged from his throat was a ragged hiss, a sort of death rattle. The sound terrified him more than anything. What sort of death was this for a man who had lived by his wits and his fists, and who had extinguished from his heart any trace of fear he had ever found? No, this was not a fitting end. Jack had been determined to conquer the wild, and he would not let it destroy him now.

He heard something, the twitch of a nearby tree branch, and stiffened.

"Hello?" he rasped, barely a whisper. "Is someone there?"

There was no reply, but then he *felt* it, that familiar presence, the weight of the wolf's regard. With a shuddering breath, he let his head loll once more to the side, and there it was, standing in the trees off to his right with its head high, some kind of small, furred creature in its jaws. Blood stained the wolf's chest. Its eyes gleamed in the smoke-dark winter evening.

Not death, but life!

Jack could not breathe. This huge wolf had seemed, before, to peer at him from some spirit world, from the wild heart of the Yukon. But now it trotted toward him, paws leaving tracks in the snow. His mother had spoken of a spirit accompanying his death, but Jack should have listened to his own heart more. This beast was not observing him but *protecting* him. She had often spoken of spirit guides, and perhaps this might be his own.

Yet the gray beast existed as more than a specter of the mind. It came to him now and dropped the small dead thing into the snow. Pinning it with its paws, the wolf tore it open, blood spattering dark against winter white, and then quickly snatched it up and edged closer. It had no fear of Jack, and rightly so. He had become so weak that he could barely move and hardly think. The blood spilled down from the dead thing. Jack tried to turn his face away, stomach growling with hunger and twisting in disgust at the same time.

The gray beast existed as more than a specter of the mind.

The wolf issued a low, warning growl. Jack went still, let the blood splash his lips and nose and throat, but pressed his mouth tightly closed. Whatever the wolf's intentions, he'd had enough of surviving on the hot blood of dead things.

Again it growled, dropping the little corpse right on his face in a move that seemed almost petulant. The wolf sniffed at Jack as though inhaling his exhaled breath. It nudged his cheek with its snout, then grunted and moved away. Halfway to the trees it stopped, tipped its head back, and howled. The sound reached inside Jack, curling around his heart, and filled him with sorrow and frustration, and a longing unlike anything he had ever known.

The wolf glanced at him again, almost as though it wanted Jack to join it, to run with it through the snowy woods, but Jack could not run. He could not even stand.

From stillness to swiftness, the wolf bolted into the trees, howling again as it vanished into the winter forest. Jack listened for as long as he could, but when the howling seemed so distant as to disappear, he felt himself sliding back down into darkness, though whether the void beneath him might be unconsciousness or true death he had not the focus even to wonder.

There were whispers in the dark. Voices. Since one of them sounded much more like Merritt Sloper than Saint Peter,

Jack decided he must still be among the living. He tried to open his eyes but could not. His lips were parted slightly, and he could feel a muzzle of ice coating long weeks' worth of beard. Only by probing with his tongue could he find the small opening that his own breath had managed to maintain in that icy mask.

"He's breathing. I told you he was breathing," said one of the voices.

Jim, Jack thought. *Goodman. Good man, Jim.* Inside, he smiled, but his facial muscles did not seem to respond.

"He'll have frostbite for sure," Merritt replied. "If he lives."

"He'll live," Jim retorted. "Look at him. Someone wanted him kept alive. Maybe a mountain man or Indians."

"Look around. Do you see any footprints at all?"

"Just wolf tracks. Wait . . . you think a wolf did this? Caught all these animals and just left the meat here? With all due respect, Merritt, such behavior is far beyond the norm for the lupine species. It isn't in their nature—"

The sound of their bickering warmed Jack. One of them dropped onto his knees in the snow beside him, and a moment later, when he heard the voice, he knew it was Merritt.

"There isn't anything natural about this," the big man said. "Now help me, Jim. We've got to get him back to the cabin and in front of a fire, or even the angels won't be able to save him."

Jack felt his head rocking slightly, but it took him a moment before he could feel Merritt's fingers probing his face. The man cupped his hands on Jack's cheeks, trying to warm them. The heat of his friend's flesh brought needles of prickling pain into his cheeks as a trace of feeling returned.

He could hear Merritt blowing onto his own hands before he repeated the process.

"Jim! Come on, man!" Merritt urged.

But still Jim hesitated. "It's like . . . some sort of massacre. Whatever's watching over him, I don't think it's angels."

"Damn it, Jim!" Merritt barked.

Jack blinked, the ice crust on his eyelids melting thanks to the heat of Merritt's hands. He tried to speak. *Bickering like a couple of old hens,* he wanted to say. But his voice wouldn't come. Instead, he managed only a moan. Now, at last, he could see them, although his vision remained blurry.

"All right," Jim said. "Help me snap off some of these branches. We'll need some kind of makeshift stretcher—"

Merritt scoffed. "Don't be daft. He's been out here long enough."

The big man scraped ice from his red beard and then

put his mittens back on. He bent down and began to pry Jack away from the snow beneath, working his hands and arms underneath Jack's frozen, blood-stiffened clothes.

"Merritt. His eyes are open," Jim said.

Looming above Jack, Merritt looked down and smiled beatifically, a young Father Christmas. "Well, well. So they are. Hang on, young Master London. We'll have you warm soon enough."

"Or as warm as it ever gets out here," Jim added, but despite the resignation in his words, his tone was far from defeatist. "Don't worry, Jack. You're not alone."

No, Jack thought as Merritt hoisted him up from the ground, snow and dead things—the wolf's offerings of life—sliding off him. *Not alone at all.*

Merritt slung Jack over his shoulder and began to trudge through the snow. Every step jolted Jack so it felt as if his bones were grinding together. His mind grew vaguer, thoughts flickering like a candle flame until they guttered out. The voices of his friends became a comforting drone that accompanied him down into the darkness, and he thought he heard a lonely howl off in the distance. But perhaps it was only the wind.

Later, Jack would say that Merritt and Jim saved his life, or—when he was feeling lyrical—that the fire breathed life back into him, and that he felt like Prometheus bathed in heat for the first time. But in his heart he knew that his friends would have been too late had it not been for the gifts of warmth and blood brought to him by the wolf. Jim and Merritt knew it as well, but none of them liked to talk about it, even as the days passed by.

The two men were devoted to their younger companion. Not only did they warm him by the fire and wrap him in dry clothes and blankets, but they massaged his extremities to get the circulation running again, and as though visited by a miracle, Jack's frostbite cost him only the tip of one toe on his left foot, which Merritt removed with a small paring knife.

They had questions, of course, some of them spoken— and answered by Jack in simple terms, including the brief story of the fall that had first knocked him unconscious and stranded him in the cold—and others unspoken. Merritt and Jim often glanced at each other when the subject came up, as though each was wary that the other might venture too far in the conversation and then not be able to retreat.

Finally, after several days' recuperation, subsisting mostly on dried beef stores and canned beans, supplemented by the meat of a small hare Jim had found outside the cabin, limping from a fight with some predator or other, Jack asked the question they could not escape.

"How did you find me?"

His voice remained a low rasp and his teeth hurt. They were all suffering from the beginnings of scurvy, he knew, and half the winter still stretched out in front of them.

Jim smiled and glanced uneasily at Merritt. His glasses shone in the firelight. He could wear them only indoors. Outside, the cold would make the metal stick to his skin and turn the glass brittle, and he couldn't risk the only pair of spectacles he had remaining to him. He'd broken his spare glasses on board the *Umatilla* during the voyage from San Francisco.

The men sat in the front room of the cabin on rough-hewn chairs, close enough to the Klondike stove that their faces were flushed. Merritt licked his lips in that way that Jack knew meant he craved a dash of whiskey, but they had none. They melted snow for water and managed tea or coffee every few days, rationing out the little pleasures to give themselves something to look forward to. But no whiskey.

"I nearly shot it, Jack," Jim said, eyes haunted as he gazed into the middle distance at some piece of memory. "If my rifle hadn't frozen, I might've killed it."

But Merritt shook his head. "No. You couldn't have. Not that one."

Jim shuddered but sat up a bit straighter, his expression

growing stern. Superstition seemed to offend him, and he looked around, hands fidgeting as though searching for something. Jack knew he wanted his Bible, but it must be in the other room by his bedroll, where he kept it most often to have it close to hand. Close to his heart.

"Don't be a fool. A wolf is a wolf," Jim said, straining his usually amiable rapport with his friend.

"Not this one," Merritt replied darkly, a challenge in his eyes. When Jim did not debate him, he turned to Jack. "It sat out there on the edge of the clearing, half hidden in the trees, and it stared at this cabin—at me—like my mother used to wait for me at the front door when I was late for dinner. That wolf wanted our attention."

Jim nodded. "On that we can agree. Big damn thing, too."

"Eventually we reckoned we had to check it out," Merritt went on. "I took the rifle, and we went over to the spot in the trees where it had been standing for hours, only when we got there, the wolf wasn't there—"

"Vanished deeper into the woods," Jim interrupted.

Merritt glanced away, as if to say there might be more to the story.

"So you followed it?" Jack asked. His fingers were still stiff and painful, and his feet still felt like slabs of frozen beef. The cold had gotten down deep inside of him, and no matter how hot the fire, he felt like he would never get warm.

"We followed it," Jim echoed.

"We did nothing of the sort," Merritt grumbled. He gave a murmur of dissatisfaction and stared at Jack. "When I say the wolf wasn't there, that's precisely what I mean. There were no tracks. No sign of the wolf at all, as if . . ." He trailed off.

Jim wouldn't look at either of them. He'd set about cleaning his glasses with the edge of his sleeve.

"Then how did you find me?" Jack asked, inching closer to the stove even as he stared at the flecks of gold and green in Merritt's eyes.

"A shadow in the forest, that's all," the big man replied. "Jim will tell you it was the wolf, but I didn't see anything but its eyes and its shadow. It kept ahead of us, pausing to wait when we fell behind. It wasn't long before it led us right to you. When we saw all that blood, and the rabbits and such all torn up, we were sure you'd been mauled by a bear."

Jim got up and dusted off the seat of his pants. "There'd been new snow. It covered the tracks. The wolf led us to you." He turned his back and walked away.

Jack and Merritt exchanged a glance, but they didn't talk any more about it. Neither of them had any desire to do so.

The weeks passed, and Jack's rescue seemed to mark a turning point in their fortunes. Their supplies still dwindled to almost nothing, but hunting trips were more often successful than not. And several times when they'd gone days without fresh meat, one of the men found a wounded rabbit or squirrel somewhere close to the cabin, leaving a bloody trail in the snow as it crawled away from whatever had wounded it. As soon as Jack felt well enough, and the cold no longer felt as though it ate at his bones, he resumed his daily walk. This time, however, he did not wander from camp in an attempt to make contact with his observer. To his great confusion, and a mixture of relief and strange sadness, the feeling of being watched had significantly abated, existing on the periphery of his mind. If the wolf—the creature he had come to think of as his spirit guide—was still with him, it did not deign to show itself or to make itself known in any other way. From time to time he would hear distant howls, but he felt no shiver of recognition. They were ordinary wolves trying to survive the white silence, no different from Jack, Merritt, and Jim.

Some days he walked up to the spot where his friends had discovered him—the patch of snow-covered earth where Jack felt certain he had actually died, if only for a handful of minutes. Yet no trace remained of the event itself. New snow had long since blanked out the bright crimson of the blood, and though he tried several times to dredge up a dead rabbit, hare, or wolverine by dragging his boots through the snow, he never came up with even a bone. Merritt and Jim had been far too superstitious to eat any of the meat on those animals, so Jack knew that his companions had not removed the carcasses. Yet the spot seemed untouched, somehow cleansed. If the others had not discovered him there and seen the dead animals for themselves, he would have thought the long winter had taken a terrible toll on his mind.

When first weeks and then months had elapsed since that day, his routine had become little more than exercise. He made his body work to keep himself limber, though as their supplies had decreased, they had all grown weaker. Now, on the day they had gauged as the first of April, he could move his teeth, loosened by scurvy, around in his mouth. They had no mirror, and for that he was glad. He wouldn't have liked to see his own reflection if his features were as gaunt and his gums as black as those of his companions.

Spring must not be far, although the white silence still reigned and the snow and ice made it impossible for him to imagine the earth ever flowering, the sun ever shining brightly, the river ever flowing again. The past few weeks had brought visitors to the cabin, drawn by the smoke and willing to travel far afield from their own camps now that the cold did not bite as deeply and their own supplies had run low. Trappers and prospectors and even Indians paid visits, hoping for a bit of anything they had run out of themselves. The best Jack and his friends could offer was a cup of weak tea and good conversation, but surprisingly that seemed to be enough. These veterans of the Yukon, of the gold fever and the wilderness life, came full of stories, and when Jack regaled them with his tales of life as an oyster pirate and vagabond, they repaid him in kind. He squirreled these stories away as a miser would pennies, hoarding them only to take them out and examine them later.

Stories were in Jack London's blood. Tales of adventure fed him when other sustenance became meager at best. And now he had one hell of a story of his own, and wanted only to survive to live the next one.

Such were the thoughts that lingered in his mind when he trod the by-now-familiar path back toward the cabin that morning. The daylight hours lasted longer and longer, and he felt reinvigorated every time the sun appeared. As he reached a turn in the path and came in sight of the clearing where the cabin stood, he heard Merritt bellowing.

"Jack!" the big man shouted. "Jack, where are you?"

The excitement in his voice was unmistakable and contagious. Something had happened, some piece of good news, and Jack could think of only one thing that would give Merritt Sloper such happiness. Jack picked up his pace, tromping along the path as swiftly as he could manage.

"Merritt?" he called, bursting from the trees into the clearing. He glanced around, confounded for a moment by the absence of anyone in the clearing. "Merritt, what is it?"

Then the door opened and Jim Goodman stepped out wrapped in one of the furs they had sewn over the long winter.

"What's all the shouting?" Jim asked as Jack hurried toward him.

"Not a clue. I heard Merritt, but—"

"I'm here!" Merritt called, and they both turned to see him ambling around the side of the cabin. The winter had been hard on all of them, but Merritt remained a big, burly man in spite of the weight he'd lost. He gave them a good-natured grin.

"Let's have the last of the good coffee," Merritt told them. "The bit we've been saving to celebrate."

Jack gripped Merritt's shoulders. "The river?"

For weeks they had taken turns visiting the river every day, waiting and hoping.

Merritt nodded. "The ice is breaking. You should hear it. It sounds like the whole planet is cracking in half. There's movement as well, shifting here and there."

Jack whooped loudly and embraced him, then spun

toward the cabin. "Pack your things, gentlemen! We're going to Dawson!"

But Jim still stood in the open door of the cabin. He hadn't moved. Jack thought, at first, that something awful had happened to him—some madness or illness. Then he heard the man's soft, shuddery breaths, and the prayer he spoke with a hitch in his voice.

"It's all right, Jim," Jack said, putting a firm hand on his shoulder. "We're going to be all right now. We made it through."

Only then did Jim lift his eyes to look at his friends. Only then did he smile, and begin to laugh, and moments later they were all laughing and whooping with elation.

Merritt clapped Jack on the back. "Go on, then, kid. Make that pot of coffee. We've earned it!"

Jack did as he was asked, not even minding that Merritt had called him "kid." And a cup of coffee had never tasted so good.

The three days that followed were some of the longest of Jack's life. With the snow beginning to melt and the sun showing its face, a sense of renewal filled him—renewal of life and of purpose. The world seemed to be awakening around him, and as the winter retreated, so did the aura of mysticism that had blanketed the land. Both

Merritt's and Jim's conflicting superstitions seemed to burn off like fog.

Trees dripped with melting ice, which glittered like diamonds when the morning sun spread across the landscape. The days grew longer, and Jack spent a good portion of every one down at the river.

He stood well back from the bank, wary of the tumult caused by the spring snow melt. As if the great machinery of the world had churned back to life, the Yukon Rriver now flowed fast beneath the ice. Cracks had formed, floes shifted, and on the third day of his vigilance, the entire river seemed to lift itself up and start downstream.

"It's beautiful," Jim Goodman whispered.

Jack had not heard him approach but was so entranced that he could not tear his gaze away from the sight. The ice buckled and broke, and the pieces jostled and collided as they were carried along. The river groaned as though the earth itself might tear asunder.

"It sure is."

The two of them stood there for over an hour before Merritt joined them, and then all three of them watched the spectacle in shared awe. The river churned so powerfully that huge chunks of ice, blue-white and gleaming, were hurled from the water onto the snowy bank, only to slide back down into the flow as the snow melted beneath them.

Jack saw a dark shape amid the ice. Raising a hand to shield his eyes from the glare of the sun off the snow, he peered at the shape and realized it was the broken and splintered curve of a small boat. A team of hopeful prospectors behind them must have become stuck in the winter freeze just as they had been, but not been as swift in getting their boat out of the water before the rapid icing had crushed it.

He narrowed his eyes to slits, trying to make out a second dark shape that bobbed up beside the first. Massive slabs of ice shifted and things flowed with the river, and for a moment he assumed the sodden, rigid thing to be an uprooted tree. Then he saw pale fingers, a marble-white arm, and understood that whoever had been steering that boat had never made it out of the ice. The winter had preserved them well, but now spring had come and the river would take them.

Jack glanced at Merritt and Jim. They were smiling and trying to converse despite the roar of the ice grinding together. His friends had not noticed the body, and he had not the heart to point it out. Spring had come, after all. For them, if not for everyone.

"Come on, friends!" he called. "Let's pack up. Another few days and we put the *Yukon Belle* back in the water. Dawson, here we come!"

———

From miles upriver they saw the smoke of Dawson's chimneys rising. Jim bailed water from the leaking boat even as Merritt tried to keep their supplies from getting wet; they had made furs to keep warm during the winter and wanted those to stay dry most of all. Sodden with water, the furs would stink, but worse, they would be dreadfully heavy. It would have been best for the men to wear them, but spring had arrived and their heavy coats and caps were enough.

Jack kept a steady hand on the tiller, though the oars were shipped. With the rush of the current, the Yukon high and churning with the spring melt, they had no need to row. The river hurtled them onward as though on the crest of a wave, and Jack sat in the stern guiding the *Yukon Belle* with his head high, breathing in the crisp air, which smelled to him of victory. He had not yet tamed the wild, he was not a conqueror, but he had survived and thus become its master.

When at last they rounded a bend in the river and came in sight of Dawson City, Jack laughed out loud. Merritt slapped Jim on the back with such vigorous bonhomie that the lanky teacher nearly tumbled overboard.

Dawson wasn't much to look at. After Dyea, Jack would have expected more from this newly fabled land than the sprawl of tents on the riverbank and the blocks and blocks of shabby one- and two-story buildings, muddy streets, and gutters running with filth. If anything, the place looked grittier and less substantial than Dyea, despite the massive extent of Dawson. But he steered toward the half-collapsed docks, and his friends dipped their oars into the water to help guide the boat, and he began to understand.

Whatever people wanted to call it, Dawson wasn't a city at all. There might be saloons and gambling halls, music and whores, a newspaper and a dentist and other signs of civilization. There might be buildings and board-walks of wood, and bank vaults filled with money. But those things were only by-products of the reality of Dawson. Smoke swirled away in the chill breezes and the sun shone down, dogs pulled sleds full of goods along worn tracks, and people by the hundreds rushed or milled about, all of them on their way to dig for gold, or pray for gold, or beg for gold, or sell their bodies and souls for gold.

Dawson wasn't a city. It was a mining camp, rough and grim and alive with greed and jealousy. And hope. Yes, that, too. *It's a wild place,* Jack thought. Dreams could be built or crushed there, entirely dependent upon destiny and courage. *But the courageous man makes his own destiny.*

With that thought resonating in his mind, he bent the tiller up out of the water, grabbed a rope, and leaped to the

Dawson wasn't a city. It was a mining camp, rough
and grim and alive with greed and jealousy.

dock. Merritt and Jim paddled against the current as Jack tied off the *Yukon Belle.*

"Quick, now, boys," Merritt said, already dumping the furs onto the dock. "Get the gear out of the boat. The *Belle*'s sinking."

Jack saw that it was true. Jim had been forced to give up bailing in order to paddle, and the water sluiced into the boat between planks, filling the bottom. Without someone emptying it out, the boat would be at the bottom of the Yukon in minutes. Jack didn't mind. The *Yukon Belle* had done her job.

"She got us here," he told Merritt as he hauled a heavy pack up onto the dock. "That's all that matters. The rest is up to us."

CHAPTER SIX

CITY OF HOPE AND GREED

FROM A DISTANCE, Dawson City had looked grim. Closer in—actually walking its streets and smelling its air—Jack realized it was worse than that. It was a wild place draped in false civilization. Like the rough clapboard buildings lining the streets behind extravagant, colorful façades, its reality was dour and gray. *Here is a place that was never meant to be,* Jack thought, and even his newfound enthusiasm seemed to wither somewhat under Dawson's gaze.

Leaving Jim back at the riverside with their belongings, Jack and Merritt ventured in, hoping to find cheap accommodation and somewhere to store their gear. The smell hit Jack hard: raw sewage, rotting food, the stench of beasts of burden kept out in the open. Beneath that, however, were the aromas of cooking food and spilled drinks, and both made his mouth water.

They passed a crude sign daubed with the words FRONT STREET, and before them lay the early results of the Yukon gold rush. Rough buildings rose on either side with timber walkways laid before them, and the buildings' frontages belied the true nature of their construction. Saloons, dress shops, a dentist, outfitters, markets, hotels, a laundry—a whole new town built in this wild place with the river as its real source of life. And yet, where Jack had expected enthusiasm and excitement to hold sway, so many people seemed possessed of a strange listlessness that he worried that an illness had swept through the city. Some of the men and women who walked along the street had a dazed expression, their haggard, thin faces drooping and their eyes vacant.

"What's wrong with them?" Merritt muttered, and Jack could tell how unsettled the big man was.

"I don't know," Jack said. "Let's ask."

"But—" Merritt tried to grab him, but Jack was too fast.

"Friend," Jack said, grabbing the hand of a passing man. He was taller than Jack, with a bald head mottled with scabby skin and a huge, drooping mustache that hid his mouth and dipped below his chin. "What's the matter with Dawson?" It was a strange question, but Jack could think of no other way of posing it.

"Dawson?" the man said. His accent was pure north-east, containing the New York lilt that Jack remembered so well. "Dawson's a ghost town."

"Doesn't look like a ghost town to me!" Jack said, try-ing to sound enthusiastic.

The man looked from Jack to Merritt and back again. "Jus' get in? Been out in the wilds for the winter, huh?"

"That's right," Merritt said.

"Come to stake your claim and find your gold, huh?"

Jack nodded. There was something like mockery creep-ing into the man's voice now, and Jack didn't like it.

But the man sighed, as if to mock was too much effort, and his eyes seemed to sigh along with him. They were weak, Jack saw. Pale. As if this rough land had leached the color even from those.

"I been here close on six months," the man said. "Never went any farther. From what I hear up the trail, there's no need. Gold? There's some. But no new strikes fer some time now. So Dawson's jus' where the weak ones finish their journey an' stay. The strong ones turn around and head home."

"We haven't come all this way to turn tail and run," Jack said, angry now. "Haven't been through all we've been through—"

"Think you've been through tough times?" the man said, his voice dropping low as he leaned in closer. "Don't compare to what you'll find here, or beyond. There are *stories*—"

"Listen here," Jack said, and he took a step forward. He felt his fury rising, his fists clenching; and a few heads turned their way. But nobody seemed particularly alarmed, or even interested, and he wondered how many fights these people saw on the streets of Dawson every day.

"Jack, come on," Merritt said, grabbing his arm.

"Yeah," Jack said. He glanced back at Merritt and nodded. *I'm fine*, that look said, but Merritt's expression spoke otherwise. Perhaps he saw something in Jack that he'd never seen before.

The man walked on, squelching through the mud. He did not once look back but stared down at his feet as if in an effort to not see anything else.

"Let's find a place to stay first," Merritt said. "Then we need to store our stuff, rest, get our strength up. See if we can find some damn fruits and vegetables to eat, stave off the scurvy. What do you say?"

"I say yes," Jack said, again nodding. But the listless man preyed on his mind, and he vowed to himself that he would not remain in Dawson any longer than necessary.

They walked farther along the street, watching men and women guiding teams of dogs and packhorses through the mud. They passed a bar and heard the noise of jollity from inside, and that raised Jack's spirits more than it should have. *At least someone here still has a grasp on the good things*, he thought, glancing around the street at faces that hovered like ghosts. He looked up at the bar's name where it was painted across the façade: DAWSON BAR. Original. As with Front Street, and the Dawson Food and Clothing Market, it seemed that those who came here lost their strength of imagination along the way, and named their places purely for functionality. Nevertheless, he promised himself a visit to the Dawson Bar later that day. It would be good to take a drink, and he saw from the look on Merritt's face—the slightly wider eyes, the flicker of tongue across lips—that he was thinking the same.

They passed a place that advertised GOLD DUST BOUGHT FOR CASH. Merritt grinned, and Jack grinned back.

"Be doing some business here soon," the big man said, and Jack nodded, looking through the shop's dusty window. A wizened little man sat behind a table in the small room, spectacles perched on his nose. Before him on the table were a pair of weighing scales and a set of weights. The man was nodding off to sleep, the rest of the shop empty. He did not seem very busy.

"Jack!" Merritt called from along the walkway. He was pointing across the street at the Yukon Hotel. Jack smiled and managed a chuckle. The name might not inspire, but the thought of a bed, a warm bath, and a good meal suddenly made him almost dizzy.

"Let's go, then," Jack said. "We'll arrange for rooms, then go and help Jim bring the stuff into town."

"How'll we manage that?" Merritt asked.

"Look around you! We'll hire a team of dogs."

"We'll need to buy them," Merritt said, voice lowering.

"Come on, now. We're not quite ready, I'll give you that. But we still have the *hunger*! Not like that poor son of a bitch." Jack waved along the street back the way they had come, but he knew that his friend was right, and he'd been thinking on that for the last few minutes. They had lots of equipment, nothing to haul it, and very little money. Either they'd be faced with working for someone else or they'd have to come up with some other means of procuring the dogs and sled they'd need to continue their adventure.

A problem for later that day, Jack decided. For now—

"Get off me!"

The raised voice came from the narrow alley between the Yukon Hotel and a neighboring building, one proudly extolling itself as THE ONLY SHAVING PARLOR AND LAUNDRY IN DAWSON.

"Give us the dog and we'll leave you be."

"He's *my* dog, *I* found him, *I*—"

"Found him, did ya?"

Jack hurried across the street and heard Merritt on his tail.

"It's got nothing to do with us, Jack," Merritt warned. And although he knew the big man was right, there was something about this place that called itself a city that was already grating on Jack's nerves. It was the curious lethargy of some of its inhabitants, the falseness of many of the buildings, the haphazard way in which the streets had been laid out, as if such things as order did not matter. But more than anything, he thought, it was the sense of defeatism that pervaded the air. He was used to rough places—the waterfront in San Francisco, his months on the road, the terrible four weeks he'd spent in jail—but such atmospheres were usually created by the people. Here, the city itself felt dangerous. For a fleeting instant, he thought of the wilderness that had been here before the first stampeders arrived.

And he wondered what the wild must think of their intrusion.

"Hey!" Jack called. "Leave the kid alone!" In truth, the kid was probably only a year or two younger than Jack, but he looked like a child.

"Get lost and mind your own business!" one of the men said. There were two of them troubling the boy. The one who'd spoken was tall and stout, with a shaggy black beard that entirely covered the lower half of his face. His eyes were hard, his skin pale and blotchy, and he wore a long gray coat, which he now shifted aside, displaying the two pistols slung around his hips. The other man was shorter, thinner, and the smile he directed at Jack chilled him to the core. It was bereft of anything approaching humanity. This man—with his short-cropped hair, neatly trimmed mustache, and wide-brimmed hat—was cold as the heart of this land, and Jack sensed a simmering brutality that made his skin crawl.

Wish we hadn't left our damn guns with Jim, Jack thought. And he said, "What's *your* business, beating on the kid like that?"

"We haven't even started beating on him, yet. Just getting around to it, in fact," the short man said, and his voice was a knife across ice.

"They're trying to take my dog!" the boy said. "My Dutch. I found him, I fed him, he's *my* friend!"

Jack nodded at the boy but said nothing.

"Jack," Merritt whispered. "They have guns."

The short man smiled. He'd obviously heard Merritt, and he shifted his black jacket slightly to reveal the revolver on his belt.

Jack laughed. It took everyone by surprise—even Jack,

because it was a growl he'd felt building—and the tall man's hands went to his pistols.

Behind him, Jack heard Merritt's sharp intake of breath.

"Leave the boy alone," Jack said casually, no sense of threat in his voice. "Come on, what's he to you? You want his dog when there are a thousand others in Dawson, I'll bet. Did you really come here to find gold and leave your good sense behind?"

The short man's smile was still there, but it stopped a hundred miles from his eyes. *He's seen some things*, Jack thought, *and not all of them on the Yukon Trail.* He wondered how many men this short man had watched die. He wondered how many he had killed.

"Archie," the short man said mildly.

"If you know what's good for you," the big, bearded man—Archie—said, coming quickly along the alleyway toward Jack, "you'll turn around and—"

Jack kicked him once, hard, between the legs. Archie folded over slightly, groaning, and Jack turned sideways and ground his boot down the man's right shin. He cried out and staggered back, but Jack knew he had started something now that needed finishing. He'd been in enough scrapes down on the waterfront to know that once begun, a fight wasn't over until one man was down, and that was doubly true with hard men like this. Glancing at the short man, confident that—for now, at least—he wasn't going for his gun, Jack surged forward and laid into Archie with his fists.

It was like hammering at a side of beef. Archie was a big man beneath his layers of clothing, and heavy, and Jack wondered how someone from the trail could still retain so much meat on his bones. He was either a good hunter or a good thief. But Jack gave him no opportunity to recover from the first attack. When Archie cocked back a fist, Jack darted within his circle of reach and shouldered him in the chest, pushing him against the side of the hotel. Timber creaked, and one of Archie's flailing fists caught Jack across the jaw.

The pain was fresh and shocking, but Jack punched through it. He kicked and swung, clawed with his hands, and when he felt Archie's hand clasping for his throat, Jack lowered his face and bit. He tasted blood, and it was sour.

The kid's dog, Dutch, was barking. And as Jack delivered the final kick that drove Archie to the ground, he heard the familiar sound of metal against leather.

"Jack, down!" Merritt shouted, and Jack let himself fall.

Someone laughed out loud, and Jack glanced up. The short man was holding his gun in one hand and resting his other on his left hip as he laughed.

Archie groaned.

Jack stood slowly, shaking his hand and speckling his trousers with the other man's blood.

"Gonna shoot me?" he asked the short man.

"Oh no," he replied. "Not *you*. You're starved and underfed, but you're strong. Jack. That your name? Be seeing you, Jack. See, I don't shoot people who might be useful to me." He glanced sidelong at the skinny kid, and his laughter halted so quickly that it did not even leave an echo. "This piece of dog dung, however . . ." He lifted his gun and pressed it against the boy's throat.

Jack knew that he didn't have a chance in hell. They were at least six feet away, and he'd have to cover that distance in the same time that the man's finger had to squeeze half an inch against the trigger. But figuring the odds had never stopped him before. And he knew that there was no other choice.

As he launched himself at the short man—a man about to shoot a kid for not handing over a mangy mutt—something roared, and the pistol fired.

The boy dropped. The shot missed him, and a splintered hole appeared in the side of the Yukon Hotel where the bullet had struck. The dog shook and growled as it bit into the man's forearm, lifted entirely from the ground as the shooter stepped back, dropped his gun, and fell onto his rump.

Then Jack was there, his momentum forcing both man and dog down into the mud. Dutch let go and withdrew, teeth bared and bloodied, but he obviously knew who the enemy was here. He never took his eyes from the short man, watching as Jack punched him several times in the jaw and nose. When the man lifted his left hand to strike back, Jack clasped the bitten right arm in both of his and twisted. He felt the sickening wetness of warm blood there, and the man bared his teeth in unconscious imitation of the dog. He tried his best not to scream—Jack saw that, and it impressed him—but then pain became too much, and he let the cry loose.

Something fell on Jack's back and drove him down on top of the skinny man. Archie. But he was not there for long.

"Up ya get!" Merritt said, and Jack rolled in time to see Archie flung once again against the side of the hotel.

The boy had picked up the skinny man's gun.

"Steady now, kid," Merritt said.

"My name's Hal," the boy said. "I hate it when people call me kid."

Jack chuckled as he stood. *He's scared witless,* he thought, but he was still impressed by Hal's composure. The gun was heavy, but the boy's hands barely shook at all. And Jack shared his detestation of being referred to as a kid.

"Going to shoot them?" Jack asked the boy. Merritt glanced at him sharply, and he saw Archie stiffen where he lay against the building. But Jack was confident that he knew Hal's capabilities. He might think himself grown-up and brave, he might even think himself strong. But he was no killer.

He handed the gun to Jack, who in turn passed it to Merritt.

"You have no idea who you're messin' with here," the thin man said. He stood, holding his injured arm across his chest. Dutch advanced on him and growled again, edging forward so that the man backed up against the wall next to Archie.

"A big dumb mule," Jack said, pointing at Archie; then he aimed his finger at the thin man. "And what comes out of a mule's backside."

Hal giggled; Merritt sighed. Jack knew what his friend was thinking. Less than an hour in Dawson City, and already they'd made two enemies. Well . . . they wouldn't be here for long. And it was yet another reason to head on as soon as they could.

"Funny kid," the thin man said.

"Come on, William," Archie said.

Jack gave a small nod. At least the big guy knew when to admit defeat.

"Be seeing you," William said.

"Sure thing, Billy," Jack said. "Go get that arm seen to. Looking at the dog's teeth, here, I'll bet he's been eating all sorts of tasty treats from off the street."

William glanced down at the dog, which growled again. Then he looked up and pointedly fixed Hal, Merritt, and then Jack with his gaze. He'd composed himself quickly, dropping the grimace of pain and replacing it once again with that cool smile.

It spooked Jack, but he did his best not to show it.

"Dawson City's a small place," William said. "But it's already got a big cemetery." With that, he turned and walked back along the alley. Archie followed, glancing around nervously at Dutch as the dog watched them go.

"Well," Merritt said, holding the gun as if he didn't know what to do with it. At last he slipped it into his coat pocket. "Well," he said again.

"Couldn't just let it happen," Jack said quietly. He looked at Hal. "You all right?"

Hal nodded, but Jack saw that he was far from all right. As well as being scared and shaking with the upset of what had happened, he was malnourished, weak from lack of food, and his clothes were hardly suited to the cold. However he'd come to be here, something had gone badly wrong along the way.

"Come with us," Jack said.

"No." Hal knelt down next to Dutch, and the dog nuzzled at his neck. There was a devotion there, and even a love, and Jack felt a momentary pang of . . . something. Jealousy? Mourning? He was not sure. But his mind flashed back to that great white wilderness and the wolf that had guided him through.

"You sure, Hal?" Merritt asked. "Those were bad men. You cross paths with them again, they'll likely do you harm."

"I can look after myself," Hal said, his bravado offset by the quaver in his voice.

"Well, we'll be staying here if you change your mind," Jack said, nodding at the side of the hotel.

"No one's come to see what the commotion was about," Merritt said. He was looking back nervously at the street, his hand still in the pocket where he'd slipped the gun.

"No one will," Hal said. "There are mounted police, but they spend more time up north. It's wilder up there. Dawson's often left on its own." His eyes darkened.

"What are you doing here?" Jack asked, and the boy looked at him with an expression Jack recognized: pride.

"Surviving," Hal said. Then he turned away, whistling for the dog. Dutch followed his master along the alley and back onto the main street. Hal paused and glanced back.

"Much obliged," he said, nodding to Jack. He offered a smile. "And good luck."

Then he was gone.

"Well," Merritt said again.

"Yeah," Jack said. "Well."

The Yukon Hotel had one large room available, and they took it. Behind the hotel there were storage barns, and for the rest of that afternoon Jack, Jim, and Merritt took turns guarding their equipment while the other two hauled it through the settlement to the hotel. By the time they'd finished, the sun was smearing the horizon, and the sounds of Dawson City had changed. The streets were still haunted by the slow, sallow ghosts of what had once been optimistic people, but now the bars were alive, and the sounds of music and revelry strove to deny the impression those people gave.

They'd told Jim about their run-in with the two men, and like Merritt, he was all for lying low that evening. But Jack would have none of it.

"If they scare us off now," he said, "they'll have won. We run into them again, and they'll already know who's in charge. They'll think twice before getting mixed up with us."

Jim was already lying on his cot, fully clothed and half asleep. Merritt looked ready to hit the sack as well.

"Come on, Merritt," Jack said. "Just a quick drink?" He

could already taste the beer on his lips, smell the tang of whiskey as it poured amber and gold into a glass.

Merritt sighed, but Jack knew the lure of a drink would overcome his hesitation. They bade Jim a good night and went down to the hotel lobby. Just before they stepped outside, Merritt grabbed Jack's arm.

"Jack, I've got to speak plainly. I'm not sure I like what happened today. I know you've lived rough, at times, but that scene with the dog . . . I confess it shocked me a little."

"But what they were doing to that kid—"

"They had it coming for sure, Jack! I'm no coward, and I'll not shy away from a confrontation. But for a while there you looked . . . wild."

"We're *in* the wild, Merritt," Jack said. He could think of so much more to say then—about looking after yourself, and kill or be killed—but instead he went out into the Dawson City night, and Merritt followed.

They found a table in the corner of the Dawson Bar and sat nursing their drinks as the world went on around them. It was not unlike a dozen such bars Jack had frequented along the harbor in San Francisco and Oakland, but there was something about this place that gave it a sharper, harder edge. It took a while for Jack to place it—it took two drinks, both of them nursed carefully and drunk with delectation—but then he had it:

Desperation. This place hummed with it; it wound its way into and out of every smiling face and laughing mouth, and Dawson City at night really was little different from how it had been during the day. The only slight distinction was that at night, the people's disillusionment came out in different ways.

"I'll never be like this, Merritt," Jack said. "I'll always have hope. Promise me you will, too?"

"Of course I will!" Merritt said, grinning. "Jack, I know what you see, but give these people a chance. Many of them have probably been here for over a year, separated from their loved ones, doing their best to find—"

"I'll bet half of them haven't even left Dawson since they arrived! Prospectors?" Jack looked around, trying to see if he could make out who spent their time prospecting, and who lived off the prospectors' needs. Perhaps he *was* being unfair: After all, they were availing themselves of the limited facilities Dawson had to offer. But Jack's spirit was free and determined, and he could not understand how someone could have come this far and then not gone that extra small step. This could well have been a bar any-where in North America, but beyond those doors and out in the wilds, there could lie a world's ransom just waiting to be found.

And it wasn't all about money. It was about grabbing life and living it to the fullest. The adventure had left these people, and having hauled themselves through the wilderness and countless hardships, they were creating new lives that were probably barely discernible from their old ones.

"Young as you are, you're a hard man," Merritt said, and that shocked Jack. He saw that his friend meant it, and it wasn't just about the fight they'd been in that day. It was something deeper.

Is it true? he wondered. *Who is Jack London?* He thought about that as he drank. And he could never have known that within weeks, that familiar question would be answered for him in a manner he could not possibly imagine.

Hollow-eyed prospectors told tales at the bar to anyone willing to spring for the price of a drink. Local merchants, lost men without the nerve to set off into the true wilderness, abandoned women, and new arrivals nearly trembling with the excitement of their dreams ... all gathered around to listen to tales of epic dogsled races, fistfights and murders, and the men who'd struck it rich. The bar breathed resentment and greed, filled with a collective yearning for gold.

Amid those tales, though, were others—the stories and legends of the north. There were Indian curses, river gods, and wandering ghosts to be found in the vastness of the Yukon, if the half-drunken tellers of tales were to be believed. Some of the stories of hauntings were told by men who did look genuinely haunted, and many of the curses were detailed by those who seemed accursed. But among them were even wilder stories, of snow beasts and forest spirits and animals who walked on two legs. One little, rat-like man spoke wide-eyed of arctic bears that drank human blood and could take on the shapes of those they killed.

Another spoke of the Wendigo, and that prompted several others to share what they knew of the legend. Jack perked up at this. He had read much about the Yukon during the journey on the *Umatilla*, including the local lore, and the tale that had most intrigued him with its grotesquerie was that of the Wendigo. The legend began with a group of men lost in the frozen lands of the north, wandering aimlessly and slowly starving. A hideous thought, but something that must have happened in reality far too many times to count. With his friends all dead, the last man alive turned to cannibalism, feasting on his companions' corpses. But his action brought a curse upon him, transforming him into the Wendigo, an eternally ravenous beast, his tainted spirit cursed by the wild to suffer endless hunger. It was said that anyone in the frigid northlands who ate the flesh of another human being—or of the Wendigo—would share the same fate.

And this first Wendigo was still there, an insane spirit that would take deadly physical form to consume the flesh and bones of men, women, and children, growing as it ate, always hungry, always raving. A deceitful thing, too, difficult to see. An imitator, taking on an explorer's form to lure its victims close. A stalker.

The legend had fascinated Jack back then on the ship, and in the smoky bar, surrounded by the hopeless and the hopeful, all of them hungering for something, it fascinated him even more now. He looked at the men sharing the bits and pieces they knew of the legend—some of which jibed with the account Jack had read and some of which did not—and he wondered how desperate a man would have to be to consume the flesh of his friends. These people, for instance. Some of them seemed desperate enough to do almost anything, and they had food, drink, and a fire to warm themselves.

In the wild, there was no telling what they would become.

The thought unsettled him even more than the rest of that day's troubling events, and after only a few drinks, Jack and Merritt left the bar, heading back across the street and past groups of people wandering without purpose.

Jack felt tired and depressed, and part of him thought it was because William and Archie had not appeared in the Dawson Bar. Jack had always been a scrapper, and the run-in earlier that day seemed to have awakened something in him. He wasn't sure he liked what it had brought to the surface—not after their long journey, which had been all about survival. He remembered riding downriver to Dawson after the ice had finally broken up, and how he had sat proud in the stern of the boat, master of the wild that had done its best to kill him.

A shadow flashed across his mind, with padding feet and a streak of gray fur. Jack frowned. And then he heard a terrible shout.

"What the hell was that?" Merritt said.

"Came from the hotel," Jack said. "Come on." *It's the boy*, he thought. *Hal came to find us, and they found him, and God only knows what they're doing to him now.* He had never quite believed that William had been about to blow Hal's head off earlier—or maybe he hadn't *wanted* to believe—but there were other ways they could punish the boy. He'd heard rumors of people being branded out here, like cattle, marked by the outlaw slavers who drove them.

He pulled his pistol from his belt as he ran and glanced over to see Merritt do the same. Lord knew Jack didn't want to be involved in any gunplay, but after what had happened earlier, they had all agreed that it was best to carry their weapons with them, at least until they left Dawson.

Jack burst through the hotel's front doors. There was no one at reception. The area was dark, and it smelled stale, like the collected exhalations of everyone who had ever stayed there. From the floor above he heard the rumble of booted feet. Then, nothing. No more shouts, no more footsteps. Just a loaded silence.

"Jack," Merritt said, "Jim had his gun on him, didn't he?"

"He did, yeah," Jack said. "But he was half asleep even before we left."

"Come on," Merritt said. The big man brushed past Jack and started up the stairs, taking them two at a time with his long stride. They'd heard no gunshots, but after that initial awful scream, no more voices either.

"There are others staying here," Jack whispered.

"It's not them I care about," Merritt said without turning around. He was at the head of the staircase now, and turning left along the corridor that led to their room. Jack kept up with him, heart thumping, senses heightened, and he tingled all over. Merritt and Jack paused outside the closed door to their room. No other doors were open.

"Maybe it was just someone . . . ," Jack whispered, raising his eyebrows with a shrug.

"Couldn't tell if it was a man or a woman. Could you?"

Jack shook his head.

Merritt tapped the barrel of his pistol against the door. "Jim?" There was no answer. He pressed his ear to the door, listened, glanced at Jack, and shook his head.

"Maybe we should—," Jack began, but Merritt stood back and kicked at the door. Jack backed away and let the big man kick.

The door swung open—it had not been latched or locked, it seemed—and bounced off the wall, springing back and giving them only a brief view of what lay on the bed.

Merritt gasped, but Jack was through the door within a couple of heartbeats. *All me,* he thought, *this is all me, all my fault, my stupid fault for getting involved.* But then he realized with a gush of relief that Jim was not dead after all. He moved slowly, turning his head to the left and back to the right again. Blood was splashed across his pillow, and one hand was raised in a warding-off gesture, his little finger bent backward at an unnatural angle. There was a gash above his left eye from which the blood still flowed.

Jack looked quickly around the large room, saw no one waiting in the shadows, then advanced on the bed. "Jim," he said, and his friend opened his good eye.

Jim gurgled something. His eye went wide.

From behind him, Jack heard the terrible meaty impact of wood against flesh and bone. Someone grunted, and by the time he'd turned around, Merritt was slumping against the open door. Archie stood behind him in the doorway, and he grinned at Jack as he brought the wooden club down on the back of Merritt's head one more time.

"Evenin', Jack," William said, slipping through the doorway beside Archie.

"Son of a—" Jack pointed his pistol, but already he knew he could not shoot. William did not carry a gun, only a wooden club, the same as Archie. And in the darkened corridor behind them, more shapes shuffled and came closer.

Perhaps if he'd known what was to come, he *would* have fired. Shot William, killed Archie, and then tried to fight his way through the men behind them. Perhaps he should have.

But right then all he knew was the present. So he dropped the gun on the bed and put up his fists, as ready to fight as he'd ever been before.

Archie laughed and dropped his bloodied club, balling his fist. William's smile was as cool and haunting as ever. Two more men came into the room—bad men, wild men, with the glint of brutality in their eyes and the scars of their rough existence marking their skin.

"Come on, then," Jack said.

And so they came.

"Come on, then," Jack said.

CHAPTER SEVEN

ONLY THE WILD

H E WAS LOST IN ANOTHER terrible storm. Snow swirled and raged heavier than he had ever thought possible. He could feel it pelting his skin, like shards of ice instead of soft flakes, and when he tried to breathe in, snow invaded his throat and lungs. It froze him on the inside, while outside he could feel little. The smell of muck and horses pervaded the air, but he was motionless in this whiteout, and there was not a sound to be heard. *This is the true white silence,* he thought, and then between gusts of snow he caught sight of a familiar shape. The wolf was running toward him, bounding through snow so deep that the creature all but disappeared with each jump. It ran and howled—though he could not hear it—but it never seemed to draw any closer.

A curtain of snow obscured his vision, and he felt so alone.

A steady, low bumping began, so slight that he was not certain whether he was feeling or hearing it. And though he tried to walk, look around, see his hands, it was only his awareness that acknowledged the blizzard, not his body. *Dreaming*, he thought, but even that did not feel quite right.

He caught sight of the wolf again, fighting its way through the snow. It seemed closer than before, but still he could not hear it. He tried to shout, but it could not hear him, either. There was just the snow, and that steady *thump* . . . *thump* . . . *thump*. . . .

It was impact, and noise. And beneath the noise there were smaller thuds, coming from farther away but adding to the rhythms that seemed to be assaulting his body and senses.

The snow started to turn brown. It melted away, taking the blank landscape beyond with it, and the sound and feel of the impacts became more defined.

He heard the loud howl of a wolf, so familiar and real that he almost felt as if he could grab hold of it. He smelled horse, opened his eyes, and could see three men ahead of him, walking toward a thickly forested hillside. The horse to which Jack had been strapped ambled after them. There was no snow on the ground; that terrible blizzard remained in his skull.

"That sounds close," one of the men said.

"Yup, but you'll never see them," another man replied. He glanced across at Jack, and it was Archie. "Well now, look who's awake," Archie said. "Stan, wait up! Got another one who can walk."

The horse stopped, stomping its feet a few times, and each stomp pounded into his head. Archie untied him, ripping ropes from around his waist and arms, and all the time he was whispering into Jack's ear, "Now's your time, Jack, now's your time, now is when you'll find out how tough you are, how hard, and I look forward to every minute of every day from now on, now that you're awake. Little bastard."

Jack's arms were afire with pins and needles, and he groaned as circulation found its way back through his shoulders and along to his hands. He wasn't sure whether his skin burned or was frozen solid.

Archie pushed him from the horse.

Jack twisted to keep his head from hitting the ground, but the fall knocked the wind out of him. He rolled onto his back and stared up at a clear blue sky, and he wondered how something so beautiful could exist in the hell he'd just woken to.

"Up!" Archie said. He kicked Jack in the thigh. "Make yourself useful. Up, now!"

Jack tried, gingerly, to obey. He closed his eyes against

the thumping rush of pain throbbing in his head. Every inch of him felt like it had been boiled and cut, whipped and frozen, and he knew it would be a while before he could truly assess his injuries.

"Up, or I'll gut you and leave you for the wolves." Archie sounded serious.

Jack looked around. They were up in the hills, forested slopes rising around them, a small creek running somewhere off to the left. There was no sign of Dawson City. He saw men carrying guns and little else, horses and dogs, and other men bearing great burdens, some of them with their legs tied just far enough apart to enable them to walk. Through the pain, he realized what had happened to him: They'd shanghaied him, and for the moment, he was a slave. And he also knew that Archie *was* serious. Away from whatever scrap of civilization Dawson City offered, out here he really would gut Jack and leave him for the wolves.

Jack stood, and it was one of the most painful experiences of his life. He bit his lip to prevent himself from fainting.

Archie chuckled and threw a bag at Jack's feet. "Just this for now. Don't want you injuring yourself." His voice turned dark. "Lost enough of you already, and the real work's not yet begun."

The column moved off again. Archie stayed close, a rifle

cradled in his arms, but Jack tried his best not to look at the big man. He didn't want to give him the satisfaction . . . and besides, he had to concentrate on every single step.

A few minutes later, walking, starting to think about where he was hurt and how badly, Jack noticed the man walking ten feet to his left.

"Merritt!" Jack whispered.

Though he must have heard, Merritt didn't look up.

"Merritt! Hey, you all right?"

His burly friend looked fine, walking as strongly and confidently as ever. There was a big pack on his back, and he carried several long shovels across his chest.

"Merritt, where's—"

"Jim's dead," Merritt said without turning to look at Jack. And through everything else he said, he could not bring himself to look up from the ground before him. "They must've hit him harder than they needed, because when he woke up on one of the horses and they cut him loose, he fell. Could hardly stand. I went and tried to help, but they beat me back. Jim was walking in circles. He'd lost his glasses, but it wasn't that—it was . . . it was his head. It got all swollen where he'd been hit, but it looked soft. They tried to get him walking straight, gave him a load to carry, but he fell again and again. Told him what they'd do to him if he didn't walk, but I don't think he even heard. Then

William—your friend William, Jack, guy with the look of death in his eyes, the one you made an enemy out of—he pulled his gun and shot Jim in the head. *'Too much trouble,'* he said, and everyone started walking again. Didn't move him aside, just walked on by as his body started to cool. I tried going back to him, but they wouldn't let me. I wanted to fight, but I didn't have it in me, Jack."

"Jim . . . ," Jack said softly. He glanced to his right at Archie, only to find the bearded thug grinning. *He's letting Merritt tell me this,* Jack thought. *He wants me to know.*

"Jim's dead," Merritt said. "And if it weren't for you an' your fists . . . Who knows, Jack? Who knows?"

"Merritt?" Jack said. *No, not me, not my fault.* "Merritt?" But his big friend did not look up, and as the day wore on, he moved away from Jack, farther up the line of human packhorses.

Jack watched and listened for the wolf, but after the cry that had woken him, there was nothing.

Only the wild.

It had taken Jack seven months, during which time he had made three friends and lost two of them—one through the cruelty of the slave drivers and the other through blame and guilt—but at last he was panning for gold. The third friend he thought might exist only as a madness of his mind. And out here in the beautiful, awe-inspiring, bru-tal wilderness of the Yukon, that wolf felt closer than ever before.

He supposed he should have expected brutality to exist here, where gold painted men's perceptions with the pos-sibility of untold fortunes. His short time in prison had made him shockingly aware of the potential for cruelty that existed in some men, and out in the wild, with the law spread so thinly it might as well be a breath in the wind, sometimes that cruelty came to the fore. He should have expected murder and theft, jealousy and greed, and dead men littering the wondrous landscape, with bullet holes or shovel-blade wounds the only evidence of their search for the yellow metal.

William was their leader, of that he was already certain. The man had shorn himself of the trappings of civilization and morality, and he wore cruelty like a new skin. Perhaps he had always been cruel—certainly he had always had that potential—but Jack suspected that coming here had changed William completely. With his hair slicked back and that mustache, the short man reminded him of a card-sharp in some western dime novel. He had the air of a man reveling in the freedom of the Yukon, and every bad thing that freedom permitted.

Archie seemed to be William's right-hand man. His

muscle. Jack had bettered him in a fight, and he knew that marked him for extra-special treatment. He had already caught Archie glaring at him many times, and Jack was aware that he would be made to suffer for that beating back in Dawson.

There were seven others. All of them were heavily armed with rifles and revolvers, and some of them had taken to carrying short wooden clubs spiked with nails. Jack saw no hope of escape or help in any of them—greedy, wild, brutal men, criminals pushed north by their crimes and pulled by the possibility of gold. He had already watched one of the slaves badly beaten simply for sitting for a rest, and that man worked now with one eye swollen shut and a limp so heavy that Jack suspected his leg was fractured.

The slaves. There were twelve of them, including Jack and Merritt. Several Indians, four black men, a few white; the slavers did not distinguish between color or creed in who they chose to labor for them. Perhaps they had press-ganged people who looked strong, although one of the Indians must have been eighty years old. Maybe they had attacked only people who had offended them in some way, but there was a Frenchman who could barely speak a word of English, and he seemed to Jack a gentle, intelligent soul.

Whatever the reasons for selection, the slavers worked them hard.

The morning after Jack had awoken on the horse's back, after marching them through the night with only one stop for a drink and a bite of stale bread, William's gang put them to work in a narrow, shallow creek. Earlier they had passed two dead men, just as dawn painted the eastern hills, the stark white of bones showing through tattered, rotting flesh. The men had been torn apart, little to distinguish one from another save the color of their boots. Tools were strewn about them—prospectors—and Jack had seen dried black blood splashed on the plants and ground. They were recent kills, and for a few miles after they marched past, even the slavers were quiet.

What did that? Jack had wondered. *Man or beast? Or perhaps neither.* The brutality of the men's deaths had followed him, a memory as solid as the deep shadows he sensed watching. Shadows too deep and too cruel to be the wolf.

At last they had stopped at the creek. The stream emerged from a fold in the land, passing out from a small, tree-clogged ravine and flowing merrily across the floor of a shallow valley. There were few trees down here—the ground looked as if it was affected by regular flooding— and most of the forested areas started a hundred paces in any direction. The creek bed was perhaps as deep as a man was tall, thirty feet across; and at the moment the stream filled less than a third of its width.

It was the perfect place for the slavers to stop. If one of their slaves did run, he'd have to climb from the creek first, then make it across open ground before he hit the trees. Plenty of time for a bullet to blast out his lungs.

They strung the men along the stream—keeping some distance between them to prevent talking—gave them each a pan, and told them to start searching for gold. When one of the men asked what share of any gold they would receive, he received a rifle butt across the throat in response.

They'll kill us before they'd let us go, Jack thought then. The realization was chilling, but hardly surprising. Somewhere in the woods there awaited twelve areas destined to be turned into shallow graves. It would not be soon, he knew. The men wanted as much gold as they could find first. But perhaps when suspicions were aroused in fellow prospectors in the area, or when the jealousies between slavers grew too great, there would come a day when the forced march began again. And this time its end would be marked by a bullet to the back of the head.

He would not be here long enough for that to happen. And, he swore, neither would Merritt.

He scooped up another panful of grit and stones from the bottom of the stream, doing his best to shut out what had happened and enjoy the simple act of panning. He focused all his attention down so that he could not see their surroundings, nor the cruel men guarding them. Thinking of his mother and Eliza, he swilled water around the pan in a gentle circular motion, spilling a little more mud and water each time until the heavier elements were a slick across the bottom. This was what he had been traveling so long to do. All that effort, all those months trapped in the cabin in the middle of the greatest winter he had ever known, coming closer to death than he had ever been before, and now he was looking for the glint of gold amid the gritty brown sediment of this Yukon creek. He tried to feel enlivened by the act, excited. But he could not. However much he kept his head down, Jack could not shake the knowledge that he was a prisoner, and any wealth he discovered would line the pockets of thugs and killers.

"If only they knew who they were messing with," he said to himself, but even he was not sure. He felt that he was beginning to understand himself better out here, as if he could perceive more of his bright outline set against a dazzling sunset. But there was still a great mystery to Jack London. That thrilled and terrified him in equal measures; he could not help believing that there were wonders in his future, that his life had led him here with some purpose, but he had to overcome this terrible present for them to offer themselves up for view.

"Jack," someone whispered.

He frowned, looking around without raising his head. Across from him up on the rim of the creek stood a slaver, rifle resting in the crook of his arm as he smoked. He was looking into the distance. Upstream to Jack's right, a black man Jack knew only as Jonas was kneeling in the water.

"Jack," he heard again, and Jonas glanced up. "Our voices flow with the stream. They can't hear. Do you see?"

Jack looked across at the slaver again. The man was closer to him than Jonas by at least ten steps, but he seemed to hear nothing.

"Stream's flowing down, so you can hear me but I won't hear you."

Jack coughed as acknowledgment, and Jonas smiled in understanding.

"Big man, Reese, he wants to make a break. Tonight after they've fed us, when they think we'll be tired and ready for sleep. He says if we're all in, then most of us will make it."

Jack frowned and tried to glare at Jonas, but he wasn't certain the man understood. They both kept panning, kept swilling. *Damn, if only I could whisper back. It's crazy! They'll slaughter us all.* Reese was a huge bear of a man, and Jack had been surprised that William and his men had dared club him into slavery. But from the little that he'd seen of Reese's interaction with the other slaves, Jack already knew that he was a bully. William must have recognized that in him, and understood that it meant Reese was no threat on his own. Bullies were inevitably cowards, who could only act with others around to support them or urge them on.

Jack glanced at the slaver and risked a shake of his head to Jonas.

Jonas frowned. "You want to stay here?"

Jack shook his head again.

"Then this is a chance. Longer we stay, weaker we get."

Jack coughed, harsher than last time in an effort to communicate disagreement.

"Back to work!" the slaver said. He came closer by several steps and kicked at the stream, splashing cold water across Jack's face. Jack wiped it quickly away and glared at Jonas, offering a single shake of the head again. But Jonas was already looking back down into his pan.

Farther up the stream, several men away, Jack could see Merritt. He was in his own world, working slowly and methodically. With Jim dead, Merritt's whole journey was soured.

I should feel that as well, Jack thought. But sad though he was, the future was still an exciting place, and he had the unerring conviction that his journey had only just begun.

Jack could not help but revel in the beauty of this place. The creek was marred by the cruelty of man, but the hills and forests surrounding them exuded the pure, untainted wildness of nature. He breathed in the scents of stream and forest, and felt the welcome heat of sunlight warming his skin.

Beyond the constant rush of water he heard occasional birdcalls, but though he listened hard, the cry of the wolves eluded him. He tried to extend his senses to find anything watching them from the forests. Just because he had heard no wolf cry, that did not mean the wolf was not there. *Always watching me,* he thought, but right then he would have welcomed some sign that this was the case. He could feel the immensity of the wilderness, the pull of the wild on his adventurous soul. It called him, and he swore that he would answer.

Jack hated these men for their cruelty, their ignorance, and their inhumanity. But more than all that, he hated them because they were stealing from him the experience he most desired: freedom to explore the wilderness and the chance to be a part of it.

The work was hard, and Jack took frequent drinks from the stream. The water was still icy cold from snow-melt, and the more he drank, the hungrier he grew. *They've got to feed us something,* he thought. *Or eventually we'll be too weak to do them any good.*

Just when hunger had begun to claw at his insides in earnest, their captors called out a pause for lunch. As the men put aside their pans, Jack glanced up at the steep hillside to the south of the creek. It was heavily wooded, and the trees smoothed the rough contours of the land. *Something there,* he thought. When he closed his eyes, he felt nothing, but part of the hillside was blurred to his senses or immune to them. A blank on the wilderness. An area of mystery, and fear. He shivered.

"Sit down and don't move!" Archie shouted to them all. "You need to piss, do it where you are."

Jack sat thankfully, pulling his freezing feet from the water. He wondered for the first time what had happened to all their equipment. Gathering dust in the storage barns behind the Yukon Hotel, no doubt. In there were his warm boots, extra clothing, gloves, and hats, and now he wore some rough clothing that William's men had given him. It might be spring, but it was still cold.

Archie made his way down the line with a bag of food. He gave each man a chunk of bread and a finger of jerky, and the slaves all bit in ravenously. Reese took his food with a nod of thanks, and though Archie did not acknowledge him, Jack knew how clever this was. *Makes them think he's subdued*, he thought. Perhaps Reese *was* a bully, but he was preparing well for his escape attempt. *Not well enough, though!* Jack glanced around at the slave drivers—their guns and knives, their cruel faces—and he knew that the slaves would need more than determination and speed to escape. If they really were to get away, they'd need to kill William and his men first.

"Why d'you think it won't work?" Jonas asked. A dozen steps away from Jack, still his voice carried. No one intervened. Perhaps the slavers were allowing the men this brief contact.

"Foolish," Jack said. "They've got guns! We have to pick our chance well, we have to—"

"Wait," Jonas said. Then he turned, and Jack knew that he was talking to the next man along from him in the other direction. He watched, fascinated, as he saw the conversation pass from man to man without the slavers knowing anything was awry. Heads dipped slightly, or tilted to aid hearing, and Jack tracked the voices even though he could not hear them.

The string of whispers reached Merritt. He nodded once, but then Archie was before him, handing him the food. Merritt took it without looking up or saying anything, and Archie moved on. Jack saw Merritt bring the food to his mouth, and just before he chewed, his jaw worked as he said several words.

The message reached Reese. He was wiping his mouth after his food, his actions slow and deliberate. His long hair hung down beside his face, heavy beard obscuring his mouth. He leaned forward and took a handful of water from the stream. As he drank, Jack saw him say a few words in response.

"Here you are, a meal fit for a king," Archie said. He'd reached Jack, and he delved into the bag for a chunk of bread. Jack found his mouth watering, and he could actually smell the stale bread above the scents of the woods and stream.

He held out his hand.

"Darn," Archie said, and dropped the bread into the stream. It floated away, already sinking as it took on water. Jack reached out for his lunch, and Archie struck him on the right shoulder. It was not a hard punch, but Jack was unbalanced, and it sent him headlong into the stream.

He came up spluttering, welcomed back above the surface by Archie's heavy laughter.

"Don't tease the animals," someone said. William. He had emerged from the tents the slavers had set up, and now he was crossing the grassy floodplain to the stream.

"This one won't bite back," Archie said, still smiling.

Jack crawled from the stream, shivering.

"Not anymore," William said. Once again Jack saw the

coldness in the leader's eyes. *It's like there's nothing in there at all*, he thought, and he was glad that his soaking provided an excuse for the next shiver that shook his body.

"Here," Archie said. He dropped a scrap of jerky onto the ground, and as he turned away he stepped on it.

Jack pressed his lips together. His heartbeat increased. *Not now*, he thought, but the temptation was strong. He could be on Archie in moments, slipping the man's knife from his own belt, then around and up into his neck—

"Reese says you're just a kid," Jonas whispered. "Says you don't know nothin'. Says to shut up and listen to him if you want to live."

Jack blinked softly at Jonas, aware of Archie still walking away chuckling. Aware also of William staring at him, eyes calculating and cold.

Jack sat down, brushed the dirt from his scrap of jerky, and started chewing.

They worked through that long afternoon. There was a break around midafternoon when another of the slavers brought around a handful of biscuits, and this time Jack had his share. To most of the men he must be just another worker; it was Archie and William who bore grudges. He stored this information away.

Several times he risked a look upstream. Past several

other men he saw Merritt working away, and he thought his friend seemed reduced by what had happened. Still stocky and strong, there was a weakness about him now, as if a part of him had withered when Jim had been shot. *He saw his friend die*, Jack thought. *That must have been terrible.*

Beyond Merritt there was Reese. Once, the big man caught Jack looking at him, and he offered a grimace in response. The two men were too far away to communicate effectively, so Jack simply turned away and started panning again, disregarding Reese's look and turning his back. *Man's a fool*, he thought. But Jack was worried: If Reese made a move that evening as he'd planned, then Jack and Merritt would also be dragged into it. Events could move on without him, and he'd have to pay for the foolishness of another man's decisions.

And if there was an uprising among the new slaves, he knew for sure who would be the first target of the slavers' wrath. Jack paused in his panning, staring down into the trickling water and seeing the beautiful, deep blue sky reflected there. Maybe Reese knew about him and Archie and William, and was relying on that to aid his own escape.

Maybe Merritt had told him.

A shadow passed before him and he shifted the pan again, spilling water and dirt back into the stream.

They worked into the evening until it became too dark

to see, and then the slavers ushered them all back into the space between the encircled tents. There were five tents in all, though Jack already knew that none of them were for the slaves. Their place would be around the fire and beneath the stars, ankles bound together and tied to heavy stakes. There was a pile of rough, uncured hides close to the fire, and he could already smell the stench on them. By morning he'd stink of death, and a dip in the freezing stream would likely do nothing to wash that away.

The slavers' dogs barked as the exhausted men were told to sit and await their food. The smell of freshly brewed coffee wafted from the can above the fire, and Jack closed his eyes and tried to push the smell away. But his watering mouth was an unconscious reaction. He remembered drinking coffee on the Chilkoot Pass with Merritt and Jim, and how the two men had seemed close even then.

"It's gonna be tonight," Jonas whispered, when he managed to get close enough.

"Stupid!" Jack said. "We need to get their measure first, figure out their weaknesses. Seen the guns?"

"Seen how much we've had to eat today?"

Jack sighed. He looked at Jonas, lips pursed, then noticed a slaver staring right at him. "I reckon we'll be moved on upstream," he said, louder.

"Yeah, toward where the first strike was made," Jonas

said. The slaver looked away, and Jonas pressed on in a quieter voice. "We've *got* to get away! Reese, he has a plan, he knows what he's doing and—"

"Reese will get you killed, Jonas." Jack saw the man's face drop, and he could perceive the desperation there. Who had he left back at home? A wife and child? A mother, like Jack's, hoping for help from her gold-hunting son? And here Jonas was, captured and put to slavery like members of his family mere decades before him, and there was a man ready to fight to free him. Jack could see the allure of Reese and his plans. He felt it himself. But he also knew that if the big man was allowed to act on his plan, then most of them would be dead by midnight.

And Jack would be the first.

Food came, handed out by a couple of men he'd never heard speak. Jack received the same share as everyone else. William and Archie must have had other things on their minds.

As the men ate, Jack slowly edged his way into the center of their group. There sat Merritt, and beside him Reese. And they were fully aware of Jack's approach.

"Merritt," Jack said, chewing on another piece of tough jerky. Merritt barely acknowledged him; a quick glance, a blink.

"Kid," Reese said, "you still being a fool?"

"I'm no fool," Jack said. "You're set to get us killed, and I'll be the first one put down." He looked at Merritt as he said this, hoping for some reaction, but there was none.

"What makes you think you're so special?" Reese asked.

"I've already beaten the hell out of Archie," Jack said. "Back in Dawson. He holds a grudge, and he's set to act on it sometime soon. Do what you plan tonight, and I'll get the first bullet." Reese grunted and shrugged, and Jack's foot flashed out and connected with the big man's lower leg. Reese glared at him. "You'll get the second," Jack said. "I'm betting William will want some sort of revenge for his slaves rebelling. Means he'll have to get all the way back to Dawson to get more, or maybe he'll just attack one of the other prospectors' camps around here, maybe one with women and kids. So your bullet will be in the hip or gut, just something to stop you cold. Then when everyone else is dead, they'll get to work on you properly." He bit another chunk of jerky and chewed. Merritt had his eyes downcast.

"We'll surprise them," Reese said. "They've got the upper hand now; we're all shocked by what's happened to us, confused. They're relying on that. We act now, it's the best chance at surprise we have. Longer we leave it, more on guard they'll be."

"Who will you take first?" Jack asked, retying his boot-laces. He and Reese could never keep eye contact for long, never let the guards know there was a conversation going on.

"Nearest one. Get his guns, then move on."

"You ever shot a man?" Jack asked, and he could already see the answer in the big man's eyes. For a moment, he actually looked scared.

"Not yet," Reese said.

Jack was aware of the rest of the men listening. He glanced around to make sure none of the slavers could hear, and they seemed safe for now.

"You need to go for the strongest first," Jack said. "Not the loudest, or the cruelest, but the one who'll coolly shoot a man in the back in cold blood. We already know one of them, but there'll be more. We have to spend time marking them."

"You're just a damn kid!" Reese said.

"And you're just a bear with no bite."

"No one talks to me like that!"

"I just did," Jack said. And he realized then what he had to do. He'd known for a while, he supposed—most of that day—but here and now, he saw the way this would play out. Most of the men were behind Reese, because the lure of freedom was greater than the wisdom of caution. So he had to prove to the men who was wisest, and who was strongest. He had to show them who could really lead them to freedom, and in the wild, that wasn't done by talking politics.

Reese was already keen to fight.

Jack took a deep breath, glanced around at the others—expectant faces, sad eyes, some of them already beaten men—and then his gaze settled on Merritt.

His friend's eyes went wide as he saw what Jack was about to do. "Jack, don't—"

Jack pushed himself forward, swinging a heavy right at Reese's head. With the thunk of fist against skull, and the excited shouting of men, the fight of his life began.

Reese had not been prepared for it. Though he acted the hard man, he was exactly what Jack had suspected: a coward enjoying the scent of leadership. Jack's flailing fists drove him over sideways, and both of them fell dangerously close to the fire.

Voices rose around them, and a cheer as Reese recovered and launched a heavy fist into Jack's shoulder. Then he bucked and threw Jack off, grabbing a burning stick from the fire and swinging it high over his head.

Jack rolled away and felt the stick strike the ground close to his feet. Sparks hit the bare skin above his wet socks. The heat was almost welcome. He gained his feet and turned, ready to hold back an attack. But Reese was just standing there, swinging the still-smoking stick left and right like a giant pendulum.

The whole camp had gathered to watch. The slaves had stood and pulled back into a tight circle, affecting the air of people avoiding violence rather than urging it on. Jack saw Merritt there, the only one who seemed to despair over what he saw.

He is *still my friend,* Jack thought. And in the midst of a fight that was partly about saving Merritt's life, that idea pleased him immensely.

Beyond the slaves, William's men were also watching. Jack saw five or six of them gathered within the circle of tents, William and Archie included. The others must have still been on guard duty beyond, not lured in by the sudden violence, and already Jack was learning how organized they were. *Don't you see?* he wanted to shout at Reese.

But Reese was coming at him then, blackened branch swinging wide again.

Jack ducked and punched Reese in the stomach. His hand sank into flab, and the big man *whoof*ed and staggered to the side, winded. Jack went after him and struck him across the head, but Reese surprised him by swatting him aside. Jack stumbled and hit the ground hard.

He heard the slavers betting on who would win the

fight. His fall must have changed the odds.

Standing, Jack braced himself for another attack. But Reese hung back. A trickle of blood ran down from somewhere under his wild head of hair, drawing across his cheek and entering his equally unkempt beard. He looked like a forest wild man of legend, but his eyes spoke of an altogether gentler upbringing. For an instant Jack wondered where Reese came from and who waited for him back home. Then the big man came for him again— perhaps finally realizing what was at stake here—and Jack stepped sideways.

The fight became more consistent, and more brutal. Reese had seen the look in some of the other men's eyes, and he knew that he had to win this fight to maintain his position at the top of the pecking order. And Jack caught sight of Merritt's lost, longing expression, and knew he had to save his friend. The first bullet would be his, yes, but the thought of Merritt dying because Jack could not protect him . . . that was unbearable.

The men were growing wild, now, like a pack of dogs—or wolves—waiting to see which fighter would dominate, and which would offer up his throat. His fellow oppressed men, and the oppressors, all cheered and jeered. But beyond that was something else. A great awareness, a paused beat in the timelessness of the mountains and rivers, as if just for the length of this fight, time had halted, held its breath, and Jack was suddenly *more* than a speck in the wilderness. He was the mountains themselves, the deep rivers holding their glittering golden secrets for those brave enough to search, and that watcher from the mountains gave him strength, and it was a strength that came from fear.

Because the thing that watched was no wolf.

Reese had strength, but Jack had youth and speed, and a brutal instinct that the other man lacked—he had hurt men before, beaten them into bloody submission in dock fights and back-alley brawls. He took no pride in that history; it had merely been his way to survive the life he had led up to this day, and it would get him through this night.

The wild in him. The wolf. They came to the surface like never before, and he thought of the pack, surrounding them, howling, and he knew there was only one way this fight could end. He beat Reese, and when the big man fell, Jack beat him some more. Defeated, Reese raised his hands in supplication. Still Jack fell upon him, nuzzling down beneath the stinking beard and clasping the man's throat between his teeth. He growled.

"Yes," Reese panted.

Jack growled again, and he heard the sudden silence that had fallen over the slavers' camp.

"Yes," Reese said, whispering this time. "I submit. I submit."

Jack released him, tasting the sweat and blood of victory on his tongue. He stood slowly. And before Archie and three other men came at him with their fists and clubs, he felt the cowed, respectful eyes of the other slaves upon him.

CHAPTER EIGHT

THE FEAST

JACK COULD NOT SLEEP. The beating they'd given him had been bad enough, and he was thankful that no bones appeared to be broken. Weak as he already was, thinner than he'd ever been, suffering again from the beginnings of scurvy and feeling how loose his teeth had become, the energy he'd expended that day should have slipped him into the deepest sleep. After panning for twelve hours with little food, then fighting Reese and taking the beating from Archie and the other thugs . . .

He could not recall ever being so exhausted, and yet sleep eluded him. He lay on his back and stared up at the stars. The night sky drew heat from the ground, and from Jack, and however many skins he draped over himself—and some of the men had thrown their own across to him— he could not stay warm. He wondered at the number of stars up there, and thought about how many other hopeful people were lying like this across the Yukon Territory, staring into the dark and dreaming of the golden days yet to come. Even though Jack's situation was far different—the bruises, his ankles tied to a stake in the ground—he still felt free. There was more to trapping a man's soul than tying his legs and beating him into submission.

Jack blinked, his eyes heavy and sore with tiredness. He heard snoring from the other men around him and hoped that Merritt was sleeping well. *Saved your life today,* he thought, and he was sure that Merritt understood. He hoped they *all* did, even Reese. He'd not meant the big man any lasting harm.

He tried casting his mind out beyond the camp, leaving the captors and captives behind, exploring the darkness to seek out whatever had been watching the fight. Even while Archie had beaten him with fists and a wooden club, Jack had felt observed by something far away, that terrible thing that held him in such curious regard. And, knocked almost into unconsciousness, he had felt like the observer. He'd felt a distance to his pain, as if he was both suffering it here and viewing it from afar.

Within him was a raving hunger the likes of which he had never experienced before. This was not only a hunger for food—good meat, which he'd not had since hunting from the cabin; fruits and vegetables, which they'd had little of in Dawson—but for something more spiritual. Something deeper.

Listening desperately for the familiar howl of wolves and, when he could not hear them, feeling lonelier than he ever had in his life before, Jack drifted off to sleep at last.

In his dream, something touched his face. It was cool and wet, and Jack raised a hand to brush it away. Something else brushed against his exposed foot, and a shape worked its way closer to him beneath the skins piled across his body. He felt both trapped and assaulted, and he started to panic as he felt the thing coming closer. He could feel the strange heat of it, and yet when it touched his stomach, it, too, was cold, and wet.

He opened his eyes. Shadows stood all around him, barely visible in the light of the weakened campfire, utterly silent. He gasped and sat up, and when the pain of his beating bit in, he realized that this was no dream.

Ten trail dogs stood around him, staring. They'd been nudging him with their noses, and now that he was awake, they simply watched. These animals were slaves to William and Archie and the rest, just as Jack and Merritt and the other men were. They'd stolen the dogs, just as they'd been trying to steal Hal's mangy mutt when Jack and Merritt had first encountered them.

He looked from one to the next, and each of the dogs reflected moonlight in its dark, wet eyes. None of them made any noise. None of them glanced away, not once, even when he brought his arms from beneath the skins and folded them across his chest. *It's so damn cold,* he thought, and he glanced at the fire. It had been allowed to burn down, and around it he could make out the shapes of his fellow slaves sleeping. Surrounding them, visible as pale blurs in the starlight, were the slavers' tents. Beyond the tents somewhere, he knew, there were at least three slavers still on guard.

Or there should have been.

"They'd have come to see what was happening by now," he whispered, and one of the dogs edged closer.

Jack pulled back. He knew how vicious trail dogs could be. But then he exhaled, sensing no threat here. They were around him but not *surrounding* him. He reached out a tentative hand, and a dog rolled its head against his open palm.

"Hey, boy," Jack whispered. "What's on your mind?"

The dog whined, low and quiet, and Jack felt its voice rumbling against his palm. The others edged closer. One of them sniffed him, another snapped at the offending dog.

What is *this?*

The moon emerged from behind scattered cloud cover.

It was half full, and its silvery sheen fell across the landscape like a dusting of snow. The tents grew lighter, the shadows beyond less dense. Jack looked around, trying to make out the moving shapes of William's guards, but he could not spot them. Maybe they were sitting somewhere, watching the silent camp and confident that, motionless, they'd spy any movement the instant it happened.

The dogs turned away. Jack felt a momentary pang of regret at their departure, and he almost called them back. But whatever part they were playing this night was over, and he was keen to see what was to come. *Something's happening*, he thought. He assured himself again that he was not asleep; the vibrancy of his senses convinced him of that. His skull hurt, and his neck, and his limbs and ribs from where the slavers had beaten him. But the pain seemed fresh and vital, as startling as the burn of returning sensation after almost freezing to death.

He looked beyond the camp, because he knew that whatever happened next would come from there. And then he saw the wolf.

It stood below a line of trees a hundred feet from the camp, up a steep slope that led out of the creek and to the hillsides higher up. It stood in just the right place for the newly revealed moon to touch it, and its mottled gray pelt seemed to shine.

"There you are," Jack whispered, and at the sound of his voice the wolf began to walk. It was making for the camp. *No!* he thought. *No, they'll see you, they'll* shoot *you!* He looked frantically for the trail dogs, but they had already melted away into the camp, returning to their hidden places like shadows beneath the sun.

Jack could see only the wolf's head and the tip of its tail for a while as it came closer, its step confident, no hesitation at all in its approach.

"They'll *see* you," he whispered, glancing around desperately for the sentries. But they were still absent. Nothing stirred among the tents; nothing moved around the fire.

The wolf disappeared behind one of the tents and then emerged close to the closed flap. It sniffed at the tent, then started across toward Jack. It was beautiful. As the creature moved gracefully, its fur caught the moonlight in rolling lines, shadows dancing across its coat like breaths of smoke. Its eyes were alight, brighter than the meager campfire, and they never moved from Jack's face.

"You're here," Jack said as the wolf stopped ten paces from him. He sniffed, and he could smell the animal scents; he closed his eyes, and he could hear the wolf breathing.

It came closer and pressed its muzzle against Jack's throat.

He snapped his eyes open, and he was staring into the

wolf's face. It opened its jaws, slowly, and closed them on the collar of Jack's coat. Then it pulled.

It wants me to leave, he thought. "But . . ."

The wolf growled, so softly, and then it darted to Jack's feet. In seconds it had bitten through the ropes binding his legs together, and in another few heartbeats it had gnawed the rope staking him to the ground. It turned its head and looked past Jack, back at the forest from which it had emerged. It growled again, slightly louder.

"Merritt," Jack whispered. "If I go and he stays behind, they'll kill him."

The wolf grabbed his hand in its jaws, a lightning-fast movement. He felt its wet tongue, the heat of its insides, and the incredibly hot points where its teeth pressed into his skin. *It's going to drag me!* he thought, panicked, and there was no way he'd be able to fight such an action. But it bit once, then let go and walked a few steps back the way it had come.

Jack crouched, wincing as circulation returned to his legs. He should have been seen by now, and so should the wolf, but he was being offered an opportunity here, the chance to get away and seek help. Hal had said that the mounted police patrolled these vast northern areas, and if he could get away and find them, bring them back, then maybe . . .

The wolf's hackles rose as it looked back and forth

between Jack and the forest. It trotted back toward the tents . . . then gripped the flap of one in its teeth and pulled.

"No!" Jack said, louder than he'd intended. Nobody stirred, and the wolf let go of the flap and stared back at him. *I can go,* he thought. *I can follow it out of the camp as easily as I watched it walk in, and once I'm away, I can do my best for these men. I can fetch help.* Right then, weighing the chance of that against the possibility of ever overcoming William's men—however much he knew about them, however good his knowledge—there was no real alternative.

Besides, this was not the first time the wolf had saved his life.

I'll leave the camp and it will be gone, he thought. *Vanished back to wherever it comes from.* He went, moving quickly but carefully, and as he passed between two tents, he could hear men snoring inside. The wolf stood before him, resplendent in its coat of starlight. He followed, and as he crossed the grasses and entered into the forest, he expected the crack of a rifle at any moment, and the impact of a bullet between his shoulder blades. But none came.

The wolf did not pause. It led him up the slope, heading out of the creek bed and toward whatever wilderness lay beyond, but Jack's flush of freedom did not last for long.

Minutes after entering the forest, he sensed that he was being followed.

And moments after that, he knew that whatever stalked the darkness was nowhere near human.

He could smell it: rotten meat, rank flesh, insides turned out. It pursued him, and he turned around to see its face. But however quickly he turned, the thing was always behind him. It made no noise, but it was always there. Jack ran. The wolf led the way, and whenever he feared it would leave him behind, it slowed down, giving him time to catch up. Not for a moment did he believe the thing following him was one of William's men. If he had believed that, he would have turned to fight. This thing kept its face hidden from him, buzzing around him like his own echo. And Jack ran.

The slope was steep, but he dug his hands and feet into the soft ground and pulled himself up. The wolf was close in front of him, so close that he could smell it again, and when he glanced back and saw fleeting movement from the corner of his eye, the wolf loosed a low, mournful howl as if Jack were already dead.

Low down in the creek behind him he saw the glow of the firelight.

The slope leveled a little, and Jack was able to move faster. If the wolf had not been with him, he believed he would have screamed, so close was his pursuer. He could smell the stench of it, almost feel it reaching for him with each tree he passed and each shadow that merged with his own. He glanced back again, and once more the thing coming after him flitted from his line of sight. He paused for a moment and turned left and right, looking up through the branches at the stars and down at the mud between his feet. Still his pursuer eluded his view.

I was safe back there! he thought. *People around me and the fire, and I was safe!*

This thing, whatever it might be, was playing with him. It could have closed in on him at any moment, and if it had meant to kill him, it could have done just that.

Jack shouted. His voice, a wordless scream of rage and frustration and fear, echoed across the creek. *What nightmares will I seed in those sleeping men's heads?* he thought, and then his own nightmare appeared before him.

At first, he knew that he must be asleep and dreaming. This was the most realistic dream ever, but he would wake up aching from the beating and shivering in fright from his nightmare, and then he would go back to the creek and start panning for gold again. The idea held a sort of comfort for him, because at least then the danger was something he was used to and could face: the brutality of man. Here, standing before him in these dark woods and staring back with eyes that he recognized all too well, the danger was far from known.

He stared at himself. Haggard, emaciated, weak, his skin so thin it was almost translucent, teeth missing from bloody gums, hair fallen out in clumps from a loosened scalp, neck and jowls hanging low and empty, and Jack London's eyes—for his they were—were older, and darker than he had ever believed possible. This was the face of a man who had seen the pit of hell and returned with its madness imprinted upon him.

Wendigo, Jack thought, amazed and terrified, and the wolf bit into his ankle. He screamed and fell, and when he looked up again, the thing had gone. He caught sight of a shadow some distance away, and as it moved downhill toward the camp, it grew, expanding into the physical and finding its true, huge, monstrous form. Undergrowth rustled at its passing. Tree trunks cracked.

And Jack knew what it would do. Everyone in the camp, including—

"No," he said. "Merritt, *no!*"

Jack ran, and this time he went downhill. He had no inkling of what he could do when he reached the camp again, and there was no real logic to his actions, but he could not leave Merritt there alone. Not with this . . . not with . . .

Why didn't the Wendigo eat me? he thought.

The wolf howled again behind him. Jack heard the

sounds of pursuit, and this time he knew what came. It had saved his life, taken him away from the camp where he would surely die . . . but he had not known just how close that death might be.

"No!" he said, voice shaking. "Not Merritt!" In the forest only barely lit by the moonlight, he ran headlong down the slope. At any moment he could hit a rock and break his leg, or run into a tree and smash open his skull. But the wolf was behind him, his spirit guide watching; though he had turned away from it for a moment, he still trusted its influence.

The monster moved through the trees before him, but it was far away now, much farther down the slope. Between blinks it disappeared, and the next moment he felt a great weight crash against his back, knocking him to the ground. The wolf rolled with him, pinning him down. Jack thrashed against it, and somehow he was up and running again, aiming for the last line of trees before the grass plain that led to the camp.

The first of the screams rose up. Panicked, terrified, cut off by a terribly wet, ripping sound.

"No!" Jack shouted.

The wolf drove him down again, its weight too much for him this time. It sat astride him, and Jack had to watch as the slaughter began. The trees obscured some of his vision, and for that he was thankful.

The moon retreated behind clouds again, and the campfire was soon snuffed out, kicked apart by something stampeding through the camp. Sparks and flames danced through the night for a moment, and some specks caught on the breeze and wafted across to the stream.

The shadow darted back and forth across the camp, moving quickly for something so large.

Gunshots rang out, single reports at first, and then a series of rapid cracks from all around. Each muzzle blast cast the shadow in a different view, a different aspect, and several of them together revealed a blink of an ambiguous shape rolling around the camp. Huge and white furred, black mawed and bloody, claws like the curved daggers of the Orient.

Beneath the gunshots, and filling the spaces between them, came the screams of dying men. Some cried out only briefly before their voices were cut off. Others screamed on and on, their cries interspersed with the sounds of crunching bone and tearing flesh.

The shape moved here and there . . . and still it grew in size. With every meal it ate, it became larger.

More gunshots, and then Jack saw two shapes running his way.

"Here!" he cried, not caring whether they were slavers

With every meal it ate, it became larger.

or slaves. One of them fell and was stomped by something indefinable, his shout ground down into the soil. The other got farther, but not much. His arms and legs flashed out as he was hauled backward, and just as he disappeared from view—his demise obscured by something huge—Jack saw his head twisted around on his torso.

He looked for Merritt, but it was too dark and confused to make out individual faces.

The chaos went on for several minutes. One of the tents was lifted high, flapping and drifting down in the breeze and coming to rest across the remains of the fire. The fabric smoldered and smoked but did not burst into flames. Someone started praying, and his prayer continued for some time. Maybe because this man was not trying to escape, the monster left him alone for a while, slaughtering those who *did* run. Eventually the prayer stopped, dwindling to a halt rather than being snuffed out. Moments later, something crunched.

Another shape made for the trees. Jack thought it was one man to begin with, but then he saw that it was two very close together. *Merritt!* he thought, desperate to see his friend's face. But as they drew nearer, he identified them: Archie from his lumbering run, and William from the way he clung to the big man's shoulders.

It was a most ridiculous sight, but Jack could not even

muster a smile. Maybe William had injured his legs. Or perhaps in the height of his panic, Archie had picked up his boss and run with him, the ultimate devotion in the face of such insanity.

The wolf still pinned Jack to the ground, and it growled at the two men drawing closer.

"This way!" Jack called, and the wolf growled again.

Archie stumbled and fell, spilling William into the long grass. Between the trees, its true bulk obscured by the canopy, Jack saw the looming shape of the monster drawing close.

Archie reached out a hand for help. William stood, pulled a gun, and shot him, then turned and ran directly for the line of trees from which Jack and the wolf watched. There was nothing wrong with his legs, it seemed, but as he drew closer, he paused, staggering to a halt.

Does he see me? Jack wondered. Surely not; it was too dark. But William's eyes were wide, his hand lifting as if to point, as the shape grabbed him up in two gigantic hands and tore him apart.

Jack buried his face in his hands. The wolf lay down on him, as if to shield him from view. But he could still hear. The screams had ended, the attack was over, but this long night would not end for some time.

The feast, after all, had only just begun.

CHAPTER NINE

UNTO THE HANDS OF BEAUTY

HEN HE COULD NO LONGER LISTEN—when the tearing and gnawing sounds made by the Wendigo at its supper became too much to bear—Jack got up and ran. The wolf allowed him to slip free. The whole world seemed to tilt beneath his feet and to blur around him, and it felt as though he had somehow slid out of waking and into a dreadful nightmare without ever realizing it, stepping into the realm of dreams. His mind could not reconcile the horrors he had witnessed with the weight of his own flesh and bones.

How could this be real?

He careened across rough ground, fleeing not only for his life but for his sanity. Half starved and badly beaten, ribs bruised, legs numb, chest burning with exertion and body trembling with exhaustion, Jack London ran for survival, and the wolf ran with him. Sometimes the beast raced at his side, other times it loped effortlessly ahead, flicking a glance back his way to urge him on.

The sound of his own ragged breathing filled his head. The darkness hung heavy, moonlight vanishing, and his vision blurred again as he swung his head to the left and saw trees looming there, though not the same woods where he had hidden before. He had left those behind. How far had he run? Half a mile, at least, yet he could still hear the snuffling and growling of the Wendigo.

The roar swept over him like a gust of wind, far closer than half a mile back . . . and he knew the Wendigo had abandoned the camp. Jack pictured that black maw, stained with gore, and opened his mouth in a silent scream.

Run, boy, run! he thought. And it did not escape him that in the grip of utter terror he had for a moment lost the sense of himself as a man and fallen back upon the perceptions of the rest of the world, whose eyes looked upon him and saw only his age. Just a kid.

And he rejected it.

He had defied the wild, died in its embrace and yet lived, challenged it to do its worst and yet survived. In the combat of man versus nature, Jack had snatched victory not from the jaws of defeat, but from the grasp of death. He was no mere boy.

On he ran. The night closed in and then retreated, again and again, as he passed through shadows and into moonlight. Branches whipped at his face when he found himself in woods, and on rocky slopes and ridges he stumbled more than once—the stones hammering at his knees and scraping his hands—knowing even as he rose that the smear of his blood would leave a scent trail that the Wendigo would easily follow.

Yet he did not stop, and if he slowed he barely noticed. The frigid night soaked into his bones; his empty stomach tightened to a painful clenched fist; his cracked ribs grated and set his jaw on agonized edge. And when at last he heard the Wendigo roar again—or perhaps only the howl of a whipping wind—it seemed farther away.

Always, the wolf raced ahead or darted back. It nipped at his hands when he faltered and the darkness at the edges of his vision flooded in. Three times he staggered and swayed, head bowed, body shaking, and three times the wolf snatched his right hand in its jaws, fangs pinching skin, waking him, tugging him onward until he stumbled into a jostling, bone-jarring run again.

How far had he come? Miles, at least, and in no discernible direction.

And then, eyes half lidded, he lost track of the wolf for a moment and aimed for the low, golden eye of the moon. One foot in front of the other—left, right, left—until the ground vanished beneath him. His right foot came down, but the ground had fallen away. His heel found purchase a foot lower than anticipated, but too late. Momentum carried him over the edge of a gully and he tumbled, limbs flailing, down the rocky slope until he came to rest at its base.

Jack tried to rise, but this time his body would not obey. Chill wind whipped along the gully and he shivered, but then he lost even the capacity for such involuntary functions.

He heard the wolf's howl nearby but could not respond to the call of the wild. Not this time. He listened for a roar that might signify the Wendigo's reply, and so listening, he drifted. Darkness coalesced at the edges of his vision, and he could do nothing but surrender to its embrace.

He woke to pain. Unlike a hundred other times when he had come slowly from an injured or drunken sleep to find a sense of dislocation, he recollected everything the instant his eyes opened. Pain had kept his memory fresh. So clear were his thoughts now, so devoid of the disorientation he had felt all during his flight from the Wendigo, that for a moment he thought he had never fallen unconscious at all.

And then he saw the girl, and the world tilted yet again.

He felt soft fur against his cheek, but it was not the

sleek coat of the wolf upon which he lay. Rather, he had
been swaddled like a child in the warmth of animal hides,
the fur plush around him, gentle on his bruised and battered form. A quartet of trees created a silent audience,
and through their branches he saw the promise of dawn
lightening the sky.

Beside one of the trees there stood the girl, watching
him as shyly as a child hiding behind its mother's apron.
Her black hair hung past her shoulders, fine as spun silk,
and in that first hint of morning, her almond-shaped eyes
gleamed like copper pennies amid the elegant lines of that
exotic face. She wore boots akin to those favored by the
local tribes and an ivory-hued cotton dress, but nothing
else. Despite the cold she had no jacket, and though she
breathed, he could not see the plume of her breath upon the
chill spring air.

In all his life, he had never seen a more beautiful girl.
She might have been sixteen or twenty—he had no way to
gauge—and the sight of her made him question the clarity
of mind he had felt grateful for only moments earlier.

His breath came slowly and easily, and though he was
aware of the pain in his cracked ribs, it felt distant to him.
A strange taste filled his mouth, and he ran out his tongue
only to find some kind of earthy grit upon it. Jack spat, and
a rich odor filled his nostrils as he tasted herbs.

The girl cocked her head with birdlike curiosity, and he understood that this was something she had done—put these herbs in his mouth—perhaps as some sort of remedy. Or had someone else done it? Surely she couldn't be alone out here in the wilderness, a beautiful young girl . . . *astonishingly beautiful, stealing his breath* . . . without even a coat?

He tried to raise himself up enough to look around but did not have the strength. His arms would not hold him, and his racked, beaten body sang an anguished song of protest at the merest effort. For a moment his eyelids fluttered, but he forced them open, refused to relinquish consciousness again now that it had been returned to him.

On his side, he let his head loll back, scanning the trees and the landscape beyond for some sign of other members of the girl's tribe or family, but he saw no one.

"Who are you?" he croaked, his voice ragged. "Did you"—he ran a trembling hand along one of the furs that covered him—"did you do this, bring me here?"

Twenty feet away, the girl moved fully out from behind the tree, though she kept one hand upon its bark as though it comforted her. When she smiled, he saw such natural innocence in her that his heart broke just from looking at her, and he cursed his weakness and injuries for preventing him from rising that very moment so that he could be closer to her.

Jack had no touchstone by which to recognize love. He had been infatuated before, and fascinated, and even mesmerized by girls once or twice, but he had never been in love. Still, he did not think what he felt in that moment was love. It felt more like sheer wonder.

He had to blink to clear his mind of her smile, and in that instant when his eyes were closed, he thought of the wolf, the spirit animal he considered his guide. The wolf had led him to safety, but now, as the eastern sky chased away the indigo night with the first light of morning, the beast was nowhere to be seen.

Only the girl. And it struck him again how odd it was that she had no coat, only that dress and her boots, and for a moment he stared at her and wondered if somehow his mind might not be as clear as he had thought. Were his perceptions skewed? Could the girl and the wolf be one and the same?

She laughed softly, raising a hand to cover her mouth, as though she had read his mind or at least seen the question in his eyes.

Jack felt himself fading, his awareness slipping. Whatever she had given him could not compensate for the exhaustion that drained him, for the need his body felt to rest and recuperate from the beating he had taken. He had heard of horses ridden too hard for too long that had simply collapsed and died, and he knew sometimes people went the same way. He did not feel death hovering nearby, but his body seemed weighted with surrender. Without help, without food, exposed to the elements, he would die out here.

Or not, as the girl and her tribe saw fit.

Yet there seemed to *be* no tribe.

"Who are you?" he asked again.

The wind shifted, a gust rustling the branches overhead, and Jack froze. The breeze carried a familiar scent: the gut-churning stink of fresh blood and rotting meat that he had inhaled last night, face-to-face with the cursed devil of the Yukon.

The girl halted, nostrils flaring, eyes wide, legs slightly akimbo, and staring at her he could only think of a deer ready to bolt.

"Run," he said. He swallowed hard, and whatever she had put in his mouth tasted like cinnamon. Terror had exhausted him, and he knew he could flee no farther. Someone had moved him in the night, brought him here, but the Wendigo had tracked him, and it was close.

Close enough to smell.

Jack felt curiously detached from himself. If the wild claimed him on this chilly spring Yukon morning, then so be it. He would force himself to stand, and if he could manage to raise his arms, he would fight, and he would die here, one more meal for the Wendigo.

In the distance, it roared.

"Run, damn it!" Jack rasped at the girl.

She did, but not away. In the space of three heartbeats she crossed the ground between them and fell to her knees, pressing the fingers of her left hand over his mouth as she shushed him. Jack tried to argue. He could hear the Wendigo coming nearer now, branches snapping not far off. It must be close, for he thought he heard its low growl and the clacking of its teeth as it gnashed its jaws.

Foolish girl. What did she think she was doing? He would plead with her, shout at her, make her run.

He forced himself to his knees, swaying, and got one foot under him. Pain swept over him with such sudden force that it felt as though he received each bruise afresh, pummeled by invisible blows. Teeth grinding, taking quick sips of air because breathing freely might make him vomit, he began to rise.

In all his life, he had never imagined a task so difficult.

The girl dragged him down. She put a finger to her lips, and he wanted to scream at her, to tell her that she might have killed them both. A dreadful exhalation burst from his lungs as he hit the ground, but the girl kept moving, pulling at the furs she had wrapped him in during the

night. Now she tugged them over the two of them, climbing on top of Jack as though protecting him with her own
body. So close, so intimate, her breath deliciously warm at
his throat, her whole body smelling of cinnamon.

"No," he whispered.

She fixed him with a gaze that quieted him, full of
knowledge and purpose. "Hush," she said, surprising him
with a word in his own language.

Jack hushed.

They lay still together under those furs, hearts beating
so close together. Despite all his pain and all his terror, the
awareness of her proximity, the feel of her body cleaving
to his, made him tremble with something other than fear.

The Wendigo roared, so close it must have been there
in the square formed by those four trees, towering above
them. The morning light might have illuminated it fully,
cast aside some of the dark mystery it had cloaked itself in.
But Jack feared that the monster might be more spirit than
solid, a curse given flesh, and he did not wish to see.

The stink of it choked him. He bit his lip to keep from
retching, and to stop himself making a sound. At any
moment it would tear away the furs, snatch up him and the
girl, and begin to slash at them with those curved talons,
to strip their flesh and gnaw their bones. *Hide here, trembling beneath a fur? The girl must be mad.*

He closed his eyes and steadied himself, taking long, slow breaths. *Inhale. Exhale. Inhale. Exhale.* Moistening his dry, cracked lips with a swipe of his tongue, trembling with the girl atop him, he listened to the grunting and gnashing of the Wendigo and heard amid those sounds a quiet chuckle, like the secret enjoyment of a madman. Once upon a time, the monster had been human, and its ravenous hungers sprang from the font of soulless human need.

It searched for them. It scraped at roots and thumped at the trunks of trees. Yet somehow, though the dawn blossomed into morning with each passing moment, and they lay there exposed, covered only by furs, the Wendigo could not find them.

Astonished, feeling every moment as though his luck would end, Jack opened his eyes and stared up at the girl, her beauty so immaculate and otherworldly. She cocked her head slightly, her eyes sparkling with something akin to amusement. Once again she pressed a finger to his lips to assure his silence, but then that finger traced through the tangle of beard that his journey had earned him.

It felt like magic, the two of them impossibly hidden.

He could feel the presence of the Wendigo as though its existence alone was enough to pin him there. But then he heard the piping of birds, and their song merged with the hungry prowl of the monster, and its own sounds changed.

The Wendigo growled in confusion, perhaps troubled at having lost the scent it had followed. Or perhaps the true arrival of morning unsettled it, for such a creature surely belonged to the night.

Branches cracked and birds took flight with a loud flutter of wings, but Jack listened to its steps receding and knew that the monster had given up the hunt.

Soon all he could hear were the birds and the wind and the soft breathing of the girl, and all he could feel was the beating of their hearts and the pain that returned to him in wave after wave.

"I have you, now," she said. "You are safe with me."

She kissed the tips of her fingers and touched them to his forehead like a blessing. A benediction. Then she threw back the furs and the bright sunshine forced him to close his eyes, and he found comfort with them closed.

His body demanded that he rest, and with the girl kneeling beside him, gently touching his hair and whispering to him in a language unlike any he had heard spoken by the northern tribes, he succumbed at last. As unconsciousness claimed him, an errant thought skittered through his mind; he wondered how this girl, really no more than a slip of a thing, had carried him to this clearing of four trees from the gully where he had collapsed the night before.

And then his thoughts were silent, the curtains of his

"I have you, now," she said. "You are safe with me."

mind were drawn, and the lights went out in his head. Only sweet birdsong accompanied him into the darkness, and the touch of her slender hands.

He woke to a fairy tale.

At first he felt only the fur against his cheek, but as consciousness slowly returned, he became aware that— for the first time in days—he was *warm*. Warmer, by far, than he had been inside the Dawson Bar. In truth, Jack felt warmer than he had since departing San Francisco the previous summer, and he lay there on the fur and luxuriated in that heat.

He opened his eyes to see a stone hearth in front of him, fire crackling inside, and he ran out his tongue to wet his cracked lips. His face felt dry and tight in the heat from the fire, and any movement, any expression, brought him pain. Still, he smiled and pulled the blanket—for someone had covered him as he slept—up to his neck.

But now fully awake, he realized that he actually felt too hot. The very idea seemed absurd, but nevertheless, he threw off the blanket and welcomed the chilly draft that eddied across the floor.

Jack sat up and looked around. Stiff and aching, he felt a hundred years old, but his pains were forgotten as he took in his surroundings. At home he would have considered this a simple cabin, but in the rough, remote terrain of the Yukon Territory, it seemed quite remarkable. Though a single room, the cabin must have measured forty feet square, and its floorboards and beams gleamed as though freshly cut, their lines as perfect as if they had been put in place by a master builder.

The huge stone fireplace interrupted one wall, but on the opposite side of the cabin stood a heavy black iron stove, its pipe rising up through the roof. There were doors front and back, and beside each one—and this surprised Jack the most, so far from what he would deem civilization—was a tall, many-paned window of warped, handblown glass. Sunlight streamed in through those two windows, and beyond them he saw forest.

Heavy furs had been stretched on the floor as rugs. At the front of the cabin there were two chairs arranged by the window to catch the best light, and beside the door a shelf laden with books. The sight of those volumes, some bound in cracked leather and others titled with gleaming gold filigree, made his heart leap.

The rear corners of the cabin were given over to living space. Nearest Jack, on the hearth side, a bed sat in the corner, head- and footboards simply yet elegantly carved, mattress hidden beneath a French floral coverlet. Opposite the bed, in the corner beside the stove, a small, round table had been draped with a white lace cloth, and two chairs were snug against it, presenting what passed in this cabin for a dining room. A cupboard held a rack of dishes, bowls, and glasses.

The table had been set for one. The smell of cooking lingered, but he had barely noticed it before. Now, though, the sight of the white bowl on the table, the fork and knife and spoon just so, made his stomach roar with hunger. A cramp fisted in his gut, and for a moment he only sat there on the floor, clutching at his belly. When the cramp passed, Jack staggered to his feet, for he had noticed perhaps the most important thing about this strange place.

The pot on the stove.

It had been set to one side so that the contents would stay warm but not cook any further. Feeling more than a little like Goldilocks, and bearing the warnings of such tales in mind, he walked gingerly across the cabin. With every step, he noticed things that he had been too over-whelmed to take in before. His boots sat on the floor by the stove. His feet ached, and his socks were thin and worn, but the boots had been set out to dry. Likewise his jacket hung on a hook by the door, as though he himself had made a home here.

But the prospect of food crowded out all other thoughts. He took a breath, staring at the pot, and then uncovered it, only to find himself awash in aromas that made him sway with hunger. Someone—the girl? Was the cabin hers? How had she brought him here?—had made a stew, and his mouth watered at the rich, meaty smell of it. A wooden spoon lay on the stove, and he picked it up and stirred, glimpsing carrots and potatoes and cabbage, but even better, dark chunks of meat that he thought must be rabbit.

Jack debated the wisdom of eating food left by a stranger, but only for a moment. Hunger overrode any hesitation. After all, what else was he to think except that the stew had been left, and the table set, for him? And he could find no logic in suspicion. No one would have gone to the trouble of bringing him here only to poison him, especially not the girl who had saved him from the Wendigo.

He frowned. Was that what had happened? She had hidden them under the furs, yes, but had the Wendigo simply missed them, somehow? It seemed impossible. The monster should have seen them and, if not, should have smelled them there. And yet it had been entirely blind to their presence.

The idea that the girl had done this nested deep in his thoughts. There must have been some trick to it, perhaps some musk in the fur that masked their scents. What else could it have been?

These thoughts crossed his mind in the seconds that it took him to bring the bowl from the table and fill it with stew, ladling meat and vegetables to make sure he got more than just broth. Returning to the table, injuries all but forgotten for the moment, he made certain not to spill a single drop. He slid into a chair, picked up a spoon, and lifted the first taste to his lips. Rich flavors filled his mouth, and then his hunger took over. He lamented the spots he left on the lace tablecloth, but not enough that he could stop himself. Jack doubted he had ever tasted anything so wonderful, and as he dipped the spoon once more into the bowl, he felt the soreness of his gums, which reminded him of the sores on his thighs and legs, both symptoms of scurvy.

Jack blinked, staring into the bowl. Carrots. Potatoes. Cabbage. Just what he needed to stave off scurvy. The girl, or whoever had prepared this stew, was not only feeding him but helping to heal him as well. Yet none of this was what struck him so suddenly as to make him pause his spoon above the bowl.

In the wild northlands, where could such vegetables possibly be grown so early in spring? The ground had thawed only weeks ago.

He dipped his spoon again and continued eating, but now his mind grew as ravenous as his belly. As he ate, invigorated by the meal, he glanced around the cabin again.

Surely the girl did not live here by herself, yet Jack spotted no trace of a man's influence in the place. The floral coverlet alone indicated only women slept in that bed, so perhaps the girl had a sister or mother who shared the home.

Yet how did she—or they—survive?

Survival. The word echoed in his mind. His spoon clinked in the empty bowl, and he rose automatically to refill it. As he spooned out more stew for himself, he continued to study his surroundings, and the same familiar feeling of unreality began to creep into his thoughts as he had had upon waking. A cabin—or better yet, a cottage—in the woods, a fire burning in the hearth, food left out for a lost stranger . . . it all smacked of fairy tales. Yet he was himself, Jack London, and his injuries and his hunger were real. The heat of the fire and the stove were real. The rich taste of the stew . . . that was also real.

This is no fairy tale, he thought.

But around him there were hints of the impossible. Fresh vegetables this early in spring, in the midst of the wild. And then there was the cabin itself, so expertly constructed. Now, though, as Jack stood in front of the stove with his bowl in his hands, what caught his attention was the absence of certain things. The cabin's walls were totally devoid of the tools of survival. In any other cabin he had visited—most in climes far more hospitable than the

Yukon, but even in the tiny shack where he, Merritt, and Jim had spent the winter—those tools had been there, or their past presence was evident.

There were no snowshoes hanging on the wall, nor any hooks to indicate there ever had been. He saw no fishing pole, no net, and no rifle with which to hunt. In fact there were no weapons at all. Surely outside, up against the cabin, there might be some kind of enclosure where firewood would be stacked and tools could be kept—a shovel, an ax, a saw. But even if that were the case, weapons would be kept inside.

Curiosity battling with his hunger now, Jack fetched his spoon from the table and walked around the cabin as he ate, bowl raised almost to his chin. His search turned up nothing to contradict his observations. Still amazed by the quality of the cabin's construction, he took another bite and then paused by the hearth, where the fire was now burning lower, to inspect the wall. The logs were joined perfectly, each of seemingly identical size, and he ran a finger along the horizontal seam between one and the next.

What had the builder used to seal the gaps? He walked the length of the wall, moving around the hearth, and noted the uniform nature of each log. There were no chinks in the walls, no gaps filled by rocks or sticks, and the spaces between the logs had not been sealed with mud daubing or sap.

Bowl in hand, Jack leaned in closer, peering at the space between two logs. He pushed a finger in and found it smooth. Brows knitted, he used the back of his spoon to scrape at the joining, and bark stripped away, revealing white, glistening wood beneath.

There were no seams. The spaces between the logs had not been sealed because there *were* no spaces; the logs had grown together. Underneath, the bark was green, and the wood glistened because it lived.

Stew bowl cradled forgotten in one hand, he turned in a slow circle, staring at the walls and doors and then tilting his head back to look at the rafters, all of it alive. He staggered toward the front of the cabin and set the bowl on top of the small bookshelf, bending to study the spines of the books. English, French, Russian, and other languages. Spinning around, with the impossible closing in on him, he stopped suddenly and looked at the floor.

Did the cabin have roots? It had to, if the trees that had been cut down to build it were still alive. Had it grown like this? Impossible. Unimaginable. But still there could be no denying his discovery. The doors and windows and the furnishings were ordinary enough, as far as he could tell. But otherwise the cabin was made of living wood.

Jack went to the front window and froze. The cabin sat in a clearing, beyond which the forest grew dense and dark. A thick tangle of wildflowers bloomed out there, vibrant purples and blues, pinks and oranges and reds, colors so rich that they erased all memory of the grays of Dawson.

He shook his head. How could any of this be real? He thought of stories he had read in which men took the wrong path in the woods and found themselves in the realm of fairies and sprites, gone only for days by their reckoning but reemerging into the world to discover that it had progressed years in their absence.

Jack clutched the sides of his head, trying too late to deny the reality of this place. How long had he slept? Where had he truly woken? How had he come to be here?

He snatched his coat from the hook by the door, putting it on as he stumbled to the stove to retrieve his boots. He stepped into them without tying them and moved toward the back of the cabin, but as he passed the window on that side, he froze yet again, this time at the sight of a thriving vegetable garden, half an acre overgrown with a mad variety of plants. Beyond the garden he saw apple and pear trees, and vines heavy with grapes.

"Son of a bitch," he whispered.

And then a breeze caressed the back of his neck. Even as he turned, he realized he had not heard the door opening.

The girl stood just inside, the sun streaming in around her, perfectly silhouetting the outline of her body beneath her cotton dress. Despite his fear and bewilderment, her beauty struck him speechless.

And then she smiled with such innocence and sweetness, only to blink in surprise, her face collapsing in genuine sadness when she realized he had planned to leave.

"What did I do wrong?" she asked, cocking her head. "Didn't you like the stew?"

CHAPTER TEN

ECHOES IN OLD WOOD

J ACK COULD NOT TAKE his eyes off her. Nor could he shake the regret that seized him when he realized that he had caused her sadness. In her voice and in her expression he saw not an ounce of guile. While both her home and her beauty were otherworldly, the disappointment and crushed hope in her gaze were unquestionably human.

He took a long breath, glanced around at the simple comfort of the cabin, and saw no danger. Magic, perhaps, for what else could he call a cabin made of living wood? But no peril. An errant thought whispered through his head, of Hansel and Gretel, a candy cottage, and a witch's oven, but he did not dwell on it. That really had been a fairy tale, and witch or not, the girl who stood on the cabin's threshold was inarguably real.

Her gaze dropped, and her lips bowed into a tiny pout. "Not enough salt," she said, and it took him a moment to realize she was still talking about her stew. She had spotted the half-eaten bowl atop the bookshelf.

Jack swallowed, throat dry. He glanced out the window at the wild garden in the back, and a realization struck him. Where would he go? He had no idea how far he had come from the river where the slavers had camped, or in which direction. His cracked ribs made breathing uncomfortable, and though his other injuries would not slow him down, one meal would not be enough to replenish the strength and vigor he had lost, nor stave off scurvy long enough for him to return to civilization. He had no weapons, no food, no supplies of any kind . . . and the Wendigo still roamed somewhere out there.

"The stew is perfect," Jack said.

She brightened instantly, her smile returning, along with the shyness she'd had when he had first seen her. But then her expression grew troubled again.

"You must be starving, but you did not finish it." Almost demurely, she gestured to the abandoned bowl.

Fighting his doubts, wary of her and of her home but recalling the way she had protected him thus far, he took two steps back toward the center of the cabin.

"That's my second helping."

"Oh," she said, nodding happily. "That's good, then."

The girl picked up the bowl and carried it to the table, passing within a few feet of Jack. He caught the scent of cinnamon as she passed, and his senses were overcome with the memory of their first meeting, of her lying atop him, body molded to his, of breathing in her exhaled breath and that warm sweet smell of her.

"Don't you want the rest?" she asked as she set the bowl down and turned to look at him.

Jack found that he did, very much. His stomach growled, and he still had the taste of rabbit stew in his mouth and wanted more. A glass of water or whiskey would also be welcome. Furs and blankets and warm fires, fruits and vegetables . . . he wanted to stay.

"What's your name?" he asked.

She turned toward him so quickly that it was almost a pirouette, the hem of her dress flying. "Lesya. I am Lesya."

"You speak English beautifully, Lesya," Jack said. "What is your native language?"

She offered him the tiniest of shrugs, and she might have blushed, just a bit. "I have always had more than one language. Tribal tongues. The words of travelers. Other languages, too."

Jack thought of the books on her shelf and wondered who had taught her all those languages. At her age, which must have been around his own, give or take a couple of years, her fluency would have amazed him were it not for the way these past few days had redefined words like *amaze* and *astonish*.

Lesya rested one hand on the back of a chair as though she needed it to keep from falling. She studied his face a moment and then glanced away.

"You haven't told me your name," she said.

"Jack," he told her. "Jack London."

"London!" she said, eyes alight with excitement. "I've heard of London."

Charmed, he caught his breath. Simply being near the girl confused his thoughts. He wanted to build something, to hunt something, to defeat another man to win her affections. The instinct filled him with new vigor, though there were no other men about to test his mettle.

"It's only a name, sorry to say. But I hope to travel to London someday."

A trace of regret crossed her face. "That would be wonderful." And then she fixed him with a hard, probing look, all her shyness fleeing. "You were about to leave. Why did you want to go?"

"I . . . ," Jack began, but he did not know how to continue. Here she stood, this impossibly beautiful girl surrounded by impossible things, and yet she behaved as if her home must be perfectly ordinary. A witch? Perhaps. But he looked into her eyes and he did not see a witch.

"*Could* I leave?" he asked.

"Of course!" she laughed. "This place is still the Yukon, although my garden is a . . . unique part of it."

"Unique how?"

Lesya shrugged, glanced aside, as if she wasn't sure how to explain.

"You saved me from the Wendigo," he said, breaking an awkward silence. "But how did you get me here?"

"I carried you," she said, as if this were the stupidest question she had ever heard.

A slip of a girl, thirty pounds lighter than Jack himself, even with the weight the long winter and the slavers' march had winnowed from his frame, and she had carried him. And she thought nothing odd about it.

"This place, your cabin . . . you know the trees are alive?"

Lesya smiled, rolling her eyes a bit as though indulging him. "Of course. Aren't all trees alive?"

"Not generally the ones used to build houses."

The girl frowned, not quite petulant but certainly dismissive. "Well, that's a pity, don't you think? This way is much better."

Hard as he tried, Jack could not think of any way to

argue the point. Could it be that Lesya did not understand the extraordinary nature of her home, or was she simply playing coy, and far less innocent than she seemed?

Again he glanced at the door.

Crestfallen, she stepped aside. "If you are so determined to leave . . . if my hospitality and my home displease you so . . . I am sorry to have brought you here. Go, if you must."

"It's only that—"

"You are frightened."

He started to nod, but caught himself. "Not frightened, just . . ." But he couldn't think of a better word.

Lesya stepped nearer to him, so close that he caught her intoxicating scent again. Her chest rose and fell with each breath, and she reached for his hands and took them in her own, searching his eyes.

"Stay and heal, Jack. Perhaps this part of the woods seems strange to you, but it's home to me, and there is nothing here to fear. You are safe with me."

Where their fingers touched, a spark traveled up his arms and raced through him. For a moment he felt the same intimacy that they had shared beneath the furs, ter-rified into silence as the Wendigo passed by, hungry for their flesh. How long since he had been this close to a girl? Too long. And he had never been so close to one as lovely and delicate, as open and earnest, as Lesya.

If she was a witch and had bewitched him, then Jack welcomed it. A girl like this did not need magic to make a man breathless and eager to please. And when she said he would be safe with her, he believed her. She had kept him alive right under the Wendigo's nose. That seemed proof enough.

"I should finish my stew," he said.

Lesya squeezed his hands excitedly and nodded. "Yes, you should. And I have wine, if you'd like some."

Jack grinned. It wasn't whiskey, but wine would do just fine.

Lesya was as good as her word. Over the days that followed, she cared for him as he recovered. He slept the nights wrapped in furs and blankets, and during the daylight hours, when Lesya wandered the forest in search of game she did not seem to have to hunt, or gathered fruits and vegetables from her garden, he spent long hours in her bed, inhaling the scent of her from the bedclothes. When they were in the cabin together, she cooked a marvelous array of meals for him, flavored with herbs and spices from her cupboard and garden. After a few days he stopped wondering at the impossibility of the things she cultivated.

Though Lesya protested, wanting him to rest and recuperate, after the third day he refused to remain indoors while she waited on him so completely. He could not chop wood, and could only carry a couple of logs at a time without aggravating his healing ribs, but she did not argue when he wanted to help her gather vegetables for dinner. That small thing helped Jack to feel immeasurably better. He needed to work, and to have a sense of usefulness, and soon his thoughts drifted back to the journey that had brought him here, and the purpose with which he had left his own home.

Lesya made him smile, and he made her laugh. At her insistence, he read to her by candlelight after dark. Her bookshelf included a copy of Dickens's *A Tale of Two Cities*, and whenever Jack read of the passionate, doomed love of Sydney Carton for Lucie Manette, they both pretended not to notice the way his voice quavered, just a bit.

Yet in quiet moments his thoughts returned to his own home. His mother, Shepard, and dear Eliza would be waiting for some word of his arrival in Dawson. Wanderlust and a thirst for adventure had led him here, his desire to conquer the wild driving him on, but he carried their hopes and expectations with him. And though that spring in the woods with Lesya felt like paradise, as first one week passed, and then another, he became torn by his desire and duty.

She must have sensed something in him, for one morning Lesya asked him to walk with her in the forest.

Hand in hand they strolled among the trees, the

sunlight streaming through above them. Beyond the clearing the forest seemed so ordinary, and Lesya must have taken different paths every day, for there were no trails worn down by her passing.

On most days, they talked as they walked. She had a way of persuading him to tell her stories of his life, and he needed little encouragement to talk of his time as an oyster pirate or dockworker. But he also spoke of his dreams and ambitions in a way that he had never revealed to anyone before, and he revealed the tale of the thirty days he had spent in jail, a hellish drama that even his family did not know. Lesya taught him words and phrases in half a dozen languages, and they discussed books they had read. But other than that she would reveal nothing of herself. Jack wished she would tell him about her life, and yet at the same time he loved the mystery of her. That she had magic in her touch he had no doubt. But he never pressured her to discuss the true nature of her house or garden, and Lesya never volunteered the information.

On that day, though, they kept their thoughts to themselves, walking as happily as lovers on an afternoon stroll in the park.

And yet·. . .

Jack felt they were not alone. A presence kept pace with them from the moment they left Lesya's clearing. He knew it was not the Wendigo, for he would have heard it, even caught its scent, if it stalked them there. And though he had been keenly aware of the absence of his spirit guide in the days he had spent in the woods with Lesya, this presence was not that of the wolf.

Something else watched them; something brooding and grim, perhaps even menacing. Yet Lesya seemed to sense nothing, and though from time to time strange shadows shifted deep in the forest, Jack saw no sign of any real danger.

And when they stopped in a different clearing, where the trees grew tall and bent inward and the sunlight shone down so brightly that it turned the spot into a golden cathedral, Lesya reached up to caress his face, and then she kissed him, and all his worries were forgotten.

On a late morning, after he had lost count of the days he had spent in Lesya's cabin—more than three weeks but not quite a month—Jack stood just inside the open front door sipping a cup of strong tea and studying the trees beyond the clearing. The night before, Lesya had traced her fingers along Jack's biceps and declared that he needed more meat if he was to fully regain his strength. Though he now felt quite recovered—more healthy even than before he had left San Francisco—Jack did not argue. A look into the girl's almond eyes, sparkling with tiny flecks of green he only ever noticed when their lips parted after a kiss, was enough to still any argument he might have within him.

If Lesya wished to cook him a special meal, by all means he would eat it, and be thankful. The days and nights with her passed by like dreams, their lingering walks in the woods giving way to time spent within the cabin walls, warm by the fire, or over the stove with the wondrous aromas of Lesya's cooking filling the place. She taught him more about spices and herbs than he had ever imagined one could know. For tonight she had promised caribou steaks, and this morning she had gone out to hunt.

Without weapons.

Jack could not help but wonder how she would trap or kill the animal, how she would carry it back to the cabin, and where she would store whatever they did not eat. But he had learned the fruitless nature of asking such questions. Lesya would only smile, as if the query itself were a silly thing, and Jack ought to know the answer without having to ask it.

Left on his own, he had made tea and sat down to attempt to read Alexandre Dumas in the original French, but soon the warm breeze from the open window and the smells of spring lured him outdoors. Now he found himself focused on the trees at the edges of the clearing around Lesya's cabin, curiosity niggling at him. *Clearing* really wasn't the word, was it? He saw no sign that any trees had been cleared to make way for the cabin. There were no stumps and none of the dips in the ground that the removal of them would leave behind. Yet the trees that lined the glen were uniform as a stockade fence, ringing the cabin and gardens in a circle.

Jack set his tea on top of the bookshelf, just inside the door, but he carried his book with him. Perhaps he'd bring Alexandre Dumas on a wander, find a fallen tree upon which he could sit in the sunshine, and read. Being with Lesya made him so consistently breathless that his desire to explore the forest had been easily sated by his rambling walks with her. But they seemed to take different routes every day, and Jack liked the idea of getting to know these woods.

He couldn't stay here with her forever, though there were times—moments when she looked at him just so, or when he held her close and breathed in the smell of her hair, or when she laughed—that he wished he would never have to go back to civilization. If this small glen was fated to be the only bit of the wild he would ever conquer, part of him could be content with that.

But only part. In his heart, he knew that he could not stay, and that parting from Lesya would be painful. Whenever he thought of his family back in Oakland awaiting news of his journey, he buried those thoughts deep. With the scent

of her still in his head, his hands still remembering the soft-
ness of her skin, he put off thoughts of leaving for another
day. Another week. Perhaps he could stay until summer.

Book in hand, Jack walked through the flower garden
in front of the cabin. The flowers seemed to bloom more
fully each day, their colors increasingly vivid, but the trees
in the forest had none of their luster. From white birch to
black pine, they cast ordinary shadows, and if there seemed
more birdsong rising from their branches than he had
heard in the wooded walks of his past, Jack ascribed that
to their distance from the intrusion of man.

Now he paused at the edge of the clearing, studying
the base of a tree. His gaze roamed from one to the next,
and he knew that the uniformity of the circle around the
house was no trick of the eye. Shifting the book to his left
hand, he pressed his right palm against the bark of a tree.
Its ridges pressed into his flesh, but the bark felt entirely
ordinary to him.

Only a tree, he thought. Whatever magic suffused
Lesya's home—for he had long since accepted that there
was magic here—a tree remained a tree. But he glanced at
its base, following the knuckled roots where they plunged
into the earth, and his gaze pursued an imaginary path
back toward the cabin. Perhaps the roots intertwined. He'd
toyed with the idea that the cabin was part of the forest,

but now he wondered if the opposite might be true, if the forest, somehow—at least this ring of trees—might not be a part of the cabin.

He chose the sunniest gap among the trees and set off, leaving the glen behind. The book felt good in his hand, the texture of the cover a comfort to him, a real and familiar tether to the civilization he had left behind. The thought brought a smile to his face. The hours he had spent in Dawson City had not inspired within him any faith in its connection to civilization, but compared to this place—presumably far from even the smallest village, a tiny place of order amid the chaos of the wild—Dawson seemed a genuine metropolis.

Jack had met the challenge of the Yukon Trail and survived the cruelty of man. He had endured the elements and the rigors of the wilderness. But when he had set out to conquer the wild, to better himself and prove man greater than the powers of nature, he had never imagined the things he would encounter. Back on board the *Umatilla*, the Wendigo had been only a story. But in the white silence of the far north, myths took on flesh and became terrifyingly real.

Even now, as he wandered along a trail that seemed to have been laid out just for him, the trees aligned on either side like the entryway to a grand estate, he shivered at the memory of the slaughter in camp that night. The screams of the men echoed in his head, and he could not erase the sight of the Wendigo, half invisible in the moonlight and the dark, snatching them up and pulling them apart to get at their insides.

If he could have considered it just an animal, that would have been easier. But he had seen it close up, had watched it mirror his own image and step through the shadows, and nothing of mere flesh and blood could have done that. No, the Wendigo was something *more*. It was a cursed thing, a legend, born of some hideous magic.

A shiver went through Jack and he paused. The breeze still felt warm, but he looked around the woods to find that somehow his trail had led him into deep shadow, where the canopy of the trees grew thick overhead. He glanced about until he saw a splash of bright sunlight and set off toward it, conscious of the general direction of the cabin.

For nearly ten minutes he pushed other thoughts from his head and just walked. His boots snapped twigs, and sometimes the ground was soft underfoot, though there had been no rain since he had first woken in Lesya's cabin. A stand of white birches gleamed in the sun, many of the trees stripped of leaves despite the time of year. They were not dead trees, but they did not flourish the way most of the forest did, and they had none of the vibrancy of the few apple and pear trees in the garden behind Lesya's home.

Jack wondered if she could save them. Only a fool would have denied the influence she had on things around her, the way the flowers and plants flourished. Even Jack had thrived in her care, returning to vigorous health, though he believed his own recovery had much more to do with her cooking than with whatever magic could keep the wood of her cabin alive.

"Get her out of your head," he said aloud.

The wind through the leaves seemed to answer back.

Accepting magic had not come easily, especially to someone who still bore an emotional burden from the spiritualism his mother indulged in. The things she had claimed to believe had brought death and the dead near to him and his home, and they had frightened and confused him. He remembered a gas lamp, and his mother's chanting voice as she called upon her own spirit guide and invited other, darker things to visit them in their kitchen.

One rainy evening, the lamp lay in bright shards on the kitchen floor. The roses on its shade had been as vivid in color as the flowers in Lesya's garden. Jack had not touched the lamp, yet it had moved, and his mother had blamed him. She had punished him.

Cursed him.

Spiritualism filled him with contempt. He hated the theatrics that went along with it, and the arrogance of those who claimed to practice it. Magic seemed only a hair's breadth from the kind of spiritual chicanery his mother had indulged in, defrauding widows and distraught daughters of their money, and so he had always dismissed it with the same casual disdain.

Until now.

Since he had first learned of the wide world as a small boy, he had yearned to explore its mysteries, to visit exotic ports and secret chambers, to dare its oceans and peaks. Now he had been forced to accept the existence of an even wider world. There were forces at work around him that had nothing to do with science but might equally be a part of nature. For he could not think of Lesya's witchery as anything but natural. She certainly considered it as such, did not even seem to understand the word *magic*.

With a smile, he sat down amid the dying birch trees and leaned against the trunk of the sturdiest. Opening the book, he delved into Dumas's *Le Comte de Monte-Cristo*. Though this sort of melodrama did not usually appeal to him, Jack had read the book in English several years before. He thought he remembered enough of the story that he'd be able to decipher this text, even with the little French he knew.

The attempt failed miserably. Though he concentrated,

scanning pages for words he recognized and trying to translate the sentences around them from context and memory, it soon became evident that today would not be the day he taught himself French.

After twenty minutes or so of this fruitless labor, he lost patience entirely and rose. The sun had reached its apex, and Jack relished the warmth. The nights were still cold, and he would never wish to be in the Yukon during winter again. But he did not mind the spring.

Book in hand, he glanced once in the direction he had come and immediately decided to forge onward. If the book would not provide distraction, then he would have to explore beyond its pages. Perhaps he would come to the outer edge of the forest and be able to get some bearing on his position. Surely they could not be more than five miles or so from the river camp where he had panned for gold with his fellow captives?

The thought brought Merritt to mind, sullying Jack's mood.

Many shades grimmer, he set off to what he gauged to be east. Things moved in the undergrowth and in the branches overhead, animals darting to and fro to escape his path. But as he walked, the journey became more difficult. Exposed roots and stones jutted from the uneven ground and the trees grew closer together, so that he found himself ducking beneath branches, scratching himself many times, and tripping more than once.

He managed not to fall, but the forest had grown so thick that it seemed nearly impassable. Realizing that it would be illogical to continue—especially since he took the density of the woods as an indication that he had been walking deeper into the forest instead of toward its edges—Jack shifted direction. Yet fewer than ten minutes later, he ran into a similar obstruction. The way had been clearer, paths easily made among the trees, but soon he found himself in the thick of the forest again.

Once more he shivered, but this time a creeping suspicion accompanied the chill that ran through him. He glanced around but saw only the shade thrown by branches and the dappling of golden light where the sun shone through.

He had come into the forest alone, but now he had company, and now that he had become aware of it, Jack could not understand how he had missed it before. Of late he had thought little of the wolf. It had aided him when he was in peril, and these days with Lesya had presented only heart-quickening joy and contentment. Yet he had wondered what had become of his spirit guide, the animal that had breathed new life into him when he lay dying in the winter snow, and had given him a rapport with the wild that he would never otherwise have found. Why had he not seen it? If he closed his eyes at night, sometimes he thought he could hear the lonesome howl of a wolf far, far off. But then the fire would lull him to sleep, or Lesya would brush her lips against his in a soft kiss, and the · wolf would be forgotten.

This, though, was not the wolf. Nor was it the Wendigo. But Jack knew it. He had felt the presence before, in the woods that day when Lesya had kissed him for the first time. He had sensed the intensity of its attention upon him— its menace—and the small hairs on the back of his neck had bristled. He had understood with utter clarity that it did not want him there.

He peered into shadows, searched the trees for the source of the threat, but saw nothing. Frustrated, he turned north and walked until the woods thinned, picking up his pace, tapping the book against his thigh. He still felt its attention upon him, the weight of its displeasure, but he would not be frightened off by something he could not see.

Again he turned east, and after several minutes found his way blocked by the clustering of trees. Nodding, frustration growing, he backed away from the tangled branches, staring at the bases of those trees. The roots grew on top of one another, twining like vines or lovers' hands.

"All right. If that's the way it must—"

He backed into a tree, the sharp edge of a broken branch poking his back. Jack spun around to find that the forest had filled in behind him. Impossibly, there were trees there that had not been there before, giant old-growth wood, thick branches blocking his way.

And now a little tremor of true fear was seeded in his heart.

He turned around several times. Protecting his face, ducking his head, he pushed between two trees, twisting through an opening. Branches seemed to twine together but he forged ahead, jerking left and right, hearing the snap of wood. A branch whipped out, scratching his forehead and drawing blood. Others jabbed his sides and whacked his shins, but Jack drove forward, bullish and determined. Through the trees ahead he caught a glimpse of the woods he had left behind, an ordinary forest with sun streaming through the branches above and plenty of room to move.

But the trees he passed only grew closer together, their limbs thicker and stronger, until at last they forced him to a stop. Without an ax or a saw, he could not hope to proceed any farther.

"Why are you doing this?" he shouted, as though expecting the forest to answer. He heard only the rustle of leaves and the song of birds in reply.

Then he tried to turn but felt the press of a knotted

branch against his back. Heart beginning to race, he twisted around, scratched by every movement, and found that the wood had caught him. Trees grew so close around him now that their branches had created a cage, thick limbs barring his way, pressing against his arms and legs, his back and ribs, so tightly that he had nowhere to go.

Jack tilted his head back and saw a glimmer of sun through the dark canopy above, and he realized there remained one avenue open to him. If he wanted to see his way back to the cabin—or perhaps make out exactly what the trees were trying to prevent him from seeing—he would have to climb.

Determined, he managed to lift his right leg and get a foothold on a lower branch. Without a good view of the sun, especially at midday, he had now lost all sense of direction. A view from high up would give him some bearings. And if the spirit of the wood—for he had no doubt he faced some sort of forest deity—would not let him explore as he wished, then he would learn something that way.

Grabbing hold of a thick limb, he hoisted himself up. Branches shook and swayed, but Jack climbed, forcing his way upward, feeling tiny trickles of blood on his skin from a dozen little cuts. Fear nestled in his gut, but he ignored it. He had been fearful on the White Horse Rapids and on the Chilkoot Trail, but had never let that stop him. Only the Wendigo had ever made him run.

"Do your worst," Jack whispered as he climbed.

The branch under his left foot snapped, and he fell, tumbling through breaking branches that stabbed at him on the way down. He hit the ground with an impact that drove the breath from his lungs. His chest burned for long seconds as he waited for his wind to return, his back stretched across knobby exposed roots.

"Son of a bitch," he wheezed when he could breathe again.

Brushing off the seat of his pants, holding his right hand over a gash on his left biceps, he rose to his feet and saw that the trees had shifted again. They were still gathered close, but now a single path lay open to him, free of roots or stones or trees, as though the trail had been cleared specifically for his use.

He knew very little about these woods, but it seemed clear that Lesya's was not the only magic at work here. That sense of menace surrounded him like invisible smoke, and he began to feel claustrophobic. He had lost track of which direction might be east, but it no longer mattered. The forest had thwarted him. Only one path remained.

If he had any hope of returning to Lesya, or ever finding civilization again, he knew he had no choice but to follow.

CHAPTER ELEVEN

THE LANGUAGE OF THE LAND

J ACK FOUND THE ENERGY to run. It reminded him of his flight through the forest from the Wendigo, but this threat was more sinister and less known. It hid in the shadows beneath trees, under last year's leaf cover on the forest floor, and behind every trunk. Even when he sensed that the threat was now far behind him, still he ran. He did not once look back. He tried to reason that this was merely because he needed to look ahead, to make sure he did not run into a dip in the ground or the cruelly sharp stake of a snapped tree limb. But the truth was, he was scared of what he would see.

He hoped that he was going in the direction of the cabin, but his usual good sense of direction was blurred and confused. Those trees had aimed him a certain way; but once away from their influence, he changed his route, cutting through a shallow ravine worn by a long-ago stream, then left again, passing a series of five fallen trees tangled like dead lovers. He was confusing himself, but he hoped that he confused whatever had been stalking him more.

And then somewhere to his right, Jack heard singing. It was the strangest, sweetest voice he had ever heard, and haunting at the same time. He thought of wind whistling through hollowed bones. His blood ran cool, yet the voice held no threat.

He found himself walking toward it, unable to avoid its allure. *The other way!* he thought. *I should be going the other way!* But the voice drew him on, and it was the words that gave him some comfort, at least. He did not understand them, but they were a language that he had heard Lesya muttering in her sleep. He pushed through a growth of low trees, closing his eyes as one thin branch scraped across his cheek.

Reaching the edge of a clearing, he saw Lesya. He paused, standing still within shadows beneath the trees, and tried to understand what she was doing. To begin with, his mind could not comprehend, and one word whispered inside him: *magic magic magic. . . .*

Lesya was the center of everything. She stood in the middle of the clearing, arms by her side and head tilted slightly as though listening, and she was as beautiful as he had ever seen her. It was her voice that filled the air. He could not see her face—she was looking away from him—but he knew that while she sang, she smiled.

Jack had heard of snake charmers, though he had never seen the act performed. He'd once seen a man beguile a bull to do his bidding, and Jack himself had learned the subtle art of guiding a dog's attention. But he had never in his wildest dreams imagined this.

Lesya had the forest in her thrall. All around her, flower blossoms seemed to face her way, and branches seemed to sway with the rhythm of her words. Around her feet, grasses swished, and some daring shoots snaked across the ground to her legs, curling up around her limbs, across her waist, and higher. She looked down at the shoots and they drew back, but slowly.

Her song changed slightly, and shadows flitted around the clearing. Jack could not quite work out what they were—animals, he thought, though they moved just too fast for him to focus on them. He would track one shape, see it disappear just when he thought he had it centered, and then another would tease the extremes of his vision. He blinked hard a few times and looked again, but the shapes were still only that—suggestions of creatures.

He could smell them and hear them, and perhaps they were as amazed at Lesya as he.

Jack frowned, thinking back to moments before when the forest had been closing in on him, crushing him, herding him in a particular direction . . . but this was nothing like that. There was no malevolence here, only reverence for whatever Lesya held within her. *That was something else,* Jack thought, and he looked back over his shoulder into the motionless forest behind him.

When he turned back to the clearing, he saw, past Lesya and in the shadows of the facing trees, something gray.

"Oh!" Jack cried out, because he thought it was a wolf.

Lesya turned around. Her singing stopped. The forest became only a forest again; movement ceased, shapes stilled into shadows, and growth and decline followed their own imperceptible timescale once more. The gray shape vanished.

And for the space of a heartbeat, Lesya's face looked blank and hard.

"There's something in the forest," Jack said, because he had no idea how to even begin asking about what she had been doing.

Lesya walked to Jack, touched his face, and looked over his shoulder into the forest behind him. She sighed.

"Come with me," she said. "It's time I told you some things."

"About you? About the forest trying to kill me?"

Did Lesya smile? Jack wasn't sure, but if she did, it was an expression he did not like. He had never seen a hint of mockery in her eyes until now.

"If he wanted to kill, he would have killed," she said. "I need to tell you about my father." She headed across the clearing without once glancing back, and Jack could only follow.

As they walked, Lesya talked. Jack listened in amazement, but also with some relief. Incredible though what she told him was, at least it went *some* way toward explaining what had been happening to him these last few weeks. *Magic*, he thought again, but it was something much older than that.

"My father is Leshii, an ancient Forest Lord, and he has lived in these forests for three hundred years. He came in the minds and hearts of Russian explorers, and he had a comfortable home here until the land slowly killed them. Hunger, the cold, violence, the local tribes—within three years of coming here, the explorers were all dead. But my father remained, because he had found a paradise. He claimed these forests as his own, protecting them, nurturing, enjoying places where the touch of man was rare."

Lesya and Jack paused by a stream, and she jumped across to the opposite bank. He went to follow . . . and paused.

"It's too far," he said, trying to picture just how she had leaped. He frowned, because the memory was hazy.

Lesya smiled across at him, then pointed down. "There are three stepping stones for you to use," she said, and Jack started across. Even before he had reached her, Lesya was talking again.

"So far from home, my father was weak. The tribes here did not know him by the right name; their belief in other spirits, and their denial of him, was weakening him year by year. Summer would come, and he would dry out to almost nothing. And then winter, and darkness, and he would grow strong again in the haunted minds of men and women. He disliked preying on their fears, but that was his only way to grow. And he paid them back by protecting their herds, and warning them when harsh winters were closing in."

"So it was he who tried to kill me?" Jack asked. He had seen magic and witnessed things that he could barely believe, but he was still far away from believing this. Yet the question did not feel foolish, and Lesya's answer was sobering.

"My father is mad, now, after so long here," she said without turning to look at him. "And I sense that with you and me, he is jealous. It's only lucky that he is so weakened by time and disbelief."

"So if I believe, will it strengthen him?"

Lesya stopped then and turned to him, her face grim. Yet her eyes still sparkled. *I could love her,* he thought unexpectedly, and he held his breath, waiting for the trees to close in and crush the love from him.

"You must let me worry about my father," she said. She came close, touching Jack's face and looking at her bloodied fingertip. "I'll protect you."

"And you?" Jack asked. "What about you? If he's your father, then . . . ?" He frowned, shook his head. *What does that make you?* he thought, but he did not say that. She was too beautiful to question.

"I had a human mother," she said. "A long time ago, when Father was still strong and could appear as a man, he met an Indian woman lost in the hills, took her in, cared for her. He knew that the time would come when their disbelief wore him down, and perhaps he thought that taking a human wife would avert that." She shrugged. "She died giving birth to me."

"I'm sorry," Jack said, and Lesya smiled sadly.

She turned and headed away again, and minutes later they emerged into the cabin clearing.

For a second, Jack felt dizzy. He leaned against a tree and looked past Lesya at the cabin. *This is all too much,* he thought. *Living buildings, forest gods, and Lesya . . . Lesya, my love, what was she doing back there in the clearing?* He feared her then, and realized that part of his confusion always had been fear. She was something he could never understand completely, and her beauty—and, perhaps, the idea that they could love—was clouding his mind.

"Of *any* human, it's you who can understand," Lesya said, as if in response to his thoughts. "There are so many wonders!"

She fell to her knees, leaned forward, and placed her hands on the earth, smiling up at Jack.

He blinked.

And then Lesya was an arctic fox, loping across the clearing and disappearing behind the cabin.

"Lesya?" he said, looking around for her, unable to believe what he had seen. His acceptance of a touch of magic was being challenged every moment by things even more unbelievable.

A caribou emerged from behind the cabin, trotting across to Jack, dodging the many bright flower beds dotted around the clearing. It paused before him and snorted, smelling of cinnamon and the wild. He blinked . . .

. . . and Lesya was there again. She was breathing hard, as if she had been running. Her simple dress still sprouted fur in several places. Every inch of her smile included him, and was *for* him. He closed his eyes, but that could not shut

*He closed his eyes, but that could not shut
out such terrifying wonders.*

out such terrifying wonders.

"Jack, there's nothing to be afraid of," she said.

Jack opened his eyes again, and it was still Lesya standing before him, the incredible, beautiful woman who he knew it would be so easy to love. "Really?" he asked, because he could not help doubting.

"Really." She came forward, her exotic, mysterious smell carried with her, and kissed him softly on the lips.

I believe you, he tried to say, but he could not speak. She had taken his breath away.

She led him back to the cabin and inside, making him lie on the bed while she treated his many cuts and abrasions.

"I lost your book," he said, realizing that he had dropped the Dumas novel during his flight through the forest.

"It doesn't matter," she said. "I've read it many times."

"Where did you—?" Jack began, but she placed her fingers across his lips as she had that first time.

"Hush, Jack. Lie back, be still, and let me tend these wounds. My father has many ways and wiles. He did not trap you this time, but where his spirit wanders, he controls those places completely. The largest tree to the smallest creature. I have to make sure he didn't plant infection in you."

"Infection?"

"Fungal spores, fly larvae, poisonous plant extracts,

rancid fluids from dead things . . . the forest is full of dangers." She smiled slightly, softly, as if thinking some private thought.

"I can wash . . . ," he began, but trailed off. She was using a soft, damp cloth soaked in some thick, warm fluid, and wherever she touched his skin, it tingled and warmed. It was a pleasant experience, and it felt cleansing. Even his cuts did not hurt so much when she touched them.

So he closed his eyes and let her clean his wounds, using the opportunity to think about everything that had happened. The thoughts swirled through his mind, different images flashing in and out, and there were so many wonders that it was impossible to focus on one thing. The terror he had felt surrounded by those trees, the blind panic that had led him to begin climbing, the rustling and whispering that had sounded so much like the forest conspiring to kill . . . all these were countered by the wonders he had seen in that clearing, and the things Lesya had told him. As amazing and unbelievable as her story had been, it was really the only explanation of what was happening to him that he could accept.

"What were you doing in the clearing?" he asked.

"Communing with the forest. I have many of my father's talents, and as a half human I also have needs."

"Needs?"

"This cabin, the garden. My father does not eat, but I must."

"I saw you . . . the fox. The caribou."

"Another gift from Leshii. He can imitate the images of wild animals and plants. But I'm flesh and blood, as well as spirit and breeze, and so I am able to transform, to become them."

"It sounds incredible."

"It's very lonely." She looked away and sighed, as if sorry she had gone so far.

I'm here, Jack wanted to say, but he could not. How could he really comfort a creature like Lesya? She looked so human, yet she was something far different, and however alluring her person, however beautiful her smile, she was not a woman. *What are you?* he wanted to ask, but again, he could not say that out loud. He had no wish to hurt her feelings.

My wolf, he thought, and for a moment his heart leaped. Was it possible that this wondrous woman had been with him all that time in the wild? But he closed his eyes, certain that was not the case. The wolf had been something that Lesya was not, and vice versa. He would have *known.* Lying there, he breathed in her scent, and it was like nothing he had smelled before.

"I can show you," she said softly.

"Show me what?" He opened his eyes, reveling in the sight of her once again.

A slow smile grew on her face. "Yes," she said, nodding. "Yes, I can show you!" She clasped his hands and pulled him from the bed. "Outside, Jack! Come with me." And she turned and rushed to the door.

Jack swayed where he stood, dizzied. But her sudden enthusiasm was catching, and he felt invigorated once more. "What are you going to show me, Lesya?"

She stood in the open doorway, the sun throwing her shadow back into the cabin. Jack imagined that shadow flexing and changing: a bear, a fox, a snake.

"I'll show you how to answer when the wild calls." And then she was gone from the doorway, back out into the open.

As Jack followed, Lesya's laughter drew him on. She took him to sit below the apple tree, and he smelled the blossom that was impossible here in the Yukon.

"This is the call of the coyote," Lesya said, and the sound that came from her mouth could have issued from no human throat. Jack drew back a little, unsettled. But when Lesya stopped and tilted her head, listening as an answering call came in from far away, he could not help smiling.

"Now you try," she said.

"Me?"

"Why not? Here, I'll help." She sidled up close to him, touching his throat with her left hand, his chest with her right. "The call starts here, in the chest. Bring it up through your throat, turn your head . . . like this . . . let it flow out rather than shouting. Try."

Jack tried, and Lesya's hands pushed at his chest, drew up to his neck and throat, turned his head, and stroked across his Adam's apple. He felt something give way within him, as though a door had opened, and then a stirring . . . an awakening. Whatever magic Lesya had, Jack had the inescapable suspicion that she had placed a small piece of it deep within him.

She continued to caress his throat as though guiding and drawing the call up out of him, and he opened his mouth to release it. The result was a poor imitation of the call she had produced, but Jack still opened his eyes wide in surprise.

"Try to *think* of yourself as a coyote," she said. "Let the call come from deep inside, rising naturally, not pulled out. And don't be shy."

"Shy?" Jack said, scoffing. The last thing he'd ever been was shy. But Lesya raised one eyebrow, and he found himself blushing.

"Self-conscious," she said. "Feel free and natural, not watched. It's only me, after all."

He smiled, nodded, and tried again. Lesya's hands and fingers did their work, but this time he felt them as movements of his own flesh and skin, not someone else's. And the call that he uttered was answered by that distant coyote.

"Did I . . . did I speak coyote?" Jack asked, staggered.

"You did," Lesya said, laughing. "Do you want me to teach you the language of birds?"

That afternoon, and for the next couple of days, Lesya showed him incredible things.

Jack's facility for learning had always been immense. A reader almost since before he could talk, during his short life he had consumed countless books, both factual and fiction. He was a sponge for information, soaking it up wherever he could get it, but his true intelligence rose from applying that information. His mind was not just a repository of knowledge but a factory in which that knowledge could be sorted and combined. He was *hungry* for learning, and in all the months he had spent in the Yukon so far, this time with Lesya sated that hunger more than any other he could remember.

She told him how to track the flights of different birds, anticipate their paths, and be aware of their habits and natures. Some of their calls he found quite easy to learn, but others were more difficult. Lesya worked on these with him, and he felt her magic opening more and more doors within him. Some of what he learned was not magic at all, however, and it was always the most obscure advice that seemed to make things click into place. *Think of butter melting in a pan,* she said, and the next time he tried whistling a northern shrike's call, he could have been the bird itself. *Smell the bloom of the rose,* she suggested, and as he whistled, he heard yellow warblers answering from the trees around the clearing.

They walked into the forest and she taught him more calls—elk, bear, bison, caribou, moose, cougar. Some he found easier to imitate than others, but it was never the shape of his mouth or throat that caused the difficulties. Lesya guided him past the physical constraints nature had given him, and deeper inside there was a spiritual contact she taught him to make with these animals. He stretched, listening to her voice to guide his way, and sometimes the contact came quickly. Once that touch was made, he would smell the scent of the animal in question, hear it sniffling across the ground seeking its prey's trail or crunching tough grass between its grinding teeth. He would see it in his mind's eye, and as he attempted its call, so his image of the creature would utter its own roar, whine, or growl. He could reach out and feel the touch of its fur or pelt on his hands, and at the same time his own skin seemed to bristle, and he felt the cool touch of unseen ground beneath his feet.

Other times, seeking out an animal was much more difficult, and he soon realized that it was some animals' stealth that kept them hidden away. He spent a long time reaching out in his search for a cougar, and as the sun dipped toward the forests and hills in the west, he began to despair of ever realizing one. He had uttered the roar of a grizzly bear and the mournful howl of a wolf, but such incredible feats suddenly seemed insignificant if he could not touch a cougar. He felt like a fool for thinking that way, and perhaps arrogant in his newfound talent, but the sense of failure at the end of that day did not sit well with him.

"Perhaps they're too far away," he said. "Maybe there aren't any close enough for me to . . ." Still he could not vocalize what he was doing, because he did not really know.

But Lesya shook her head, her lovely hair swaying as it caught the dusky light. "There's one watching us right now," she said.

Jack caught his breath, staring at her. "Where?"

Lesya closed her eyes and whispered, "Find it with me."

Jack tried. He stretched, reaching out with his senses, and this time where he sensed nothing, he probed deeper. Lesya closed her hand around his, he felt her claws, and then he touched the cougar, growling low in his throat, looking down into the valley from the high mountains and focusing on the small clearing and the people there.

He gasped, opened his eyes, and sat back against the tree.

"So you see," Lesya said, but she said no more.

"Yes," Jack said, nodding. "But I'm still not sure I believe."

"You wait here," she said. "I'll go and cook dinner. Something special tonight to celebrate, and a glass of wine to seal what we have become." She walked away, and Jack watched her go. *What we have become*, she'd said.

Jack frowned, chilled.

What we have become.

Jack waited in the clearing and watched the sun set. All the while he was thinking about what had happened to him, and what they had done. He felt renewed, remade as a larger, more elaborate version of his old self, and the things he had achieved were amazing. *No one will believe*, he thought, but that idea did not concern him. This was not something to share, an ability to wear on his sleeve and boast about on cold nights around warm fires. This was intensely personal, and it reinforced his connection to the wild.

As the sunlight splashed across the wooded, hilly

horizon, broken into shards by trees and ridges, he cast his mind out again as Lesya had shown him, trying to sense past the forests she inhabited. He felt a thrill of fear doing so, because in all her teachings she had never gone beyond a certain point. *It's dangerous,* she would say, or, *It can't work that far.* But Jack was a man who had to experience such things for himself.

Even Lesya's word was not the same as experience.

So he probed outward, eyes half closed and half open so that he could watch the cabin. The oil lamps were lit in there, and he saw shadowy movement within as Lesya went about preparing their meal. *Maybe she will sense what I'm doing,* he thought. But he could not let that scare him off. Part of what he felt for her was fear, yes, and there was still something about her that he could not quite perceive as clearly as he'd have liked . . . but he remained his own man.

He pushed out, out, past familiar forests to less-known lands. And then somewhere before him was a presence he knew so well—the wolf! It started at his intrusion, howled; and it was so far away that he could not hear it on the dusky air.

Jack smiled, delighted, and tried to connect with the mind of the beast he had come to know as his spirit guide. But then he frowned. The contact remained, but the wolf was pacing back and forth across his mind, skirting the boundary of Lesya's domain as if keen to enter but unable. He sensed concern and fear, and a pent-up frustration that was almost violent in its potential.

"What is it?" he muttered, and in his mind the wolf growled.

"Jack!" Lesya called.

He sat up and opened his eyes fully, looking across the clearing at the cabin.

"Jack!" Her voice sounded urgent.

"Yes," he said, trying to affect tiredness. "I was dozing."

"Dozing," she echoed. "Well, the food's ready now, if you'll rouse yourself." She disappeared back into the cabin.

Jack stood, stretched, and tried to feel his way back toward the wolf. Perhaps because he'd been disturbed, or due to the fear of discovery, he felt somehow blocked now, unable to probe with his senses anywhere beyond the boundary of this small clearing. It was as if the traces of magic that Lesya had put inside him were not within his control.

Why don't you come to me? he thought. And he remembered the wolf's growl, and its pacing, and he realized that was *exactly* what it was trying to do.

Lesya had prepared a dish of fried meat—Jack thought mutton, though he had seen no sheep in the area—

with roasted vegetables. It was exquisite, and his stomach rumbled as they sat in the chairs and ate. Lesya was quiet, contemplative. She even looked beautiful like that, and Jack knew there was no expression that would ever steal her beauty.

"What is it?" he asked at last. Plates emptied, mugs filled with wine, they sat on deep soft rugs by the open fire, leaning in to each other. They were both staring into the flames.

"I don't want it to go wrong this time," she whispered.

Jack frowned. *Is she talking to me?* The flames flittered; a sap bubble in one of the logs spat with a loud snap.

"Jack," she said, turning to him at last. "I love you."

His heart thudded, and he blinked several times to clear his vision.

"And you have to stay with me now."

"What? Stay?" *I don't belong here,* he thought. *This is not my home, home is somewhere I need to be,* and other such thoughts jumbled over each other, as if Lesya's use of that single word had opened a door in his mind behind which . he had been holding his true nature prisoner.

How long had he been here, now? Many weeks, surely. All along he had been pushing to the back of his mind the knowledge that in time he would have to return home, and as recently as days ago he would have said he wished he could remain with Lesya forever. But something had changed.

Something that sent ripples of unease through him.

"Yes, Jack," she said, leaning in so that her nose was almost touching his. Her eyes were wide, and he saw a sheen of perspiration across her top lip. Was Lesya truly nervous? "Because I love you, and you love me, and I've told you so many secrets."

"Love," he said, savoring the word like the fine wine in his mug. *And just where does that fine wine come from?*

"This place . . . it's magical, and it's mine, but . . . I get so lonely." She looked away, frowning.

"Lesya, I'm not sure I can—"

"He'll kill you," she whispered. "If you go out into the forests alone, he'll kill you. I've felt his rage growing out there, his jealousy, and he might be weak, but madness gives him strength."

"You told me you'd protect me from your father," he said.

"And I will. But not if you go out there on your own."

And there it was. A threat. It felt to Jack as though a curtain had been drawn back to reveal parts of Lesya she had never before allowed him to see. He nodded slowly, turning back to the fire so that she could not read his eyes.

Lesya leaned against him again, resting one hand on his leg and molding herself to him. Her scent overwhelmed him, her hair was a sensuous breath against his neck and cheek, and he could hear the steady rhythm of her breathing. *Love,* Jack thought, and he tried to ally that word with what he felt for Lesya.

Not if you go out there on your own . . .

"What are you thinking?" she asked, and she sounded almost desperate.

"Nothing," Jack said.

Prisoner, he thought.

Next day after breakfast, Jack took a walk to the edge of the clearing. He felt Lesya's disapproval, and all the way he could sense her eyes on the back of his head, watching, waiting. But even though the past few days had exposed many wonderful things to him, and he felt more whole than he ever had before, Lesya's warnings last night had set a distance between them.

He sat beside a rock and looked back at the cabin, and when he waved, Lesya waved in response. She went about tending her garden. And she never turned her back on him.

I'm being guarded, he thought. *She's always watching.* So he leaned back against the rock and looked at the sky, closing his eyes and willing himself to relax. The thought of running flitted through his mind, but then something else crossed its path.

Jack's eyes snapped open. He breathed deeply, opening

his senses, welcoming in the smells and sounds, the feel and taste of the air, all as Lesya had shown him. And he knew that ten feet behind the rock stood a wolverine.

He tried to breathe evenly, heart racing with excitement. *Now's the time to try*, he thought, and he probed outward with his mind, welcoming the creature's senses as his own. It paused in its sniffling, sensing his presence even though it could not see or smell him. Jack froze. Then the creature let out a startled cry, and turned and fled back between the trees.

Jack was exhausted. Sweat dripped down his face and sides, and he suddenly felt as if he'd run for miles. Panting, he leaned against the rock and closed his eyes again.

When the footsteps approached, he knew that she wanted him to hear her.

"It takes time," she said.

Jack opened his eyes. "After yesterday, with the cougar, I thought—"

"I helped you with that, Jack, remember?"

"Yes," he said. "I remember." *It takes time.* But perhaps he no longer had any. And this fresh reminder of the passage of time brought home to him the situation he was in.

He smiled at Lesya and knew that his escape must be soon.

That night, Jack ventured out into the forest alone, and Leshii came to kill him. The Lord of the Forest planted trees around him, trapping him in the darkness, sending branches and trunks tumbling toward him, and all the while he heard Lesya in the distance singing her sweet song. He called to her for help but she did not hear, and Leshii manifested as a darkness among shadows. He was as old as she'd said, and mad, and he was a jealous god.

Jack tried to reach beyond his wooden cage with the senses he had just learned, but he was only a man.

And when Leshii reached out with sharpened branches and plunged them into his feet, Jack opened his mouth to scream.

He gasped in a breath and stared at the timber ceiling of the living cabin. *Trapped in a wooden cage!* he thought, and Lesya moved in her sleep beside him. *Thank God. Only a dream.*

Breathing hard and fast, still feeling pain in his feet from where Leshii had pinned him down in his dream, Jack tried to calm himself. *Only a dream. Only a . . .*

Something moved.

Jack tried to sit up, but now he felt a weight on his legs, holding him down. Something shifted beneath the blanket, and terror curled itself into a tight ball in his belly. Breath caught in his throat, and he reached down with a trembling hand to tear the blanket away.

In the moonlight that streamed through the window he saw the thing that held him down, sliding and crawling across his lower body, rooted in the house's living floorboards. The figure raised its head, and he saw the face—made of twigs and leaves, moss and mulch—and he knew who it was who held him now.

Leshii.

Flexing tendrils wrapped around Jack's feet and ankles. He opened his mouth to scream, but Leshii raised one twig-like hand and held a knotted finger across his own lips, shushing him. *Shhh* . . . It reminded Jack so much of when Lesya had first rescued him from the Wendigo that the scream froze in his chest. Leshii's eyes, dark holes framed by leaves, opened wide . . . and then turned to the side.

The god of the forest had not come there to kill him. But then why *had* he come?

Lesya woke and began shrieking at her spirit father, and then Jack's own scream came at last, more startled by her fury and the way Leshii's eyes suddenly darkened with dismay than from the heart-clenching terror he'd felt moments before.

CHAPTER TWELVE

THE LIVING GRAVEYARD

SHE TRIED TO CALM HIM. After Leshii had fled the cabin with a rustle of leaves and the cracking of split wood, Lesya had gone to the doors and windows and muttered something that might have been a spell. Then she came back to Jack and took him in her arms, hugging him to her, sitting on the bed so that he could lie with his head in her lap.

The smell of her was strong, but it was no longer merely sensuous. Now, it was dangerous and dark, secretive. Jack accepted her soothing words and gentle rocking, because in truth he needed some form of comfort. But as night bled away and dawn pushed into the cabin, he could not find sleep. He stared at the sliver of bark he had pried from the wall, and the flesh of living wood beneath. He felt Lesya's own fears transmitted through her voice and touch.

And he knew he had to escape.

———

That morning, Lesya cooked bacon and eggs, and they had a feast for breakfast.

I've never seen a pig around here, Jack thought, though he supposed there might be wild boar. *I've never seen chickens.* But these eggs could have been from any bird. Ducks were everywhere, and she only had to know where they nested.

"I'm sorry about my father," she said. "It's the first time I've seen him manifest like that in a long time. I thought he was far weaker, much more distant."

"Is that why you're afraid?"

Lesya stared at him, a soft smile on her beautiful, almost flawless face. "I'm not afraid, Jack."

He nodded and continued eating.

"If he comes again—"

"Thank you," Jack said, and he smiled back. "He did scare me, and if you hadn't woken when you did . . ."

"He might have killed you."

"Yes. So thank you, Lesya. I accept your protection, and I'll do whatever you think is best." He looked through the window and did not have to feign his fear. *I'm still not certain about any of this.*

Lesya leaned across the table and stroked his cheek. "I do love you, Jack."

He smiled at her and touched her hand but did not

reply. Her eyes flickered away, and for a moment he felt a flush of sorrow for her. *I could* love her, he thought, *even after everything.* "You're very special," he said. She sighed and set about clearing the dishes.

"I'm going to the spring to wash," Jack said.

"I'll heat some water in here, if you wish."

"The cold will do me good!" He rubbed his eyes, shook his head. "Help wake me up, chase away the bad dreams."

Lesya nodded. "Very well. And later, I can show you how to track snakes and stinging things."

Jack pulled on his boots and went to the door, and there he had to pause. *This is my escape,* he thought. *And if I succeed beyond all my hopes . . .*

He turned around to look at Lesya for the final time. She was standing by the stove, watching a pot of warming water and running her finger around her plate, collecting bacon juice and egg yolk. Her simple dress hung just right, and her hair, still tangled from sleep, framed her face. She was quite beautiful, the most gorgeous woman Jack had ever seen and would ever likely see again, and this was exactly how he wished to remember her.

She looks so normal, he thought, though he knew she was far from that.

"Something wrong?" she asked, suddenly aware of his observation.

"No," Jack said. "Just thinking that I love you."

Her smile was wondrous.

And with everything he intended to do, still Jack could find no lie in what he had said.

He walked across the clearing toward the spring. It was close to the looming line of trees, but not too close. His heart was thumping; his legs quivered with anticipation of what was to come.

At the spring, he started unbuttoning his shirt. He glanced back at the cabin. Lesya was just visible behind one window, her pale face gleaming with sunlight reflecting from the glass. He waved, she waved back, and then she retreated farther into the cabin.

Jack ran for the trees.

Everything changed suddenly. The potential of what he'd been planning was now an actuality, and the danger was real and pressing. With every pounding footstep, he expected to hear Lesya's warning screech from behind him: *Jack, beware my father.*

Jack had already chosen to ignore that, if and when it came. It was a gamble that held his life and future in the balance, but since Leshii's appearance the night before, things had become clear to him. He had family waiting for him in California, and that was where his real life lay. This, everything he had seen and done here . . . this was make-believe.

The air around him remained silent but for Jack's steady breathing. A few birds took off from the clearing somewhere to his right, and he resisted the temptation to reach for them. He was on his own flight.

It was only as he passed between the first of the trees that he heard Lesya's voice. She did not shout or rage but screamed, a high, incredibly loud sound that chilled Jack to the marrow and set him running faster than ever before. Tree branches lashed at his face, he ran through a spiderweb that felt as strong as string, and his heart seemed to double its beat. Sweat broke out all over his body.

The scream came again, even louder than before, and at its end he heard, *"Jack!"*

He was committed now. He dodged between trees, looking and feeling for anything abnormal in the forest around him. *What will she do?* he thought. *How will she punish me if she catches me?* By running, he was denying her love and making a lie of trust he had placed in her this morning. At first she had seemed a sweet woman, but now Jack no longer knew. Someone with such power . . .

A tree ahead and to his right started to fall. He heard the cannonlike crack of its trunk rupturing close to the ground, and then the entire canopy above him was in tumult as the huge tree came crashing down. He dodged left, darted right, and then realized that whichever way he

went, he would not escape its reach. In a hopeless gesture
he brought up both arms before his face . . .

. . . and the tree stopped falling.

Another had grown beneath the shattered trunk,
uppermost branches splayed in order to catch the falling
tree. This new tree had two trunks and a thick bole, and
its upright limbs seemed almost to ripple in the sunlight
streaming through the forest.

Jack ran on. A powerful breeze suddenly roared through
the forest, picking up leaves, whistling past his ears, filling
his senses with violent movement. *Lesya!* he thought, but
then a strong hand seemed to close around his right arm,
and he felt the callused skin of an old man.

He looked down. Nothing was holding Jack, but still he
felt compelled to follow.

There was another scream from behind him—much
closer now—and he heard the sounds of pursuit. Heavy footfalls in the forest, the crack of trees snapping aside beneath
the onslaught of whatever pursued him, and then he reached
the edge of a ravine, teetering, just gaining his balance . . .
before being pushed over the edge by another strong wind.

You must see, a voice seemed to whisper as he fell. Jack
tumbled, wrapping his arms around his head and denying
the voice, because it had sounded so old and inhuman that
he could not accept it, could not acknowledge that he could

ever hear something so beyond his ken. He came to a stop at the bottom of the ravine, sitting up slowly as the sounds of his chaotic descent faded, and then the voice came in again.

You must see.

Jack scurried back from the voice, though when he looked, there was no one and nothing around him. Nothing but trees.

And then he saw, and realized why he had to see.

Because these trees bore unnatural fruit.

While he was down in that ravine, desperate to leave, to *unsee* what he was seeing, Jack London heard two great powers fighting for him. In the forest above, trees fell and were shattered, the ground shook, and occasionally he heard Lesya's terrible screams echoing through the battleground. Leshii, her spirit father, held her back while Jack saw. And with every heartbeat, greater understanding emerged.

Where there had been magic, now there was horror.

Where Jack had felt the strange stirrings of love, now there was disgust, terror . . . and pity. For everything that Lesya had done, he still felt sorry for her, because she was something not meant to be. A creature of spirit and flesh, she was unnatural, an aberration from the natural order of these wild places. All she was doing was trying to survive, just like him. And she must have been so lonely.

He counted fifteen trees in the ravine that had not grown here naturally. Each tree held a body within its grasp, growing *around* the body as if it had been there when the seed was planted. In some, faces pressed out of the bark. In others, the shapes were barely visible: a limb here, a foot there. These were Lesya's previous companions, men who had found and become bewitched by this beautiful woman and her impossible cabin. Some of their clothes he thought might be Russian, others French. A couple were Indians, a couple black, and he thought that they were all dead and somehow preserved from rot by Lesya's magic.

Until one of them blinked.

Jack cried out. He had been numbed to the horror up to now, but those blinking eyes saw through his defensive shield and lit the terror within. He backed away from the trapped man—only a face and the left arm still outside the tree trunk—and another tree halted his retreat.

He turned around and stared into the green eyes of a changed man. The man opened his mouth slowly, though no noise escaped, and grubs rooted among his few remaining teeth. There were terrible sores and lesions inside his mouth, and though the flesh was open, the blood was not red. It was a viscous, thick sap.

There was no sign of recognition or awareness in this man's eyes.

Like the Wendigo's eyes when it faced me in my own guise . . . unnatural and wretched!

Jack ran again, blind panic driving him now. He clawed his way up the side of the ravine, his fingers digging into the soft bank and his feet pushing. All sense of direction was gone—he could have easily been climbing toward the raging Lesya, not away from her.

Plenty more trees in the forest, came a whisper in his mind, and he could not identify the voice. Perhaps it was fear taking on a life of its own. But wherever the voice came from, it made something very clear to Jack: What he had just seen would be his fate if Lesya caught him.

Because she would never trust him again. And though she possessed an outward veneer of civility that the Wendigo never had, at least that monster was honest in its raging hunger. Lesya lied, and beneath that lie she, too, consumed.

Clearing the top of the ravine, Jack turned to look back down. The canopies of those monstrous trees were natural and lush, and from up here he could barely see the grotesque realities merged with their trunks. Panic had him, but he looked around quickly, panting, listening to the sounds of chaos. Judging that he had climbed the correct side of the ravine, he turned and started running once more.

The forest was still thick here, but it was a place he had

never wandered with Lesya. She had kept him away from that dreadful ravine, of course, so now he was running almost blind . . . and around him, the forest was coming to life. Animals large and small ran with Jack, and for a second he was confused. *Am I scaring them into flight?* But then he realized that was not the case, and that their direction would provide a good indication of the route he should take.

The whole forest was afraid.

Rabbits and foxes ran, birds and insects flew, and in the distance he heard the heavy rumble of what could have been a bear hurrying through the trees.

More horrific sounds erupted behind him. A wicked groan, like a tree being uprooted with all its roots intact; the thunderous crack of a thick trunk breaking in two; a loud scream, ending with a sob that could have only been Lesya.

"I'm sorry for this," Jack whispered, and he wondered whether she heard. She could have been that bird, that insect, that loping lynx that he'd just glimpsed to his left. If she *was* a lynx, she could run him down. If she was a bear, she could savage him. Through his panic, Jack suddenly realized that he did not have to be alone.

As he ran, leaping fallen trees and amazed at the creatures fleeing with him, he tried to cast his mind forward. At first he felt nothing, and he wondered whether his treachery would strip him of the abilities taught him by Lesya. But then he felt things slowly changing, even as he fled. Concentrating on the wooded landscape around him, he also sensed the breeze and smells and sights of an open grass plain.

He heard a wolf's growl, and Jack sent his own voice back.

And also as he ran, it seemed as though a trance was being lifted from him. The forest stripped it away, and his exertion, and the distance he was putting between himself and the cabin—the place that had been his haven, and had become his prison. His sister Eliza smiled at him from memory, Shepard grabbed his hand and extracted promises Jack had not kept, and even his mother was there, not quite smiling but no longer cursing him. *For them, if for nothing else*, he thought. *For them*—

A writhing creeper tripped him. He struck the ground hard, winding himself, rolling until he crunched hard against a tree trunk. Terrified, he looked up at the looming growth, expecting it to uproot itself and bring its earthy underside down on him. But while he considered danger from the tree that did not come, the creeper twirled intimately around his leg . . . and then pulled tight.

Jack shouted out in pain. He clawed at the creeper, tugging, scratching, but the more he touched it, the tighter it coiled.

He noticed only then that the sounds in the distance

had stopped. No more roars or screams, no more echoing noises of unimaginable combat. All the animals had fled, leaving him behind, and the forest became quieter than he had ever heard it.

Quieter than the grave, he thought, and he wondered what it would feel like to be part of a tree, having his blood drawn to make way for the living plant's sap, and how time would seem so painful as it ticked away infinitely slowly. . . .

A shape moved far away between the trees, a pale blue.

More creepers snaked across the ground and enveloped him. A breeze came, shifting leaves and windblown seeds that should not have taken flight until autumn. He smelled cinnamon, and soil; the fresh odor of Lesya's breath, and the familiar rot of old leaves. He tried to cast his senses outward again, but he was small, he was *nothing*, little more than an echo on this landscape of incredible things.

"Help me!" he shouted, but the forest stole his voice.

And then Lesya was there before him, emerging from the trees—changing from the spirit of the forest she had been—and she was transformed. Still beautiful, but terrifyingly so. Still smooth skinned, but possessed of a radiance that honored no natural law. Her eyes shone with fury, her mouth was downturned in a grim parody of the smile she had always worn in his presence. She no longer carried her beauty like a gift, but rather as a natural consequence of

"Help me!" he shouted, but the forest stole his voice.

what she was. It was her rage, however, that marred her with the only shadow of ugliness.

"I thought you were the one," she said.

"Lesya—"

"I thought there was *love*!"

"I don't belong here in this place; I can touch the wild but—"

"I showed you things," Lesya said, and her voice grew gentle again. She came closer, walking in that way that had always enraptured him, hair flowing, head tilted slightly to one side. "I gave you a part of myself, a gift of magic I will never be able to regain. I showed you things I've never shown anyone else before."

"I know who else you're talking about," Jack said. And he wished he hadn't.

"Leshii!" Lesya growled, and the trees around them shivered, the ground shook, and the air itself seemed to draw away in fear.

Jack gasped, struggling to draw a breath as she approached him. Her hands were clawed before her, and the usual pinkness beneath her nails had turned a pale green.

He closed his eyes, saw Eliza and Shepard again, and his mother, and he knew that if he died, she would try to talk to him through one of her terrible séances. And confused by panic and terror—both emotions heightened to a point Jack believed no man should be able to bear—the fear hung heavy with him that his mother would succeed.

And then a roar, and a sound like the earth breaking, and it was Lesya's startled cry that made him open his eyes again.

At first he could not understand what he was seeing. There was a blur of motion, shapes darting this way and that, and the first thing he sought was Lesya. She was not where she had been standing, so he looked left and right, following the other flashes of greenish motion.

Lesya was being driven back. Trees sprouted, fell, and died in seconds, as if he were seeing their whole immense life spans speeded up to an unimaginable degree. And with each new growth between him and Lesya, she was pushed back farther.

"Father!" she shouted, and then she started screaming in an old, forgotten language that Jack had never heard before. And though the words made no sense, the way they were delivered was familiar to him—she was pleading and threatening, pleading and threatening, following that pattern over and over as Leshii pushed her away.

A man emerged from behind Jack and knelt by his side. He was impossibly tall and thin; he had living, waving grass as a beard; and his thick vine hair hung down almost to the ground. The skin of his hands was worn bark. He was the forest come to life.

"You saw," he said, reaching for the creepers around Jack's legs.

"Leshii," Jack breathed, almost breathless.

"Leave," the man said. The creepers disintegrated beneath his touch.

"What about Lesya?"

The Lord of the Forest blinked, and in that expression Jack saw how much it pained him to appear like this. "Leave," he said again. Jack nodded his thanks and left.

Once again as he ran, chaos erupted. He kept his eyes on the ground before him and resisted the temptation to let his senses wander, because he needed all his wits now. The fight continued behind him, but it never sounded any farther away.

He could have been running for minutes, or maybe an hour, but every second of that flight through the forest was haunting and unreal. All the animals had fled way ahead of him now, so the only sounds were his footfalls through the mulch and mud of last year's leaves, and the crushing, thumping, cracking sounds pursuing him. He listened carefully, waiting to see if they came any closer. . . .

And without warning, the forest ended, and he stumbled out onto a grassy slope heading up toward a low hillside.

Jack gasped in surprise. "I thought I was in there

forever," he whispered. Behind him, the sounds of pursuit quietened, and all was silent. *Is she gone? Now that I'm out, has she accepted my escape and gone back to that lonely cabin?*

He turned, looking back at the dark forest that seemed to halt so suddenly. And then Lesya appeared before him, manifesting from the trees and shaking a few errant leaves from her hair.

"I'm truly sorry," he said.

She laughed. She stepped out from beneath the trees and onto the grassland, her smell preceding her, befuddling Jack's senses. And then she shrugged herself down into a cougar and pounced.

Something flowed past him and struck the leaping cat. Other shapes streaked in from left and right, and Jack thought, *Wolves!* They growled and grunted, flitting back and forth, and then he realized what they were doing— herding Lesya, in her cougar form, back toward the forest. She lashed out at one, dragging it down, disemboweling it with one snap of her jaws and jerk of her head.

His wolf was there then, nuzzling at his hand and trying to pull him away.

"I don't know how much more I can take," Jack said, and the animal pulled until he turned around and started walking again.

It left him to join the fray. Jack watched for a moment,

seeing Lesya shimmer briefly back into her human form, her expression one of complete surprise as she stared at his wolfen guide and protector. The last time he saw her was when she flexed back into a cougar again, and her grin changed to a roar as she entered into battle once more.

Jack ran and ran. He had no idea where he was finding the energy, but he did not question it. He aimed south and west, not really knowing whether that was the right way to go, but every step in that direction took him closer to home. The more he ran, the more important that seemed to him.

He felt that perhaps he had betrayed home with his weeks in the cabin with Lesya. Already that time was starting to feel like a dream, but he had the cuts and bruises to prove otherwise. The landscape around him was familiar in its ruggedness, and yet none of it seemed touched, or corrupted, by Lesya's influence. It was only now that he was away from her forest that he realized her hold on it had been almost visible. It was not anything so obvious as a color, or a sheen, or the way the shadows fell, but he relished the fact that he was in the true, untouched wild once again. There was more than enough magic in nature for him.

Eventually he could run no more. Halfway across a wide plain he sat in the long grass far away from any trees, then fell onto his back. Looking up at the sky, he tried to project himself as Lesya had shown him, probing outward with his senses, seeking his wolf. He expected it not to work—perhaps it had been her influence all along—but then he heard a growl, smelled matted pelt, and felt the heat of blood on his stomach and legs.

"No," Jack whispered. He sat up and looked north, back the way he had come. *No.*

He had never believed that the creature following and protecting him would be susceptible to injury. But injured it was, and he could feel the haze of its pain with every beat of his own heart. Perhaps it took an unnatural thing like Lesya to hurt something made of smoke.

The temptation to turn back was immense, but that would serve no good. However badly injured, the wolf had fought for him. He could not pay it back by throwing away his freedom.

Exhausted, cold, hungry, aching from his wounds, and feeling worse than he had just after the Wendigo attack several weeks before, Jack headed into the wilderness once again.

CHAPTER THIRTEEN

A RETURN TO THE SCENE

MEN AND WOMEN by the thousands had been lured north by the promise of gold, but the potential for sudden and extraordinary wealth had been only one factor in Jack's decision to journey to the Yukon. He craved adventure, and it sang a song he knew he would never be able to resist. Yet what truly fired Jack London's imagination was the *test*. He had perceived his journey as a great challenge, and yearned to pit himself against this harsh, forbidding land. He had come north with every intention of mastering the wild.

Now a question plagued his every step: Did merely surviving make him the master of the wilderness? His journey from Dyea to Dawson had been a triumph of will, with the threat of death lurking around every corner, but now he looked back upon those months of hardship and hunger with fond longing. From the moment of his arrival in Dawson City, when he'd run afoul of the men who would enslave him and his friends, he had begun to learn more about the wild than the frozen winter on the Yukon River had ever taught him.

Gold prospectors died in the wilderness by the dozens, never to be heard of again. The Wendigo had slaughtered slaver and slave alike in William's camp by the river. More than a dozen men had been seduced into the intimacy of Lesya's private forest and now endured a living hell among the trees. Yet Jack London had survived them all.

And he wondered why.

His route was mostly forested, with a few stretches of undulating grass plain here and there. When he reached a deep ravine cut through the forest by a roaring stream, he started the descent without hesitation. The walls were uneven, treacherous, and overgrown with brambles and other trailing plants, yet Jack climbed down with a confidence he had rarely felt before in such a situation. At one point the wall of foliage to his left erupted as a goshawk burst out, fanning him with its wings as it took flight, majestic and wondrous. He paused only for a moment; if it had so chosen, the bird could have tumbled him from this low cliff.

At the bottom, wading across the foaming stream, he felt himself being watched. It was a gaze he had not felt

before, and he turned slowly to see who or what had him in
its regard this time.

It was a black bear. Thirty feet away up the stream,
front paws parting the water, it stared at him, motionless
and calm. The only movements he saw were its nostrils
flexing and contracting as it took his measure.

Lesya! he thought, but only for a moment. This was not
her; he was way beyond her influence now. He tried to prepare himself, readying to give himself a bear's voice, a bear's
mind, and he shivered at the task. But then the bear turned
and walked away along the ravine, and Jack watched until it
disappeared around a fold of protruding cliff.

As he moved on and started climbing the opposite
wall—handholds found his hands, firm rock carried him
upward—he found himself feeling lonely. It was not the
company of men he wished for, nor even after Lesya the
company of a woman. But the thing that had been with
him for so long on his journey . . . that shade, that protector . . . Jack London missed his wolf.

All of his life, he had rejected his mother's spiritualism.
To believe, even for a moment, that she could communicate
with the dead would have crippled him with terror. Had
he believed in her antics as a boy, considered her anything
but a charlatan, he would have been haunted every waking
moment.

Yet now he knew magic to be real, knew there were spirits in the ether, and not all of them were human. He knew that a curse could create a monster and damn a man to unthinkable suffering, for such had been the fate of the Wendigo. And he finally believed that his mother could talk to the dead.

Jack's spirit guide had been his companion and protector since he had set foot upon the Chilkoot Trail. Now he worried for the wolf. In helping him escape Lesya, it had been wounded. How that was possible he did not know, but he had *felt* it happen, and he worried about what that might mean, and whether it would ever appear to him again.

And what of the wolf? What was it, truly? Did it originate within him, or without? Either way, perhaps it explained the wanderlust inside him. Perhaps he would always be lured into the wild places of the world.

He had eluded the Wendigo and learned to speak in the voices of animals. He had loved a madwoman who was half myth and had taken some of her magic into himself—some of the secret language of the wilderness. His travels had changed him, so a part of him now would *always* be wild. But if he had been so fundamentally altered, did his survival mean that he had *mastered* the wild? Or had it mastered him?

Jack wasn't sure it mattered anymore.

———

Guilt drove him on. Lesya had entranced him, and Jack had allowed many weeks to pass by. With the fate of his mother's home hanging in the balance, and with his family likely agonizing over what had happened to him, he had walked hand in hand through the forest and eaten the fruits of the wood witch's secret garden.

Now he marched east, guided by the sun, determined not to let anything stand in his way. The night of the Wendigo's attack, he had fled west from the camp by the river, but he had collapsed and fallen unconscious in a gully, only to come around some time and distance later, with no way of knowing how far Lesya had carried him.

It can't have been that far, he thought as he hiked across rugged terrain. *The Wendigo tracked me there.*

In truth, he had no idea what either Lesya or the Wendigo might be capable of. The wood witch might have whisked him a hundred miles, and the monster still caught up, but Jack had to rely upon his instincts now. And his instincts told him that Lesya's forest had not been that far from where he had fallen, otherwise she would never have found him.

At last Jack came to a place he thought he recognized: surely this was the gully he'd fallen into while fleeing the Wendigo. After descending into and climbing from the gully, he fell into a steady rhythm. The forest was thicker here, the hills shorter but more rugged, and he had to concentrate to make his way safely and without going off course. He saw many animals, all of them watching him pass. Most of them should not even have been seen—even in this wilderness, the wildlife was learning to be wary of man.

After several hours he gauged he had walked eight miles or more. As tired as he was, Lesya had fed him well in the previous weeks, and now his body tapped into the reserve of strength that nourishment had provided. Gone were the symptoms of scurvy and starvation, and yet somehow he had still been whittled down to the hardened core of himself, the niceties of home stripped away.

Late in the afternoon, he saw the silver ripple of a river through the trees far ahead and redoubled his efforts. When at last he reached the riverbank, he knelt to quench his thirst. Jack splashed water on his face, and with the scraggle of whiskers he had accumulated, it felt like the face of a stranger.

It was his first real pause since fleeing Lesya, and it was only now he realized that he had left without supplies. He had no food, no weapon with which to hunt, not even a flint to start a fire. Jack had his boots and the clothes on his back, but no jacket to throw over himself when the night turned cold. And yet he knew if he needed to catch a rabbit, he would find a way. If he closed his eyes a moment, he could feel rabbits close by, and other animals as well, and he felt confident he could lure dinner if it came to that.

But the idea of tapping into the wood magic that Lesya had taught him made his insides curdle. He wanted to be rid of her completely, to cleanse himself of her enchantment, to stop feeling the queasy love that had insinuated itself into him. Even now he wished he could erase the past few days and return to the bliss he had felt before Lesya's loneliness had revealed its dangerous edge.

So instead of pausing and making camp, he followed the river south. Though he persisted in thinking of this rushing water as the Klondike, it was merely a tributary. It would lead him eventually to the deeply flowing river, and then a trek along the bank of the Klondike would bring him back to Dawson City. There, he hoped his supplies still languished in the storage barns of the hotel where he, Merritt, and Jim had been beaten and pressed into the service of bad men.

Their memory made him melancholy. His friends and enemies were all dead. Souls bright and souls dark, they had passed from the world, and each had had a hand in forging the person Jack had now become.

Less than an hour later, he walked into the ruin of the slavers' camp.

An eagle cried as it flew above him, as if in recognition of the dread he felt as he explored the scene of the massacre. Perhaps without even being aware of it, Jack had reached out to the bird, and it did share his trepidation. Yet the eagle flew on, arcing across the sky toward the tallest of the distant pines on the other side of the river, and Jack remained.

The creek flowed by, its voice either mournful whisper or mocking chuckle—he could not tell which—and Jack wandered the site. Tents and bedrolls were strewn about, along with shovels and the pans they'd been using to sift for gold in the river. There were boots and torn jackets, all stained with long-dried blood. Brown splashes of old blood spattered the rocks and many spots around the camp. Charred evidence of two campfires had been kicked and scattered. Saddles and saddlebags lay where they had fallen, but no horses, and no mules.

No bodies at all, in fact, and that was the worst of it.

Jack picked up a discarded shovel and strode the camp with it, looking beneath blankets and torn clothing. He found nothing he could bury. When Jim had died, the slavers had left him for the animals, but no animal could have done this. The Wendigo had murdered all the men

of the camp, and now nothing remained of the prospectors or their slaves. Either the damned thing had eaten
them, flesh and bone, or it had removed their bodies to
store them for future consumption. And any bits of viscera
left behind during the slaughter had since been found by
birds or beasts who roamed the area.

Only the blood remained. And perhaps the ghosts of
the men who had died here, with nothing to mark their
passing.

I should have been here, Jack thought. It was a foolish idea. The campground still echoed with the screams
of the dying. The Wendigo would have torn him apart,
just as it had the others. It had swept through the camp,
almost invisible in the dark, and so fast that it had seemed
as though the night itself had claws and fangs. Jack had
been staked to the ground. If the wolf had not freed him
and urged him to attempt an escape, he would have been
trapped there when the monster came.

As the shadows grew long and the light began to fail,
Jack performed a methodical search of the camp. The temperature had been plummeting all day, and he scavenged a
second sweater and a heavy coat, and more than one pair
of gloves.

Some of the packs had been torn into by scavengers for
the food within, but he found plenty of dried jerky, tins of

beans, and other things he barely glanced at. What interested him most was the tin of coffee he procured from a canvas bag, along with flint and a metal pot. There were other pots, boxes of matches, tobacco, and myriad other things he would sort through in the morning when deciding what to bring with him when he broke camp. He chose the most formidable-looking of the intact packs, which he emptied in anticipation of repacking after he'd made himself supper.

The prospectors' weapons had done little good against the Wendigo, and the cursed creature had had no use for them. They were scattered all through the camp along with everything else. Jack chose the best rifle, a pair of Colts, and a two-shot derringer, as well as a pair of bowie knives and a small hatchet. Ammunition went into the pack before the encroaching night robbed him of the ability to tell which bullets went with which guns.

When he began dragging leather saddlebags over to the pile, he found them surprisingly heavy. Inside, he discovered the reason: two small bags of gold in each saddlebag, making four total. Staring into the unlaced opening of the first bag, he smiled to himself and felt like crying. He'd promised his mother and Eliza gold from the Klondike, sworn to Shepard that he would not return without it. Black-hearted men had killed for this, and luckless innocents had died. With all that spilled blood, Jack should have left the gold right where it was, except he had suffered for it as well, and he'd be damned if—now that he had it in his hands—he would go home without it.

As night fell, Jack built a fire, heated a tin of beans, and ate it with some jerky. In comparison to what he had grown used to eating in Lesya's company it was a rough meal, but there would be little better between here and home. Afterward he made coffee—the real reason for the fire; he'd eaten cold beans many times before—and then leaned against a saddle he'd hauled over beside the flames. He'd made himself a bedroll as well, but he wasn't ready to sleep yet.

On a second saddle, he carved an epitaph to the men who had died there beside the creek. The wind whipped up and the cold began to hurt his hands, but Jack did not stop until he had etched the complete message into the leather.

20 OR SO MEN KILLED ON THIS SPOT.

SOME GOOD, SOME BASTARDS,

AND ONE MY FRIEND, MERRITT SLOPER.

MAY HE REST IN PEACE,

AND THE BASTARDS GO TO THE DEVIL.

Jack woke before dawn with snow accumulating on his face. He wiped it away, his skin prickling with the cold, and blinked flakes out of his eyes. Before falling asleep he had stoked the fire as high as he could against the encroaching chill of darkness, but the temperature had continued to plummet overnight.

He sat up, removed his hat and brushed the snow from it, and looked around at the thin coating of pure white that had blanketed the land. How long had he spent with Lesya in the forest?

The days and nights had passed with a strange fluidity while he had been with her. It had seemed to Jack like no more than a couple of months, and yet at the same time the days had felt endless, as though each had been its own eternity. He had read folktales in which wanderers in the woods might emerge and find they had been gone from the world for years. Jack had no sense that the world had changed that much, but the snowfall proved that time had passed more slowly while he'd been with Lesya than it had beyond the reach of her influence.

Still, he did not believe that winter had arrived. Yesterday the wind had been calm and the sun bright and warm, the temperature in the midfifties at least. In the afternoon the temperature had slid precipitously. The previous winter, out in the white silence, he had grown used to temperatures no human should have to endure, and this morning's snowfall was warm in comparison.

No, this was not winter. Jack refused to believe even that October had arrived. Late September, then, and an unseasonably cold day. It wouldn't be unheard of this far north, snow in September. The flakes were fat and moist, the temperature only barely cold enough for the storm, perhaps thirty degrees.

It's beautiful, Jack thought. The sight of the gentle snow falling over the river as morning lit the horizon quieted his troubled mind. The snow would fall, and winter would come, and in the spring there would be rain that would wash the blood from the rocks, cleansing the horror from this place. He found some peace in that.

Unwilling to take the time to attempt a new fire in the damp snow, Jack ate two pieces of jerky and took a cup of water from the creek. He pulled on two dry, clean pairs of socks he had found in a pack and then retied his boots, grateful for the coat and gloves he had scavenged from the camp. Before falling asleep the night before, he had stowed what food and supplies he could carry in the pack he'd chosen, and now he shook the snow off his bedroll, wrapped it tight, and tied it to the pack. The two Colts hung in gun belts one on each hip, the knives in sheaths; the derringer hid in an inside pocket, the hatchet was in his pack, and he carried the rifle over one shoulder. Over the other he hung the saddlebags containing the slavers' gold.

Weighted down like that, he was tired before he'd walked a hundred yards, but there was nothing he was willing to leave behind. He could not be sure how far from Dawson he might be, or what he would encounter on the trek.

So he trudged in the snow, following the creek to the river as he had planned. Jack had thought that the arrival of morning would warm the air enough to turn the snow to rain or that it would cease completely. Instead, the day grew colder, the wind more fierce; and the snow fell faster.

A horrible suspicion began to develop in Jack's mind: that the storm might not be entirely natural. He traveled the morning on edge, peering into the storm for any sign of threat. Despite the cold, his exertion and the heavy coat made sweat trickle down the small of his back, and his labored breaths plumed their steam with every step. Jack barely noticed such details, and even the growl of hunger in his belly did not distract him from his vigilance. Every tree took on sinister aspect, and where the river passed close by woods, he scanned the trunks and branches for some sign that all was not as it seemed.

Could Lesya come this far from her secret wood? Surely she would be able to do so, but would her magic extend so far from her father's influence? Jack didn't know, and did not care to find out. His chest tightened with dread at the very thought of what would become of him should she discover him and drag him back to her cabin, or to the grove she had made of cursed lovers, the abominations those men had become. He had been hard at work trying to expunge the image from his mind, but he knew that it would always haunt his dreams.

For hours his concentration was fixed on every shadow, until at last he became utterly certain that indeed some presence observed him on his journey. It watched from the trees, or hid in the whipping snow, or submerged in the frigid, rushing river. He could not decipher its location, but he *felt* it there.

Lesya? Or . . . and a spark of hope rose within him . . . the wolf? Other possibilities occurred to him. The Wendigo had been thwarted before, but it still roamed the wilds, and who knew what other spirits and legends prowled the land?

Jack marched on, long past the time he should have paused to rest. Yet doubt lingered in the back of his mind. His senses had been heightened over the course of the year—by the guardian presence of the wolf the prior winter, and the ominous awareness of Leshii in the forest inhabited by his spirit—but did he dare trust them? Did he sense peril in the storm only because it was what he expected to find?

The question dogged him, but did nothing to relieve the tension. Once he stumbled and glanced up quickly at a line of nearby trees, only to have one of those dark figures *move*, vanishing deeper into the wood.

He bent against the wind and kept trudging, casting wary glances at those trees, but nothing else moved. Soon he had left that wood behind. An open, rocky slope led up and away from the riverbank, and the only shapes in the snow were low bushes and stones that jutted from the ground. The snow clung to the bushes, though the rocks were mostly bare thanks to the buffeting wind.

Sure he felt eyes upon him, Jack spun, seeing nothing other than the whipping snow. The weight of all that he carried dragged on him, and he shifted the saddlebags from one shoulder to the other. He unslung and cocked the rifle. His fingers were cold inside the gloves, but despite the frozen ache in his bones, he would still be able to pull the trigger. What good bullets would do, he had no idea. He had survived this long, and he meant to get home to the people who were waiting for him. He owed it to Shepard, and Eliza would be heartbroken should she never see him again.

"Show yourself!" Jack shouted, but the wind carried the words away.

Again he turned, and this time caught something moving just out of the corner of his eye. It disappeared again into the storm. He held his breath, listening, but heard only the wind and the river.

He was not alone in the snow. Something paced his every step.

Jack moved closer to the water's edge, glanced around, and came to a halt. Still standing, he closed his eyes and exhaled to let his spirit expand the way Lesya had taught him. He felt for animals at first, and found sleeping owls, skittish hares, furtive wolverines, a single black bear, and in the distance a small herd of caribou.

But the *thing* was there as well, and though he could not touch its spirit the way he could the animals', he sensed it clearly now, and he knew it meant him harm. Lesya might be a madwoman intent upon punishing him for what she considered his betrayal of her, but the wood witch was a lost soul, stricken by loneliness. The thing that pursued him now felt far more sinister and more savage than he believed even mad Lesya could be.

Jack heard snow crunching underfoot. Opening his eyes, he swung the barrel of the rifle in a wide arc, his back to the river. Once again he thought he saw a shape just at the edges of his vision, perhaps closer than before, but it vanished when he tried to look directly at it.

He raised the rifle to his shoulder and fired into the snow, listening to the shot echo through the storm. No other sound returned, no cry of pain or surprise. But he had not really expected to hit the thing that stalked him. Jack hoped only to make it wary, perhaps keep it away for a while. If luck smiled upon him, he might stumble upon some prospector's cabin or a small Indian settlement on the river.

He ratcheted the bolt to bring another bullet from the magazine. Luck seemed far too much to hope for, so he would rely on the Lee-Metford rifle instead. There were seven more shots in the rifle, and he had other weapons. He would fight to the death—fight death itself, should it come to that—but nothing would keep him from getting home after this extraordinary journey.

Bent against the storm, still he picked up his pace, wary with every step. He searched the storm for further signs of his stalker but saw nothing more. Perhaps the rifle shot had given it pause after all.

Ahead, through the storm, he saw the dark silhouettes of more trees. This stretch of woods seemed to come right to the edge of the river, so he would have to pass almost among the trees to continue southward. Yet he had no other choice. If he waited for the storm to end, his pursuer would overtake him. So Jack kept walking, studying the trees as he approached, watching the branches and the spaces between for the tiniest movement.

The wind shifted, gusting at his back now, propelling

him along, and he felt a moment of relief that the storm had turned in his favor.

And then he caught the scent that the shifting wind had brought, a familiar smell that nearly froze him with terror: the stink of rotten meat.

The Wendigo had found him.

CHAPTER FOURTEEN

THE SPIRIT OF BRUTALITY

J ACK LONDON RAN FOR HIS LIFE, and the Wendigo followed. He did not look back—he had seen it before, at night, and although now the storm might shield his view somewhat, he had no wish to witness this thing touched by daylight. But though he did not look, his other senses were alight, and he knew that the monstrous form now had him in its sights. The shifting of the breeze meant that its stink had already caught up with him; its pounding footsteps crunched snow and splintered plants; and the air itself seemed to taste different. No longer cleansed by the wintry storm, the air Jack breathed was tainted by death.

He could turn and shoot, but he was certain that would do no good. Still, he kept hold of his rifle because he didn't want the thing to think he had given up hope. How many travelers, explorers, and stampeders must it have witnessed panicking before its onslaught, shedding bags and weapons left and right as they ran blindly toward their deaths? He had no way of knowing and no wish to find out. And if he were to die here today, he would do so with dignity.

I've got to make the trees, he thought, a plan fluttering at his mind.

Whatever fate Lesya had intended for him, he had much to thank her for, not least the food he had been eating since she had found him. If it hadn't been for that, he would have collapsed or even died by now, and terrified though he was, deep down a small part of Jack reveled in the strength he felt, the speed he ran. He wondered if all victims being chased down by predators felt this way, just for a moment.

Jack reached the cover of the trees and immediately changed direction. He sensed outward and felt a fox cowering in fear a hundred steps away, and closer by lay a regular trail trodden by the fox and its family to and from the river. He steered himself along this trail, summoning his fledgling abilities and uttering a foxlike bark as he went. The land sloped up from the river here, and his pace slowed . . . and then from behind he heard the ragged snap of trees and branches splintering as the Wendigo came.

It could have taken me at any time, he thought, switching direction quickly, leaping over the hole in which he knew the fox family cowered. *It's been stalking me through the storm, and it could have closed in and ripped me apart.*

He leaped a gully and then darted to the left, away from the fox trail. He kept the musky warmth of the fox in his mind as he ran, and the growls rumbling in his throat were not his own. In the pressures of pursuit, his plan had no concrete form: He simply sought to confuse the Wendigo. If he could do that, perhaps the chance for escape would present itself.

Jack darted right and left again, trying to keep low to the ground. He dodged a large fallen tree, rejecting the temptation to hide behind it. Even if he could camouflage himself completely, he knew that the monster would find him. He might be able to smother himself with leaves or the imagined attributes of a fox, but his talents were still young, and he could never hide the true smell of his blood or the sound of his human pulse.

He paused, concentrating to shift his attention from fox to rabbit, and then started running again. *Can it smell or know those things?* he thought. *Does it even acknowledge them?* From all he knew of the Wendigo, it sought human flesh and none other. Animals might be a distraction to it at best. But he had to try.

At the next fallen tree, Jack paused and looked behind him for the first time.

The Wendigo was raging up the slope. It came between the trees, thrashing and whipping its great limbs, and for an instant it looked like a living tree itself. Its size certainly matched, and each time it lifted a leg to step forward, a sharp tearing sound reverberated through the woods, like roots snapping as their owner hauled itself from the ground. The air around it seemed splashed with blood—it misted in the atmosphere, sprayed the boles of surrounding trees—and Jack realized the sound came from wounds constantly opening across the thing's torso.

He sought its face, amazed at its pain, but such a sight was lost among daytime shadows.

It roared. Perhaps it saw or sensed him watching, and after a beat it paused, taking in great bellowing breaths as it sniffed him out. Branches ruptured as it turned its head left and right, leaves fell, and then Jack felt its full attention fixed upon him.

He tried to breathe but could not. And as he turned and started running again, he realized his terrible mistake: *I can never outrun this thing!*

Soon, he knew, he would have to stop and fight.

But first he needed to marshal his thoughts, and for that he needed a place to hide away.

He explored out and ahead of him as he ran, trying also to use Lesya's lessons and the small gift of magic she had placed within him to summon the traits of wild animals. Jack realized just how little he knew about the strange talents she had cultivated in him because, in the terror of his flight, there was no way to truly assess just how effective they were. There would be no second chances today.

Clasping his rifle, the weight of gold hauling him down, he struggled on. Soon he sensed a cave somewhere ahead of him, and the fading smell of what had once inhabited it. He moved quickly in that direction, glancing around nervously in case its former inhabitant was choosing that moment to return. But such fears were foolish, and he almost laughed out loud. He glanced around at the pursuing Wendigo— saw only trees swaying down the slope, its bulk blurred through the forest—and then he went for the cave.

The remains of the black bear's den were still there, and Jack quickly rolled among the detritus. He imagined himself as the bear, growling and grumbling low in his throat, hands pawing at the ground, fur bristling in cautious anger at what approached. And as he heard the Wendigo come closer, Jack grew still.

It paused somewhere beyond the cave.

Jack breathed heavily and throatily, like a bear, trying not to let his fear taint that sound. *It won't believe this for a heartbeat*, he thought, his confidence failing just as the monster's legs stepped into view.

The cave mouth was low and festooned with hanging plants. But even if they had not been there, Jack would not have been able to see the thing's upper body and head. It was so tall, its legs were like bleeding tree trunks, thin, knotted, punctured here and there by deep wounds. Its feet were like irregular slabs of meat, with splintered bones protruding where Jack approximated its toes to be. Blood and other fluids flowed from sores and wounds, and there were strange, spiky growths at several points up and down its legs. They might have been hairs, but they were as thick as Jack's fingers.

He realized that he was holding his breath, and with realization came a gasp. The Wendigo grunted, legs twisting as it turned its upper body somewhere above Jack's line of sight. *It heard me,* he thought, and suddenly the cave mouth became very distant and precious. It was the only splash of light he could see in his ever-darkening world, and it was also the place through which death would visit. So he squeezed his eyes closed again, casting himself back into Lesya's woodland clearing, and it was her beautiful face he saw before him as he concentrated on gathering the smells and sounds of a black bear around him. She smiled and nodded her approval, and when Jack said something back to her, it came out as a growl.

He opened his eyes. The Wendigo seemed frozen

beyond the bear cave, and he imagined its head tilted to one side as it listened for another sound. So Jack growled again, a low, throaty sound that also held a trace of fear. He imagined that any bear seeing this thing would be scared.

The Wendigo roared—a sound filled with pain and wretchedness—and then stalked away.

Jack breathed a sigh of relief and crawled quickly to the cave's mouth. *There's no way I'll lose it for long,* he thought. *It will soon sense the deception, it'll smell it out, and then when it comes back for me, I'll have lost the element of surprise.* What he was about to do felt foolish and perhaps would doom him, but then he was also tired of running. Eventually the thing would chase him down and fall upon him, and he would die knowing exhaustion and fear, and nothing else. At least this way, he would begin the fight with the upper hand.

He crawled from the cave mouth and stood slowly, leaving the saddlebags at his feet for now. The Wendigo was uphill from the cave, grabbing at tree trunks to haul itself higher. Its head was a monstrous parody of a human head, and for a beat Jack thought it was made of many bodies rolled and twisted together. He blinked quickly, trying to dispel that idea, but it would not leave him.

Squatting, aiming the rifle, he calmed his breathing and rested the sights on the back of that massive head.

When the Wendigo next paused to reach out for

another tree, Jack pulled the trigger.

The report was staggeringly loud, bringing home to Jack just how quiet the woods had become. He and the Wendigo were being watched, in silence, by the forest creatures. Perhaps it was a scene they had seen many times before as this monstrous, cursed thing pursued a flesh-and-blood human across the landscape, and in that case the animals knew what the likely outcome would be. For tales of the Wendigo to be so prevalent, *some* of its victims must have survived. But it was still regarded as myth and legend . . . so the number of survivors must be few.

Jack was certain that the bullet struck home, but its only effect was to reveal his position to the Wendigo. The huge thing belied its size as it spun around and came at Jack. No pause, no moment to reflect or to pin the human on its senses . . . it charged downhill like an avalanche of flesh and bone, and the greatest fight of Jack's life had begun.

What made me think I could defeat this thing? he thought as he dropped the rifle and stood his ground. But really he knew. It had less to do with the deceptions and imitations that Lesya had taught him, and more to do with the sense of togetherness he felt with the wilderness, and had been feeling more and more since the ship had first docked at Dyea. There was a rightness to this, and Jack was long past denying whatever destinies he had set in play by embarking upon this journey.

He had not conquered the wild, nor tamed it. He had become a part of it, and it a part of him.

Jack roared. There was no particular animal sound contained in his voice, and neither was it distinctly human. It was a cry of the wild, and he put every ounce of the energy he had left into uttering his fury and rage. It shivered through his whole body as he aimed his scream at the sky; his hair stood on end, his skin prickled, and his bones seemed to vibrate in time with the screech.

The Wendigo slowed from a run to a walk, but still it came. Its misshapen head tilted to one side, and those mad eyes regarded Jack like a fellow madman. And who was he to argue? He screamed again, this time directly at the monster. And when it seemed to pause in its tracks for a beat, Jack accompanied the scream with a step forward.

The Wendigo stepped back. It uttered a surprised cough, then crouched down and stretched its head forward. It sniffed, great moist nostrils opening in its head. Jack fisted his hands by his side. His heart was thrumming, blood pumping so fast through his body that he felt delirious in this unseasonable storm.

The Wendigo's eyes betrayed their true madness then. It screeched at the smell of Jack's flesh and blood, slavering, and its hands whipped forward, knocking branches from the trees around it as it reached for him. The arms were longer than he had guessed, its fingers even longer, and though Jack fell back, he still felt the cool kiss of its fingertips abrading his face. Blood dripped down over his lips and mouth.

He darted out his tongue, tasted his own blood, and thought, *This is what it wants.*

The Wendigo came for him, and Jack pulled his knife from his belt. He ducked its swinging arm, leaped, hacked at its foot, stepped back again as it lifted one leg and stamped down. It would happily crush him before eating him; his blood would be just as hot.

He darted around behind it, ducking something that could have been a branch or tail, leaning in toward the monster, sweeping left to right with the blade and feeling a warm pulse of blood as the metal parted skin. The Wendigo seemed hardly to notice, such were the wounds and sores already leaking across its body, and it reached down for Jack.

He ran between its braced legs and turned sharply to the right, tripping on a tree root concealed beneath the snow. Now it would tear him apart slowly before upending his halves and emptying his insides into its mouth. He could picture it in his head as he scrambled away, lunging past a tree, staying just out of reach.

The Wendigo came for him, and Jack
pulled his knife from his belt.

The stench of the Wendigo was horrendous: rotting meat, death, decay, filth, rancid fluids streaking its hide. And the sounds it made were just as repulsive: the growls as it sought him, yes, but also deep, distant grumbles from its stomach, the reverberations of an eternal hunger that could never be sated. Somewhere in there, the bones of Jack's friends and enemies alike ground together.

As it reached around a tree for him, he lashed out with the knife again, and this time the Wendigo screamed.

Jack gave over his reactions to instinct, casting aside conscious thought and allowing his primal nature to the fore. Most men eschewed this leftover of their animal past because they believed it beneath them, but now Jack felt the full import of his ancestors back through the ages, their thoughts, their intuitions, and their will to survive. Thousands of years behind him, wild men and women challenged nature and mastered it, and now Jack was doing the same.

The knife was his tooth and claw, speed his ally, fearlessness his drive. The threat of death was ever present, and there were no guarantees that one heartbeat would see the next. But such danger gave Jack power, because nature's prime movers were life and death.

The fight became a blur. The Wendigo screamed, and so did Jack. The sky and earth changed places, tree branches whipped across his face, the overpowering breath of the monster dried his eyes and entered his mouth. His hand was hot with blood and the slick touch of insides. Though he still held the knife, he could no longer feel his hand on the grip, as if he and the blade were bound together.

He thrust, slashed, and stabbed, rolling across the bloodied snow that layered the ground, and feeling the land shift around him as he darted left and right, squatted down, leaped. He used the solidity of the wilderness from which to launch fresh attacks, and at one point—minutes into the fight, or maybe hours—the Wendigo's scream came again, this time sounding different.

Somewhere in there, Jack heard fear.

He increased his assault, fury and rage giving way to a brutality he had never known existed within him. He was a wild man for a while, defined only by the present and giving no thought to the past or future—he was not Jack London, he had no family, and tomorrow was an unknown place.

At some point, Jack realized that the screaming and screeching had stopped. He was still moving across the damp, warm ground, stabbing and ducking away again, and it took him a while to realize that the ground was not the forest floor. He was soaked with sweat and blood. He could smell a fresh death. And he stood upon the tumbled corpse of the Wendigo.

Jack gasped and stood upright, looking all around. He

was standing on the monster's chest, left foot in a puddle of thick, dark blood. Around him were splayed the thing's limbs, all of them slashed and flayed, one hand almost severed at the wrist, its fingers clasped around a tree trunk and digging into the bark. To his left lay the thing's head, thrown back with its monstrous mouth open. Steam rose from the mouth. Steam also wafted from the ruin its throat and neck had become.

Something whistled, bubbles burst, and Jack heard the Wendigo's final breath.

I can be myself again now, he thought, but he was not certain of that, because things still did not feel right. His heart thundered in his chest, and his hand refused to drop the knife. And that smell . . .

The stench of rotting flesh was gone, and in its place the mouthwatering aroma of fresh food. Something was cooking—he could smell its sweet, meaty aroma, the tang of sizzling fat—and beneath that, the subtler scents of roasting root vegetables. He sighed and sank down, closing his eyes, transported back to Lesya's clearing, where he watched her preparing and cooking the kill of the day. Every breath he took brought in a richer smell, and his mouth watered uncontrollably.

"I thought I was no longer hungry," Jack whispered, but the smell of food all around him exposed the lie in that. He must have been hungrier than he had ever thought possible. Perhaps Lesya had been starving him as well as teaching him her earthly tricks? Maybe she had only planted the suggestion of food in his mind, stripping away layer upon layer of his fat as the days went by, seeking the hollowed core of him. . . .

All around him, the sounds of the forest started up again. There was richness in the birdcalls, and an exuberance to the rustlings and whines of small mammals from the undergrowth. Insects flew, flies buzzed, and Jack was starting to feel like the center of everything. He saw several birds perching on branches snapped during his fight with the Wendigo, and he tried to listen to the song they were singing. He stretched his mind, seeking to join in their harmony, but something dark loomed before and around him, blocking his senses and denying contact with anything outside.

"I'm Jack London," he said, but the words seemed to hold little meaning. His stomach rumbled and roared as if in sympathy with the terrible hunger he had sensed in the Wendigo. His throat was parched. *Flesh will serve my hunger,* he thought. *Blood will quench my thirst.*

The ground was shifting beneath him, trees growing all around. He looked about in confusion for a while, and then he saw that the corpse of the defeated monster was shrinking. Flesh and skin wrinkled and fell away. Blood pulsed from the raw meat as limbs contracted, the chest and stomach caved in, and the thing's head tilted to one side.

Soon, whatever was left of the Wendigo would be gone. Jack would have to set snares and traps, hunt a rabbit, skin and gut and cook it, and before he could do all that, maybe the hunger would take him, and he'd die an ignominious death beneath these wild skies.

But not if . . .

He fell from astride the shrinking corpse, reached out with his right hand, and cut a flap of bloody flesh and skin from the thing's chest. Holding it up to the light, he examined the meat. It was heavy and dark, and still dripping with rich blood. He put it to his nose, just a finger width away from his nostrils, and inhaled. It smelled sweet; uncooked, but its rawness held no dangers.

Jack sighed and opened his mouth, closed his eyes, tongue lolling.

His stomach rumbled so intensely that it hurt. He groaned and inhaled, and the sick stench of rotten flesh hit the back of his throat. Before he could prepare, he vomited, falling aside and dropping the handful of bad flesh. Vomiting again as he rolled away, Jack felt his hand open, and he discarded the knife at last. He came to rest against a tree, gasping at the sky, blinking, and then he sat up and looked around the blood-soaked clearing.

The Wendigo lay dead at its center, and its rot was accelerating. A million flies seemed to buzz around the corpse as its flesh turned black, its skin withered, and it returned horribly to the shape of a man.

Jack had no wish to go closer and see who the man might resemble, so he scampered back to the bear cave, trying not to dwell upon what he had almost done . . . and almost *become*. He picked up the rifle and loaded saddlebags, groaning at the ache that had set into his muscles during the fight. The rifle was a reassuring weight again now that the Wendigo was dead, because the dangers he might face would be much more natural. He needed a drink. There was a splash of water in his canteen, and back down the hillside he'd fill up again at the river, and perhaps he'd be able to take a few shots at a rabbit on the way, skin and gut it, cook it this afternoon. . . .

He fell to his knees. *I almost ate!* If he'd eaten the flesh of the Wendigo, he would have become one himself, a spirit cursed to haunt these wilds and prey on the innocent flesh of future travelers. His hunger would be forever, his suffering eternal, until he met someone brave and strong. Someone with a knife.

Jack had never known himself to be as wild and brutal as he'd been during his battle with the Wendigo. At the time it had felt so right, but afterward that wildness had almost led him to eat the flesh of the vanquished. Something had stopped him, some vestige of humanity, and for that he would forever give thanks.

"I'm Jack London," he said aloud, "and I'm a human being." The forest answered him with a brief silence, but as he went back downhill toward the river, it returned to life. Normal, unhindered life.

The storm lessened as he came to the river, and he could still see his footprints in the light snow covering from where he had been fleeing the Wendigo. It felt like weeks before, but he guessed it must have been only hours. He could see the Wendigo's prints as well, and that gave him pause. Already the chase and fight seemed like a nightmare, and to see physical evidence here of the creature's existence was shocking all over again. He looked at the blood coating his hands and trapped beneath his fingernails and wondered what would happen were he to swallow some of that. He began to panic. He could feel the crust of drying blood across his face and throat, too, and he must have taken some of it into his mouth, *must* have, when it was spraying and splashing so liberally back there in the wood.

He fell to his knees at the edge of the river and scooped up handfuls of freezing water, splashing it over his face

"I'm Jack London," he said aloud.

and head, gasping in shock at the cold but also welcoming its cleansing effect. Diluted pink splashes of blood speckled the snow around him. He washed, scrubbing his hands, scooping beneath his nails with his knife, scrubbing so hard that wounds opened in his skin. He kept washing until his own blood flowed; then he headed back along the river with his belongings, desperate to find somewhere to camp for the night that would give comfort and warmth. He needed to rest, and he needed to dry his clothes. This was not winter—not yet—but if he was to march from the Yukon before true winter did fall, he needed to get moving.

He enjoyed putting distance between himself and those woods. Back there, Lesya haunted her forest, and closer to him the corpse of the Wendigo still lay. Perhaps it was rotted down to nothing by now, but there would still be bones, and the ghost of its hunger would always haunt the spaces between those trees.

Feeling that his adventure here was over, Jack once again walked back to the ruined camp where he had seen the Wendigo kill so many. And before darkness fell, he uncovered the fire pit with his foot and went about rebuilding it.

CHAPTER FIFTEEN

OUT OF THE WILD

JACK WARMED HIS HANDS against the flames, and the darkness was held at bay. This fire felt clean and fresh, and this darkness, though filled with the sounds of the wild he knew so well, carried no threat. He had faced the worst that these lands could throw at him, and he had survived.

Yet he felt no real sense of victory. Right then, he felt nothing at all. He was an injured animal licking its wounds, and shock still held him in its sway.

And his wounds were many. Once he had settled down and lit the new fire, Jack took the opportunity to examine his body in detail for the first time, and he was amazed at what he found. His hands were badly lacerated and bruised, some of the cuts possibly from his own blade, others ragged tears from thorns and snapped wood. He spent some time picking splinters from his flesh by the flickering light of the fire, and some of them were half the length of his fingers. The pain was bright and stark, and he did not hold in his groans of discomfort.

One side of his face felt stippled with scabs, and never before in his life had he wished so much for a mirror. He could trace the wounds with his hands, but trying to place them on the face he knew so well—young, impetuous, confident—was all but impossible. His skin felt so much older, and he knew that his expression must appear likewise.

His arms and legs were badly bruised, three of the toes on his left foot were turning dark, and most of his toenails had fallen off. His stomach rumbled. His ribs ached, and he thought perhaps he'd broken a couple. He coughed into his hand and examined the spittle beneath the firelight, taking some time to convince himself there was no blood there.

As the moon revealed itself and the stars came out, Jack at last began to shake from shock. He wrapped himself in the few blankets he had found around the ruined camp—dried as best as he could before the fire—and knew that he would never be able to fall asleep.

Moments later, though, he drifted away, his head resting on the saddlebags full of gold. And as if that mystical yellow metal informed his dreams, he found himself back in better times.

———

He knew that he was dreaming, but he had no control over the rush of images that nursed him through sleep. They were recollections from his past, and stuck here bleeding and injured in the wild lands of the north with the cold season rapidly approaching again, he recognized them as some of the most important moments of his life. Here he was walking the roads, riding the rails, and exploring America from the underbelly up. He was poor but happy. He had little but missed nothing. He met some hard people in his dream, and a few who were plain cruel, but Jack always came out the other side wiser and older, and knowing humanity more. Knowing *himself* more. This was all about growing up.

The sea rolled beneath him as he left America for the first time, venturing out into the Pacific hunting seals, blood and guts up to his knees, the clear sky glaring down at the hunters' brutal deeds, and the boys and men around him were a quiet, vicious breed. Jack kept to himself but watched them all, and in his dream he could identify each and every one of them: Jeff, the quiet man who would surprise him later with his knowledge of books; Peters, the European who only admitted to speaking English when it suited him; and the man who called himself Graybeard.

People shouted as they hunted him down, his sloop filled with poached oysters, and he knew that when they eventually caught him he'd go over to their side and hunt oyster pirates himself. Perhaps that was a darker part of his history, and this memory—riding the waves as he dodged the fisheries officers and plied his piracy through sea fogs and channels known only to him—was the finer, more honest side.

He dreamed of other things, other places, and every memory made him feel better. He was reliving a harsh life well spent, filling himself once again with knowledge from beyond the wild Yukon, and in a way he thought this was his mind preparing himself for the return.

And then his dreams moved on, and he saw more. Defending the boy Hal in Dawson City. Watching in terror as the Wendigo slaughtered friends and enemies alike in the very camp where he now lay dreaming.

Lesya.

Jack shouted himself awake before the last of the dream, not wishing to reach the end in case there was no more. His life up to now had been remarkable, but there was plenty more to live, and a million places yet to see. He would not lie here and let his life play itself out across his mind, marking relevant points here and there until it reached its end. There *was* no end, not yet, and he would fight and rage against the darkness as long as he could.

He sat up and stared across the moonlit landscape, dreading the approach of death but feeling more alive than he had in a very long time. The last time he'd felt this invig-orated had been that time at the top of the Chilkoot Pass, when Merritt and Jim had first sat with him and shared cof-fee, with the golden future stretching out before them.

Jack piled more logs onto the fire, stood, and howled at the moon. He did not use Lesya's teachings or the traces of her magic to find his inner wolf voice but rather let it rise of its own accord. It was an exhalation of pure freedom and joy, and when it was answered from somewhere far away, Jack paused and sank slowly to his knees. *There you are*, he thought, because he recognized the voice in that reply. Wounded his spirit guide might be, but so long as Jack still drew a breath, it would always be waiting for him out here in the wild, and he needed no magic to find it, only his own heart.

Because the wild was where he had truly found his spirit.

He went hunting the next morning and caught a small rabbit. He did not shoot or trap it, but simply sat still beside a fallen tree for a while, making small rabbit noises and imagining himself down there in the grass with the creatures. One of them emerged from the scrub and jumped on the tree, star-ing at him and wrinkling its nose as it tried to discern his scent. Before it could sniff below the pretense, Jack reached out and grabbed the creature, breaking its neck before it knew what was happening. He experienced a moment of strange dislocation as he shed the rabbit senses—it was as if one of his own lay dead in his lap, and a sadness crept over him—and then he returned to camp, gutting and stripping the rabbit expertly before spitting it over the fire.

As the rabbit cooked, Jack went about tidying the camp. There were shreds of the dead men's belongings scattered among the grasses, and the detritus of the massacre littered the ground. He wanted the place to be as far back to nature as was possible before he left, both in honor of the men who had died here and as acknowledgment that the Wendigo was no more. It was a part of the history of this place now, and the site of its great feeding also had to move on.

He left the saddle upon which he had scored that grim epitaph atop the pile of collected debris. It seemed a fitting marker, and though it would last no more than a year or two in these harsh climes, in his mind he would read those words forever.

Eating the rabbit seemed to purge the memory of the Wendigo's flesh from his mind. His hands were greasy with cooked meat, his stomach full of it, and his hunger was sated by the time he collected his goods and set off for Dawson City. He went east and south, determined that the shreds of civilization would be in that direction, and over his shoulders he carried the saddlebags heavy with gold.

The previous day's brief snowstorm had passed, and though snow still lay on the ground here and there, the sun was quickly melting it away. Autumn had arrived, true, but the harshest weather was still several weeks distant. For the first time in a long while, Jack felt that he was now safe, and that his immediate future was mapped out before him—a return to Dawson, a journey back across the Chilkoot pass to Dyea, then passage south to San Francisco. Once there, he would try to track down Jim's and Merritt's families, and the gold he carried over his left shoulder was for them. The gold on his right . . . that was for his own family. There was enough there to cover the money that Shepard had invested in the journey and, if not to get his mother out of debt, at least to stave off the moneylenders for a time. It would be plenty. Jack had other ideas about how he could benefit from his adventures.

His own terrible tales of the north he could never tell. But there were surely a million others that he could. Stories he had heard. Lessons learned. Glimpses into the heart of the wild, but not into that wild's shadows.

Around noon of that day he encountered a small group of men and women heading north. He sat and waited by a rock when he saw them, starting to build a small fire in the hope that they'd have food they would share. He kept his guns at the ready, but by the time they drew closer, any worries had evaporated. They were stampeders—their gold pans rattled and swung from their packs—and their ready smiles put him at ease.

"Afternoon, friend," one of the men called, and Jack suddenly felt his throat burning. These were the first ordinary people he had spoken to since the Wendigo attack on the camp, and that had been . . . how long ago? He had trouble mapping the time between then and now, but he knew it had been months.

"Afternoon," Jack replied. "Strange time of year to be heading out from Dawson."

"We know what we're doing," one of the women said. She dropped her pack next to Jack, and he saw the weapons on her belt—knives, and two pistols.

"The winters up here don't much care whether you know or not," he said. The woman glared at him, but she soon averted her gaze. *What does she see?* Jack thought. *What stares at her from these eyes?*

"Only a short trip, this one," another man said. "We been out four times from Dawson now and found nothin'. This is our last try before we head on home."

"Good luck to you," Jack said.

"You found any luck?" the woman asked. She glanced down at his saddlebags, then back up at his face. He smiled and she looked away again. He felt that he should not be enjoying such power, but he couldn't help himself.

"Some," he said. He glanced away from the group, back the way he'd come, and for a moment he pondered on luck and what it meant.

"Then can you point us the right way?" the first man asked.

"No," Jack said. "Back that way, what little good luck there was found itself outweighed by the bad."

The six people were quiet for a moment, shrugging their packs off and sinking to the ground. Two of them went about finishing and lighting the fire, and soon a pot of coffee was brewing. Jack handed over his metal coffee mug, and a man placed it on the ground next to their own. Jack nodded his thanks.

"You look like you've been out there for a while," the same woman said. "Seen men like you before. Got a wild look in your eyes, like you've seen things that shouldn't be seen."

Jack shrugged and looked into the fire.

"Seen men like that who were mad, too," she continued.

Jack merely shrugged again, but this time he let a smile touch his lips. *Who's to say?* he almost replied, but he didn't want to alarm these people. They seemed good-natured enough, and they were sharing their coffee, but all of them carried guns. And he could see that none of them had any inkling of the true nature of things out in the wild.

They sat together for a couple of hours, drinking coffee and talking about gold, and the wilderness, and the equally wild place that was Dawson. One of the men grabbed Jack's attention when he talked of crazy people in Dawson spending their time in the bars spouting "rubbish about flesh-eating monsters and dead men." When Jack asked what they looked like, and whether the man knew their names, the woman asked, "Friends of yours?" That one question weighed on the atmosphere around the campfire, and it never quite recovered.

Jack was the first to rise and wish them well. He sensed eyes upon him as he lifted the heavy saddlebags, but he never once felt any threat from these people. They were like children watching an adult readying to hunt—ironic, considering his own youth—and Jack felt that the least he could do was spare them a word of advice.

"West is best from here," he said. "Into the low hills."

"We were told northwest," the woman said. "Up into the wild forests and the valleys between mountains."

"No," Jack said, and he glanced at each one of them to get his message across. "Those places are cursed." Then, shrugging off the few muttered questions that came after him, Jack turned his back on those naive explorers and went on his way.

He walked far that day, and at dusk he camped by a stream where there were the remains of several other campfires. He shot a duck and ate well, and lying beneath the stars, he listened to the night sounds closing in. None of them frightened him anymore. The cry of a wolf accompanied him into sleep, and in his mind he howled back, adding his own voice to the history of the wild.

He walked from dawn to dusk the next day, coming across the remains of several camps, and the farther southeast he went, the more Dawson seemed to exert its influence. These wilds were no longer just that—there was a taint of humanity on the places he walked through now—and much as he looked forward to his journey and eventual arrival back with his family, still Jack mourned the passing of this part of his life. It felt as if he were leaving a part of himself behind, and that night he sat by the campfire and howled, once more, like a wolf. There was no answering call—the wolves kept far to the north and west of here, away from the guns of civilization—but neither was there a reply in his mind. He went to sleep sad that night, and he carried that same emotion with him the next morning when he approached Dawson at last.

The final sight he'd had of Dawson had been the inside of that wretched hotel room, where Archie and William had come at him with clubs and fists. That felt like a life-time away, but as he caught sight of Dawson in the distance, huddled beside the river at the bottom of a gently sloping valley, he knew that places like this would never change. Built on ambition and the quest for adventure, they would always be corrupted by greed and cynicism. He would enter Dawson now with his eyes open, but he swore that he would maintain hope in his heart. Not all men were bad. Merritt and Jim had shown him that.

Dawson was bustling as Jack entered, and he drew only a few casual glances. He was one of many men and women returning from the wilds, and though he had seen more than most, his physical appearance at least seemed unre-markable. Indeed, the time he had spent with Lesya—able to shave, wash his clothes, and eat enough food to stave off hunger and illness—seemed to have fended off some of the worst effects of the wilderness, and some of the people he saw looked like little more than walking skeletons.

One man had a toothless mouth, lips rotted away by sores, one of his eyes milky white from blindness. Another had lost both hands to frostbite, and he wandered the streets muttering words to himself that no one seemed keen to hear. Jack passed them by and approached the Yukon Hotel, its familiarity both depressing and comfort-ing: comforting because it was somewhere he had been happy with his friends, if just for a moment; and depressing because entering seemed like turning his back on his own incredible adventures.

"Jack London," he said to the man behind the counter.

"London," the man said. "Huh. That's no easy name to forget. Sorry, friend, but the boy you seek is dead."

Jack blinked several times, trying to keep a straight face. One second he felt tears threatening, the next, laughter. And then the man's face sagged and his eyes grew wide as he realized who he was talking to.

He was given one of the last rooms in the hotel, a small, dingy place that nonetheless had a bed and a basin. The hotel man brought him some food and arranged a line of credit for his stay.

"I'll only be here for a couple of days," Jack said. "I'm heading home."

"Well good luck to you," the man said, and he sounded genuine. "Enough people make it this far and just stay."

"Have many returned?"

"Some."

"And gold?"

The man shrugged. "Some."

"It's a fool's game," Jack said, and as the man turned to leave he nodded in agreement. "Wait!" Jack called, suddenly remembering. "Do you still have my gear?"

"I . . ." The man stood in the open doorway, eyes averted, mouth working even though no noise emerged.

"You don't," Jack said. "You sold it."

"I thought you were dead."

"And what gave you that idea?" Jack asked harshly. "A man goes for gold, and you steal everything he has to his name?"

"After you left, there were whispers around town about who'd taken you. You and your mates. And after so much time went by, I just assumed . . ."

Jack was angry, but he was also suddenly very tired. He waved at the man, closed his eyes, and said, "You can pay me back tomorrow."

"I'll pay you what I can. And for the record, I'm glad to see you back. Good to know you're not the only one who got away from those murdering bastards."

"Not the only one?" Jack said, eyes snapping open again.

"Your big friend, Sloper. Spends his days drinking in the Dawson Bar."

"Merritt," Jack said, and he did not even notice when the man shut the door and clomped downstairs. *Merritt is alive!* For a few heartbeats he could not move. Then he rose stiffly from the bed and stood swaying in the center of the room. He tried to cast his mind back to the Wendigo attack, the slaughter, the screaming and blood, and though he'd been pressed down at the time—the wolf on his back, preventing him from going to try to help Merritt—he'd convinced himself since that he had seen Merritt killed. He could never remember the actual moment but had thought perhaps it had been his mind protecting him from the awful bloody truth.

"Merritt Sloper," he said, and the name sounded good spoken aloud. He smiled. Then he went to the basin, splashed in some cold water from the jug, and swilled his face.

Above the basin was a mirror, and without thinking Jack looked at his reflection.

A stranger stared back at him. This stranger had the same wild hair, laughing eyes, and askew smile—a grin still on his lips at the thought of Merritt's survival—but he was someone Jack had never seen before. This was a far older man than he had last seen in a mirror. His skin was weathered, and grazed all down one side of his face. And those smiling eyes were also cautious, as if constantly expecting to see something terrible beyond the smile.

"I'm Jack London," Jack said, and his reflection said the same.

Turning away from that version of himself, he shrugged on his coat and headed downstairs.

He crossed the street and paused outside the Dawson Bar. The last time he'd been here had been with Merritt, the same evening that Archie and William had jumped them in their room and cracked them all across the heads. Then, the bar had smelled of desperation, a place between destinations where some people lived their lives in a state of perpetual suspension. He'd looked down on those people, swearing to Merritt that he'd never be like that, and he felt some satisfaction that he'd gone on to have such adventures, though such adventures had been brought on by events rather than choice.

What gave him pause now was what the hotel's owner had said. *Spends his days drinking in the Dawson Bar.* Merritt was a big man with an expansive heart, and Jack had no wish to see him reduced in such a way.

If worse came to worst, then it would be up to Jack to rescue him.

He barged through the doors into the bar. Looking around, he spied Merritt quickly, slumped over the same table in the far corner that he and Jack had occupied months before. A whiskey bottle sat on the table in front of him, half empty, and the man's grizzled features seemed somehow blurred by drunkenness. Jack recognized well enough the appearance of an alcoholic, but Merritt seemed to be cursed even more—here was a man driven to drink who did not enjoy it one bit.

Opposite Merritt sat Hal, the boy Jack had rescued from Archie and William. He looked up as Jack stood by the doors, his eyes went wide, and he whispered, "Jack London."

"Dead," Merritt said. "Taken by the monster." Several people close to Merritt groaned, and a couple even laughed, throwing casual abuse his way. "You'll laugh!" Merritt said, voice rising. "When it has you by the legs so it can chew on your guts, you'll . . . you'll . . ." He slumped to the tabletop again, mumbling something into the pool of dribble spreading from his mouth.

"No, Merritt," Hal said. He stood up from the table and smiled. "Jack's here!"

Merritt looked up at Jack. A few other people seemed interested, but Jack only had eyes for Merritt, this wreck of his friend.

"Jack London's dead," Merritt said.

"I'm here, Merritt," Jack said. "And it seems to me you're the one who's almost lost."

Jack sat at their table and accepted Hal's offer of a drink. The boy regarded him with wide-eyed fascination, hardly able to talk, and when he did, it was in hushed, almost reverential tones. Jack sat quietly for a while, letting Merritt examine him from a drunken distance. The big man had changed so much, but then Jack remembered that so had he. The stranger in the mirror still haunted him.

At last Merritt slipped into a troubled sleep, the hubbub in the bar around them went back to normal, and Hal stared blinking at Jack.

Jack had to remind himself that Hal was only a couple of years younger than him. He looked like a kid—he *was* a kid—yet Jack was happy to see a friendly face.

"So what is it?" Jack asked at last. Though he spoke to Hal, he watched Merritt, hoping that his friend would wake with recognition in his eyes, but he was far gone. Perhaps tomorrow.

"Well . . . Merritt has such stories," Hal said. "He talks about . . ."

"Monsters?" Jack said.

Hal nodded.

"Well, he'll find a lot of ugly things at the bottom of a glass."

"He was talking about them as soon as he got back, long before he started on the booze."

"Trail madness." Jack took a drink, closing his eyes and savoring the harsh taste.

"Then he ain't the only madman from that trail," Hal said.

Jack glanced at the kid. Held the glass up, breathed in the whiskey fumes. *I saw them all die!*

"That bastard Archie's back in Dawson," Hal said quietly. "Ain't nearly so brutish now—had that shot outa him, by all accounts. But he's hooked up with the same types, an' there's talk that they're goin' out again."

"Archie," Jack said. "You're sure?" *William shot him, left him for dead, the Wendigo killed William, and then . . . ?* But the memory ended there.

"Sure I'm sure." Hal nodded, but he couldn't hold Jack's gaze for more than a few moments.

Jack sat back, looked around the bar, and took another drink. It seemed his adventures might not yet be over. Hal poured him another, music played, men and women drank and smoked, and though depressing in many ways, the familiar surroundings managed to relax Jack at last. Merritt snored softly on the table beside him, and this could have been a bar anywhere.

Later, after Hal and Jack had all but finished the whiskey, Hal leaned in close. *Here it comes,* Jack thought. *Here's what he's been trying to say all evening.*

"So tell me what happened," Hal said.

Jack frowned for a while, staring into an unseen distance, and he strove to hear a wolf howl that was far from there. Perhaps it was the whiskey, but he smiled.

"All right, Hal. I'm headed home, and once I leave Dawson, I'm never going to tell the story again," he said. "So you'll be the only one to hear it. And it will be up to you what you believe."

And into the early hours, Jack London told his tale.

CHAPTER SIXTEEN
———————
BROKEN CIRCLES

ORNING BROUGHT NO EPIPHANY. When he had learned that Merritt was still alive, he had wondered if the big man would still hold him responsible for Jim Goodman's death, or if the tensions that had strained their friendship in the days before the Wendigo's attack would remain. He could never have guessed that Merritt's reaction would be so much worse than anger or resentment.

When they encountered each other over breakfast in the hotel parlor, Merritt still did not recognize him. He continued to insist that Jack London had died that night in the slavers' camp. When Jack pressed him on it, the big man seemed to become confused and sad and angry in almost equal measures, and then his eyes grew distant in a way that had nothing to do with the alcohol in which he'd been stewing his brain for weeks. It wasn't madness, however. Jack had met his share of madmen. Rather, he thought that a part of Merritt remained in the north, in the ruined camp on the bank of the creek, that he had never entirely returned.

Jack feared he never would, but he resolved to treat Merritt with care. Further shock might be more than the man could handle. Picking at the biscuits and gravy on his plate, Merritt tugged his bushy red beard and seemed to start at sounds no one else could hear. Still broad shouldered and imposing, he had thinned since their ordeal in the wilderness, and though only a few years Jack's senior, he now appeared much older.

Over the rim of his coffee cup, Jack watched his friend closely. Merritt needed to be woken out of his fog, the parts of his thinking self brought back together, but it had to be done with caution.

If, Jack thought, *it can ever be done at all.*

After breakfast, he went to see the hotel's owner, who turned out to have the somewhat unlikely name of Mortimer Dowd. The man glanced up from the morning's mail—which he was sorting into piles for the hotel's guests—and a sheepish look came over his face.

"I supposed it was too much to hope that a decent night's rest would make you forget," the man said, straightening the bow tie he wore, seemingly to give the Yukon Hotel an air of sophistication—or even merely civilization—that it could never establish on its own merits. *Like a prostitute with a parasol,* Jack thought, but did not say.

"And a good morning to you, Mr. Dowd," he said.

The man's gaze flicked down to the twin gun belts Jack wore. He had almost hesitated to don them again this morning but quickly decided they would be his companions on the journey home, along with the other weapons he had brought back from the slavers' camp. As it was, he felt uncomfortable leaving the saddlebags in his hotel room. He hadn't breathed a word about the gold he had found to anyone, not even young Hal the night before, but there were some men in Dawson who hungered for it so badly that he would not put it past them to somehow sense its presence.

"I'm truly sorry," Dowd said, glancing at the guns again. "But the way your friend Sloper talked, and from the whispers I'd heard 'bout what went on up there . . . and it had been so long since you left—"

"I'll put it to you plainly, sir," Jack interrupted. "I'm no stranger to bloodshed, and I can think of a couple of dozen ways to hurt or even kill you just with the things here in this room and with the blades and guns I'm carrying."

Dowd swallowed, wetted his lips, and shook his head in a silent plea. Back in the spring, when Jack had first encountered him, the man would likely have laughed and hurled him bodily into the street—or tried. This morning, he did not dare make the attempt.

"Come now, Mr. London—"

Jack laughed. *Mr.* London, indeed, and him still years off from twenty. The laugh must have had a hysterical edge to it, for Dowd dropped the mail he'd been sorting and moved to put a dark wooden table between them.

"I've done a little thinking, Dowd. I've had enough of blood and enough of trouble, so you can breathe easily."

The man blinked warily, untrusting.

"Honestly," Jack said. "I don't have the time or the inclination to give you the thrashing I'd like to deliver, or even to argue about how long you ought to have waited. My friends and I paid you to store our things. Instead, you sold them. I understand your reasoning, and can't really say I blame you, much. But that doesn't excuse the act."

Dowd, now realizing no violence seemed likely to erupt, nodded cooperatively. "I agree. And again, I can't say how sorry I am. If I still had the money, I'd pay you back every cent, but I put it into improvements on the hotel."

Jack cocked an eyebrow and glanced around. If any improvements had been made to the shabbily constructed and decorated establishment, he had not noticed them. But no matter. . . .

"I'm going home," Jack said, and the word felt strangely, and somehow wonderfully, unfamiliar on his lips. "I'm sure you'll be happy to see the back of me, so I want you to help make that happen as soon as possible. For the next couple of days, I'll be visiting several shops in town to put together the supplies I'll need to get me to Dyea."

"Certainly," Dowd said.

Jack smiled. "You'll be paying for everything."

Dowd frowned, and it seemed as though he might suddenly find the courage to argue.

"The cost will be far less than what you garnered by selling my things," Jack observed. "And the farther I am from Dawson, the easier you'll breathe."

Now Dowd actually smiled. "There *is* that."

"Then we're agreed?" Jack asked.

Dowd thrust out a hand to shake. Jack did not so much as glance at it.

"Not so fast. There's also the matter of my bill."

Now that he believed he would be quit of Jack soon, and without any bullet holes or other wounds incurred in the meantime—and at a tidy profit, all things considered—the man stood straighter, almost magnanimous.

"Think nothing of it, Jack. If you'll be only a few days, there'll be no charge for your room or your meals. It's the least I can do."

"It would be," Jack agreed. "But you're also going to make Merritt Sloper's bill disappear."

Dowd blanched. "For how long?"

"Is he paid up to today?"

"Until Friday," Dowd replied.

Jack took a breath. Today could have been Sunday or Thursday, for all he knew, but he wasn't about to admit that.

"He doesn't pay you another dime until I leave Dawson. Not for a drink or a meal or a bed. Not even if he wants you to shine his shoes."

Reluctantly, lifting his chin in slight defiance, Dowd gave a tilt of his head that Jack took as acceptance. "Will Sloper be leaving with you?"

"I hope so."

After a moment, the man held his hand out again. This time Jack shook it.

"I didn't come here to make enemies, Mr. Dowd," Jack said, softening a little. "I came for an adventure, and got more than I bargained for."

"Consider yourself fortunate. Most get less."

Before he could stop himself, Jack laughed. It broke the tension between them.

"I really didn't think you were coming back," Dowd said.

"I know. For a long time, neither did I."

———

Over the next few days, as Jack made his preparations, he saw Merritt half a dozen times in the street, on the hotel stairs, or in the Dawson Bar, but somehow Merritt could no longer see him. Twice Jack ventured to speak to him, but his words fell on deaf ears. Merritt did not acknowledge his presence with even the slightest twitch or glance, until Jack began to feel like a ghost haunting the shattered man and decided to leave him alone.

But when all his preparations had been made, his departure scheduled for the following morning, Jack knew he simply could not leave Dawson without talking to his friend. Merritt's mind had slipped. He gazed at some middle distance, never quite aware of the solidity of the world around him, and Jack feared that if he did not do something to bring Merritt back into the real world, he would be lost inside himself forever, just as gone as if he had died at the Wendigo's hands.

Yet Jack knew his previous efforts to get through to Merritt had been spectacularly unsuccessful. His chances, he determined, would be greatly improved if he had someone there Merritt *would* acknowledge.

Thus he found himself, that Monday afternoon, standing just inside the city's newspaper office. Hal sat behind a makeshift desk writing in longhand, his fingers stained

326 THE SECRET JOURNEYS OF JACK LONDON

with ink from the printing press that sat somewhere in the rear of the building, silent for the moment. His dog, Dutch, lay on the floor beside the desk, ears pricking up at Jack's arrival.

"A pretty girl," Jack said.

Hal glanced up, brightening instantly. "Jack!"

The boy—no longer a boy, really, if he even had been one before—jumped from his chair and rushed over. Dutch raised his head, watched them a moment, and then rested it on his forepaws again, utterly uninterested in that way only dogs can ever manage. But Hal had enough enthusiasm for both of them. He thrust out his hand with such energetic bonhomie that Jack could not have refused to shake it, despite the ink. Only after a moment did Hal frown at him.

"What's this about a pretty girl?"

"At the saddlery: blond hair, pale as winter—"

"Sally Corrigan."

Jack nodded, noting the light flush that came to Hal's cheeks when he spoke the girl's name. "She told me where to find you. You hadn't mentioned working for the newspaper."

"It's a recent development," Hal said.

Jack took a deep breath, his smile faltering. "Can you spare a few minutes?"

"Of course. What—?"

"I'm leaving tomorrow. Before I go, I mean to talk to

Merritt. I thought it might help if you were there. A face he'll let himself see."

Hal nodded, glanced back at his desk, and then reached into his pocket for a key. "Stay, Dutch," he said to the dog, then looked at Jack. "He'll be at the bar by now. If we hurry, we can get him before he's too drunk to see *either* of us."

Jack didn't expect Merritt to be the only one in the bar, not in a place as blanketed in lost hope as Dawson, but still it startled him to find the place murmuring with life, ale and whiskey flowing freely. It would be much louder, and much busier, when night came on and the darkness reminded lost souls, and even those still hopeful, how far they were from home. But, still, there were twenty-five or thirty people in the bar, a handful of them eating the meager fare the place offered because they couldn't be bothered to seek a proper meal elsewhere. They'd put down roots in the place.

Roots. The word put images of Leshii and his beautiful daughter into Jack's head, and he shook them off like cobwebs. The sooner he left the vast emptiness of the north behind, the better.

"In the back," Hal said, nodding toward the farthest corner.

It seemed strange to Jack that Merritt would take up a

post there, at a small round table on the opposite side of the room from the actual bar. He would have to get up and trek over to the counter to order himself another drink, and there were plenty of stools to be had within arm's reach of the bartender. He seemed almost to be hiding, there in the corner, and there in his glass, as well.

Hal led the way and they threaded through the tables, passing men mostly sullen and women falsely garrulous, all of them waiting for something to happen to shake them from their stupor and trying not to wonder what would become of them if nothing ever did.

Jack craved simple, unaffected, genuine laughter, and he knew he would find it back home in California. But he would not have earned it until he had thrown the heavy gray cloak of this place from his shoulders. He wanted an ordinary girl with bright, intelligent eyes and a smile both shy and full of promise. The Yukon held some of the greatest beauty he had ever beheld, but it was an uncaring place, and he yearned for a warm Pacific sunset.

But not yet.

"Merritt," he began, as they approached the table.

Hal held up a hand to stop him from saying anything else. The kid who was no longer a kid slid into the chair opposite the man with the shaggy red beard, who had once been Jack's friend. Jack hung back, watching, and after a moment, Merritt looked up at Hal.

"Thought you got yourself a job," Merritt said. He cocked his head as if he weren't entirely sure Hal was there.

"I quit early today," Hal said. "Figured I'd come over and see if you wanted to have some dinner with me."

Merritt ran his fingers through his overgrown beard. "Bit early for dinner."

"But not for whiskey?"

That actually got a smile out of Merritt, but it lasted only a moment before it became a sneer. "Never too early for whiskey. Not here, so far from the world."

"This is part of the world, Merritt," Jack said.

Hal shot him a look meant to silence him, but Jack had run out of time to wait for Merritt to recover from the trauma he had endured. He grabbed a chair from another table and dragged it over, and now the three of them sat together. Merritt, as always, seemed not to see him.

Jack rapped his knuckles on the table. Merritt flinched.

"There you go," Jack said. "I'm not a ghost."

"I don't know who the hell you are," Merritt said. "But you watch yourself in here. Man could get a knife in the belly as easy as a drink in this place."

Jack smiled. Progress. Merritt wouldn't look him in the eyes, acted like the chair had just dragged itself over and nobody sat there, but he had responded. That was a start.

"Merritt, you've got to stop," Hal said. "You've gotta see. It's—"

"Hush," Jack said.

Hal clammed up and gestured for him to continue.

Jack reached out and grabbed Merritt's arm. The big man recoiled at the touch, the chair scraping on the floorboards, and his chest started to rise and fall with ragged, panicked breaths. But Merritt didn't go for a weapon.

"This *is* part of the world," Jack repeated. "It may not be a pleasant part. Ugly things happen. Maybe things that seem impossible. But you haven't stepped outside the world. You can go back to houses and restaurants and shops, to cities and towns, to the friends and family you left behind. I can take you back, Merritt, if you'll let me."

Merritt gave Hal a desperate sort of smile. "I'm gonna get another drink, Hal. Can I buy you one?"

"Look at him, Merritt," Hal said, pleading. "Just *look* at him. It's really him. It's Jack."

Merritt roared then, rising up with such force that he knocked over his chair, and amber liquid sloshed out of the glass on the table.

"Goddammit, kid, Jack is dead! Don't you listen? Don't any of you ever listen? It got him. Gobbled him up just like the rest!"

Nearly everyone in the bar turned for a curious glance,

but only a quick one. Really, none of them cared if violence erupted as long as it didn't involve them.

Jack started to rise, reaching for him, but Merritt lifted a shaking hand to his face. He gave a quiet laugh that set Jack's teeth on edge and made him fearful that he had been wrong—that Merritt might be truly deranged after all, not just scared and heartbroken. Then Merritt righted his chair and sat back down, a horrible sadness on his face. He wiped at his eyes.

"I'm sorry, Hal," he said. "I know how you hate to be called 'kid.'"

"It's all right," Hal said.

Merritt rapped the knuckles of his right fist against his skull. "No, it isn't. It's all just like broken glass up here, now. And I don't like to talk about . . . about him. I let him down, Hal. Those bastards, William and Archie, they killed Jim and I blamed Jack for it, when all he'd done was stand up to them. He tried to be my friend, tried to look out for me even after they took us, and I turned my back on him."

Then he just stopped, clamping his mouth shut, lips pressed together. A single tear ran down Merritt's face as he reached for his glass. With a thumb he caressed the glass, but he did not lift it to drink, only gazed off now into that middle distance, into nothing, maybe into a past where he blamed himself for the horror that had befallen him.

Hal sighed, started to rise.

"No," Jack said.

"Jack—"

"I'm leaving in the morning," he said, staring at the big man. "Do you hear me, Merritt? I'm going home. You could come with me. Look at me, damn you! I'm not dead! You didn't kill me. And you were right to be angry. I knew they were dangerous men the first time I set eyes on them. I should've been more careful. But I'm back now. We're both alive."

Merritt did not even blink. It seemed almost as if whatever tenant had been living inside him had gone out for the night.

Emotion welled up inside Jack. He'd been bruised and battered, yes, but he had emerged otherwise unscathed from the terror and slaughter of that night, and he would not leave Merritt like this. He rose from the chair and slid over to block Merritt's view, bent low to try to catch his eye, but the big man would not focus on him.

Anger and remorse drove Jack onward. He reached out both hands and gripped Merritt's head between them, forcibly swiveling the man's head to face him. Merritt tried to back away, but his chair hit the rear wall of the bar and

Jack managed to keep a viselike hold.

"Leave me—"

"Look at me, damn you!" Jack rasped. "I'm your friend, Merritt. I'm Jack London, and I'm not dead. The Wendigo got nearly everyone else, but it didn't get me. I'm here with you, right now!"

Merritt tried to twist his head away, but Jack held on, bumping into the table and spilling more whiskey. He bent over, putting his face only inches from Merritt's.

"Look at me!"

And at last, Merritt did. The man's eyes narrowed and his eyebrows knitted, and he took long, steadying breaths.

"You resemble him," Merritt whispered. "I'll grant you that. But if I've learned anything, it's that things aren't always what they seem."

Jack let him go, thinking that perhaps there would be no getting through to him, that the parts of his mind that were broken could never be put back together again.

Merritt reached for his glass. Jack snatched it from the table, kept it out of his reach.

"You told me once that coffee was your one indulgence. I know you've found another one, but think for a moment about the smell of fresh coffee, and not the swill they serve here. Coffee beans from South America, brewed dark and rich, with fresh cream on the side and a chocolate pastry."

Merritt started to shake his head slowly, not looking at him, but then his slack, distant expression crumbled and his shoulders began to tremble as he took hitching breaths, which turned into quiet sobs.

CHAPTER SEVENTEEN

THE CALL OF THE WILD

T HEY DRANK COFFEE AFTER ALL, a pitiful brew, and followed it with small glasses of brandy whose sole purpose was a toast to Jim Goodman. Hal had never met him but raised his glass just the same. Merritt would not discuss in any kind of detail the night that the Wendigo had attacked their camp, but when Jack explained that he had slipped his bonds and escaped into the woods, Merritt nodded in sudden understanding.

"It was you, then, who saved me."

"How's that, now?" Jack asked.

Merritt smiled. "It went from man to man, finishing off those who still lived. How so much . . . meat . . . could fit in its belly and gullet I've no idea, but I lay there hoping it would grow full before it reached me. Two others were still alive, as far as I knew. Tom Kelso and Geoff Arsenault. I heard Geoff screaming and I knew that would be the end. I could see Kelso's eyes. The man had been playing dead, like me, but when Geoff started screaming, Kelso's eyes got wide, like a deer that freezes when you come upon it in a clearing. I knew he would bolt, and—God help me—I prayed he would. That the thing would chase him and forget about me.

"But then it caught some other scent and ran off. I guess that must have been you it was after. Kelso and I didn't wait around. As soon as we couldn't hear it anymore, we were up and stumbling along the stream a ways, and when we were too tired to run, we threw ourselves in the water and let it carry us south, only crawling out when we feared we'd drown."

Jack watched his haunted expression as he told this tale and knew that the memory of the Wendigo still hung like a dark cloud over Merritt's soul. He glanced around to see who might overhear, but the big man had been talking of monsters so long that no one paid him any mind.

"Kelso left Dawson the same day we got back into town," Merritt continued, haltingly. "But I—"

"It's dead, Merritt."

Hal already knew the story, and he nodded.

"How?" Merritt asked.

"I killed it. It's just bones and dust now, my friend."

Merritt searched his eyes, and when he at last knew Jack spoke the truth, he let out a breath and actually smiled. "You've quite a story to tell, I take it?"

Jack shook his head. "If it's all the same to you, I'd rather not."

Brow furrowing, Merritt nodded. "I understand completely. In fact, I'd be happy enough never to speak of it again."

"Then we never shall."

They did not have to shake on the vow. A glance between them and a nod of understanding was enough. They had put that chapter of their lives behind them, now. The Wendigo had finally, and truly, been put to rest.

By now the bar had begun to fill, and the noise level had risen so that they could no longer converse without raising their voices. Smoke clouded the room, and two women launched into a shrieking match over a scruffy man who Jack would have wagered could not possibly smell as filthy as he looked.

"I've made arrangements at the hotel for dinner," Jack announced to his friends. "The owner is happy to accommodate us. I suggest we retreat to the quiet of that dining room. The food isn't much of an improvement over the slop in this joint, but if he tries to serve us rat instead of rabbit, it won't be hidden in a stew."

"You make a compelling argument," Merritt admitted. He pushed back his chair and started to rise, and then he stiffened, staring through a smoky gap in the crowd.

Jack turned to follow his gaze and felt his heart go still in his chest.

Three tables away, the man they all knew only as Archie tossed back a shot of whiskey and slammed the glass onto the table. One of his companions said something and Archie laughed, a grinning wolf leer on his face. Whatever he had found funny, it had been something cruel; that was evident from the glint in his eyes. Through the haze of smoke and in the low light, he had not noticed them. Even now, as they all stared at him, Archie remained oblivious.

All his attention seemed focused on the two young men at his table.

Young men, hell, Jack thought. *They're boys. Little more than children.*

They were new to Dawson City, of course, the lust for gold bright in their eyes, along with the pride at being treated as equals in the company of such gruff men. For now Jack searched the faces of the others at Archie's table, and while he did not recognize any of them, he knew the look of them. They were predators, like Archie, like William. A bullet in the chest had not killed Archie, and the sight of the Wendigo had not terrified him enough to shed his own greed.

And as Jack realized what Archie's plans were for the two boys—that he was still in the business of enslaving others to do his prospecting—the big, hairy bastard got up, clapped the boys on their backs, and exhorted them to accompany him. What lure he used Jack didn't know. Over the roar of the place, he could not hear. But the boys seemed game enough. They rose and joined Archie, as did one of the other men at the table, and without a glance back, the four of them started to weave their way out of the Dawson Bar, where the dark of night and a grim future awaited.

Jack got up to follow.

Merritt grabbed his arm, and he spun to stare at his friend.

"Don't tell me not to get involved," Jack said.

Anger colored Merritt's cheeks. "Not a chance. I just don't want you getting there before me."

"Or me," Hal said.

Jack fixed him with a hard look. "No. You stay."

The young man bristled. "Not a chance."

"Don't be a fool," Jack said. "Merritt and I are leaving Dawson tomorrow—or at least I hope he's leaving with me?"

Merritt nodded in agreement. "Apologies, my friend, but Jack's right. You've started to make a home here. You have your job at the newspaper and that girl whose name always makes you blush. If you come out there with us now, you'll have to leave with us tomorrow, or they'll kill you when we're gone."

Hal looked as though he might argue further, but then the realization sank in and he relented. "I'm going to have a drink. Come back when it's over, and we'll go have that dinner."

"Agreed," Jack replied, and then he and Merritt departed.

As they left the bar, he and Merritt walked right by Archie's other partners, who did not give them so much as a glance. They stepped onto the darkened street, the moon a scimitar overhead, providing only haunted, golden gloom. Archie and his confederate had herded the two boys off to the left—toward the river and away from town— and as Jack gazed after them, he wondered again what the black-hearted man had used for a lure. Girls? Gold? A free room? It didn't matter. All they would get from Archie was a knock on the back of the head and a short life of violence and hard labor.

"Come on," Jack said quietly.

He began to run, guns slapping his hips, his heavy coat dragging on him. He heard Merritt coming up behind him, drew one of his guns, and handed it over.

"If I've learned anything, it's that things aren't always what they seem."

"I don't want it," Merritt huffed, far too used to sitting on a bar stool to be exerting himself so.

"It's to keep the other fellow out of it," Jack explained.

And then they had no more time to talk. Archie and the others had heard their approach. In dim moonlight that transformed them all to ghosts, the two slavers and their young prey all turned to see who pursued them.

Archie—little more than a hulking, bristling silhouette—reached for a weapon as Jack and Merritt caught up.

Jack drew his remaining gun and cocked it, and Archie froze.

"We don't got nuthin' worth stealin'!" one of the boys said, putting up his hands as if it were a robbery.

"Shut up, idiot!" hissed Archie's sidekick.

Merritt moved half a dozen feet from Jack, off to the left, gun trained on the tall, thin slaver. The man had a long jaw and sunken cheeks that gave him a strangely horselike appearance, and he had a terrible, malevolent light in his eyes that came as no surprise.

Archie's hand still hovered near his hip.

"Let's see," Jack said. "Pull back your coat, slowly."

Archie did as instructed, drawing open his coat to reveal a long, wicked-looking blade hanging in a sheath on his hip. When he saw the knife, Jack grinned. He felt it bubbling up from inside him and he could not help it. It was a savage, wild grin, and it must have unnerved the others, for Archie's equine sidekick muttered something and the two boys started whispering to each other.

"Take off your coat," Jack said.

"Who the hell are you?" Archie replied.

That surprised Jack. He moved a little closer, turning to face the moon more fully, and though it took a few seconds, Archie's eyes widened in astonishment.

"I figured you for dead," the slaver said.

"No. I'm very much alive," Jack declared, and it had never felt so true.

Archie nodded slowly. "That's good. I always regretted not getting the chance to kill you myself."

Now he did take off his coat, shrugging out of it like a man about to do a job that badly needed doing. Jack knew how he felt.

"What do they want?" Horse Face asked.

Merritt cocked his gun. "Just those boys. Send them on their way and there'll be no trouble."

"But we—," one of the boys began.

"Shut up," Archie snarled.

Jack looked at the boys now. In their frightened eyes he saw Hal again, from months earlier, and yet Hal had been defiant. He had never been as scared as these two lambs. Jack had seen boys like this plenty of times growing up, had defended them often, but they nearly always came to a rough end.

"You two should never have come here," he said. "You're far more likely to find blood than gold. You should go home."

"And you can go to hell!" one of them said, baring his teeth like a little dog guarding his dinner.

Ah. Maybe they'll be all right after all, Jack thought. *If the wild gets into him, maybe he'll survive.*

"These men would enslave you," Merritt said. "They'll beat you and put you to work for them, and any gold you find would be theirs. They did it to us. Most of the men who were with us are dead now."

Jack was glad that Merritt said it. The boys were less afraid of him, and from the way they shifted away from Archie and Horse Face, it was obvious they believed him. Merritt had always had that honest quality.

"Get out of here," Jack told the boys, gesturing with the barrel of his gun.

Archie sneered in disgust and fury but did not try to stop them. The boys fled back up the street, toward the bar.

"You think that makes them safe?" Archie asked.

"I think next time they'll see you coming," Jack replied, and in his own voice he heard a familiar growl. His heartbeat sped up in anticipation, and though he knew that if he looked around he would not see it, he felt the wolf nearby.

The wolf would *always* be nearby, because he carried it within himself.

Jack holstered his gun and slipped out of his heavy coat, letting it fall to the street. Archie took half a step forward, but Merritt leveled the Colt at him and the slaver thought better of it. With the two slavers watching, Jack unbuckled both gun belts, carried them over to Merritt, and laid them on the ground.

Then he moved toward Archie until they were only about four feet apart. Horse Face was forgotten—Merritt would cover him. Jack locked eyes with Archie, feeling the wolf rising. He reached down and patted his knife where it hung sheathed on his belt.

"Now we're even," Jack said. "You have a knife, and I have a knife."

"You could've made me throw my knife away," Archie said.

Jack grinned again. "I don't want you to."

He took a step toward Archie, and the man took a step back, his gaze uncertain now, as if he sensed something in Jack that confused him. Frightened him. And it had nothing to do with guns or knives.

That gave Jack pause. He felt the wolf in him, the wildness, and knew he had gathered its deadly calm and cunning into himself along with its ferocity and speed.

Archie had sensed it as well.

But Jack didn't want that. The wolf would kill this man, and Jack would become a murderer. Even if they had the same weapons, it would be murder. He had left the wilderness behind, and if he meant to return to civilization now, he had to leave the wild as well. All along he had been asking himself, *Who is Jack London?* Now he looked into Archie's skittish eyes, and he knew.

He took a deep breath and let it out, pushing the wolf away. It might be his spirit guide, part of his very soul, but it was not him. Another cleansing breath, and the grin vanished from his face. He stood up straighter.

Jack didn't need the wolf to beat Archie. He needed the boy and the young man he had been, the wharf rat and bar fighter and back-alley scrapper.

"If you end up with my knife in your gut, and flies buzzing around your corpse when the sun comes up, who's going to cry for you?" Jack asked.

Horse Face looked confused, but Archie flinched.

"That's what I thought," Jack said. "So I'm going to give you a choice. You can fight, or you can forget about those kids and pan for your own damned gold. Maybe you'll get lucky, strike it rich, but you'll do it yourself."

"Archie—," Horse Face began.

Jack shook his head, never taking his eyes off of Archie.

"Don't listen. He's a greedy son of a bitch, just like you. Your last partner shot you. I shouldn't have to remind you, but it seems like you need reminding. Anyway, those are your choices. Walk away, or fight. But if you fight, know that I'll win. And though I don't want to kill you, we've both got knives, and people die in knife fights. It's the way of things."

For several long seconds, Jack wasn't sure which way it would go.

Then Archie seemed to deflate. He smiled a little, almost in admiration, and he picked up his coat.

"You must be joking," Horse Face said, striding toward him. "You're not really gonna let this—"

Archie punched him so hard that a tooth shot from his split and bloody mouth, catching the moonlight as it landed in the dirt. Horse Face hit the ground, tried to rise, and then only lay there, dazed.

Dragging on his coat, Archie walked away without so much as a backward glance.

"You had me scared there for a minute," Merritt said. Jack picked up his gun belts and buckled them into place.

As he put his coat back on, Jack gave Merritt a reassuring smile but said nothing. He had come to the Yukon to conquer the wild, and finally he had done so, though not in a way he ever would have dreamed. It had become a part of him, deep inside, and no matter where he wandered in the world, he would carry the wild with him, and would always hear its call.

Part of him would forever be the wolf, but first and foremost, Jack London was a man. A son, a brother, a friend. He had responsibilities, a truth that had been lost to him in the wild.

It was time to go home.

A NOTE FROM THE AUTHORS

The Secret Journeys of Jack London is a work of fiction. As such, it has taken some liberties with the truth. Most of the supernatural events are entirely invented, but readers may be surprised to learn that Jack's mother actually was a medium who held séances in the family home, and that the story of her offering him up to the spirits is a true one, at least according to biographer Alex Kershaw in his *Jack London: A Life*, which was one of our primary research sources. In this first volume, we have combined numerous elements, including details and characters from London's actual first journey to the Yukon, fictional parallels to the events of *The Call of the Wild*, and supernatural legends of the Alaskan and Canadian wilderness. For instance, the Wendigo is a traditional North American legend, a cannibalistic spirit that could possess humans, particularly those who themselves indulged in cannibalism. Who's to say the actual scars Jack London brought back with him from the Yukon *weren't* caused by a confrontation with the Wendigo? Likewise, the scary, mysterious Leshii exists in Russian folklore: a wood spirit who plays tricks on people to make them lose their way in his forests. As far as we can, we've researched and tried to stay true to these legends. They're fascinating enough without us needing to change them.

We've also tried to make the settings and hardships Jack and his friends encounter as genuine and realistic as possible. Dyea and Dawson City were real places, true frontier towns, and were as wild and lawless as we've portrayed them here, populated with equally downbeat inhabitants. And the Chilkoot Trail really was as we described it—steep, deadly, and treacherous, littered with abandoned equipment and the corpses of dead horses. These men and women stampeders were hard people facing hard times, all in the search for the elusive gold . . . which, in truth, was found by few.

It should be noted that we have wilfully altered the timeline of history in one vital respect. Most of Jack's actual adventures in the north and at sea took place when he was in his early twenties. We have taken some small license in featuring him as a seventeen- and eighteen-year-old (and somewhat larger license, in the sense that this means the gold rush takes place several years earlier in our fictional world than it did in reality). Altering Jack's age is not a great leap of artistic license, however, considering that at the age of thirteen he had bought a sloop from an oyster pirate and became a pirate himself, and at the age of seventeen he had signed on as a sailor on a schooner and traveled to Japan. By then, Jack London's life-changing journeys of adventure, danger, and excitement were well under way.

ACKNOWLEDGMENTS

Our gratitude, first and foremost, to our agent Howard Morhaim, who always sees the big picture, and to the excellent Jordan Brown and everyone at HarperCollins. Big thanks to Greg Ruth for illustrations that perfectly match the soul of the novel. Thanks to Fox2000 and the folks who made it happen: Peter Donaldson, Adam Rosen, Michael Prevett, and Riley Ellis. Thanks to Jeremy Lassen for wanting to buy it, and to Jason Williams for saying no. (Smile) And finally, a nod to the attendees of the "wild" Thai diner in Toronto in 2007, at which table the seed of this story was planted.

MLib

5/12